Outstanding praise for the

"Yates effectively captures the hor
tender interactions between h..
—*Booklist* on *Leave Myself Behind*

"The next Holden Caulfield . . . Bart Yates's main character
and narrator, Noah York, has Caulfield-style teenage authen-
ticity. Noah's voice is more than just honest or original; it's
real." —*The Plain Dealer* on *Leave Myself Behind*

"In his assured debut, *Leave Myself Behind*, Bart Yates wrung
bittersweet romance and wry humor out of brutal fag-bashing
and family secrets. His sad, witty follow-up, *The Brothers
Bishop*, begins like a snappy beach read, but soon treads
equally dark thematic waters. [Yates] . . . finds hard-won joy
in hot-button issues. His compelling debut novel was no
fluke." —*Out*

"With *Leave Myself Behind*, Bart Yates gives us both the
laugh-out-loud *and* refreshingly sincere coming-of-age
story we've been missing all these years." —*Instinct Magazine*

"One of the strengths of Yates's writing is his ability to work
out complicated plot points and weave together the threads of
the story in a dramatically effective manner." —*Bay Area
Reporter* on *The Brothers Bishop*

"Brilliantly written and funny as hell." —*Edge Boston* on *The
Distance Between Us*

"Absorbing. Brims with quiet intensity." —*Publishers
Weekly* on *The Distance Between Us*

Books by Bart Yates

LEAVE MYSELF BEHIND

THE BROTHERS BISHOP

THE LANGUAGE OF LOVE AND LOSS

THE VERY LONG, VERY STRANGE LIFE
OF ISAAC DAHL

And writing as Noah Bly

THE THIRD HILL NORTH OF TOWN

THE DISTANCE BETWEEN US

Published by Kensington Publishing Corp.

THE LANGUAGE OF LOVE AND LOSS

A NOVEL

BART YATES

JOHN SCOGNAMIGLIO BOOKS
KENSINGTON BOOKS
www.kensingtonbooks.com

JOHN SCOGNAMIGLIO BOOKS are published by

Kensington Publishing Corp.
900 Third Avenue
New York, NY 10022

All Kensington titles, imprints and distributed lines are available at special quantity discounts for bulk purchases for sales promotion, premiums, fund-raising, educational or institutional use.

Special book excerpts or customized printings can also be created to fit specific needs. For details, write or phone the office of the Kensington Special Sales Manager: Kensington Publishing Corp., 900 Third Avenue, New York, NY, 10022. Attn. Special Sales Department. Phone: 1-800-221-2647.

The JS and John Scognamiglio Books logo is a trademark of Kensington Publishing Corp.

First Kensington Hardcover Edition: June 2023

ISBN: 978-1-4967-4126-4 (ebook)

ISBN: 978-1-4967-4125-7

First Kensington Trade Paperback Edition: June 2024

10 9 8 7 6 5 4 3 2 1

Printed in the United States of America

ACKNOWLEDGMENTS

My editor, John Scognamiglio, is insightful, savvy, kind, wise, and a consummate gentleman; he's also the best damn cat-herder in the business. Thank you, John, for everything.

There are no better writers than Gordon Mennenga, and I have been blessed to have him as the first reader of all my books ever since I started this insane journey more than twenty years ago. Thank you, Gordon, for your incredible talent, honesty, and generosity.

I've leaned so heavily on Marian Mathews Clark through the years that it's a wonder she can still stand upright. She's a first-class wordsmith, but what I value even more than her crafts-manship and attention to detail is her unwavering friendship. Many, many thanks, dear one.

My gratitude also to the core members of the Iowa City Show-and-Tell Club: Tonja Robins, Pena Lubrica, Dave Dugan, and Allison Headey, for continued support and inspiration— but mostly for their exquisite food and company. Ridiculously inadequate thanks to Lisa and Edward Leff, for stellar conver-sation, music, and good Scotch in the wee hours of the night; Abe Assad, for his singular wit and divine idiocy; Jaclyn Dean for only vomiting on my shirt that one time; Candace Noble for forgiving me as I butcher the French language that she loves so well; Adrian Repasch, my terrific website designer; and Michael Becker, for having zero taste in friends.

And thanks as ever to my family: Great souls, one and all.

CHAPTER 1

The next time Mom wants me to come home, remind me why I'd rather roast my own balls over a campfire.

First off, the only transportation I can afford is the Greyhound bus—aka mobile purgatory—and I always get trapped, just like now, with a total wack job for a seatmate. Every single person who's ever sat next to me on the bus has a quaint, harmless-sounding name, like Edith, or Lawrence, or Eunice, but they smell like a cat box, or they pick their noses when they think I'm not looking, or they fondle my knee while telling me about last night's wet dream, or their ongoing struggle with herpes, or how they came to believe that the lady driving the bus is really Benito Mussolini. Where do these hapless, lonely lunatics come from? Mom says crazy people talk to me because I have a kind face—masking my inner Visigoth—but I think it's because I'm too much of a chickenshit to tell them to shut the fuck up.

My seat partner this time around is Brenda, a massage therapist with a lazy eye, ratty sandals, and breath that smells like a putrid blend of hummus and peanut butter; she just finished informing me, in painstaking detail, about her rare collection of

Peruvian salt shakers. She's pleasant enough, I guess, and harmless, but she's also boring as hell, and keeps leaning in close and spraying spittle at me with alarming regularity as she talks. Every time she does this I pull back but she doesn't take the hint; her face is never farther than three inches from mine, no matter how I contort myself to escape.

By the way, just so you don't think I'm a total dick who hates everyone—though you wouldn't be the first to draw that conclusion—there was a little girl in the seat across the aisle from me earlier this afternoon, with a haircut like Einstein's and big serious eyes like a Saint Bernard, who kept singing snatches of "This Old Man" under her breath while solving a maze in a *Highlights* magazine, and I fell in love with her the instant I saw her. I also really liked the old guy with no teeth who kept using the restroom in the back of the bus, because the third time he passed my seat he grinned when we made eye contact and said, "Do me a favor, kid, and trade bladders with me."

Anyway, another reason I dread going home is because my nominal hometown—Oakland, New Hampshire—is so mired in the past that it makes Pompeii look trendy. Nothing has altered there for eons, nary a parking meter nor pothole. It's a pretty little town, but it's so sleepy I'm not sure anyone who lives there actually has a pulse. (Save for Mom, of course, who has the heartbeat of a hummingbird.) During the two years I lived in Oakland as a kid I didn't mind the dullness so much, but now it drives me batshit, as does the absence of anything resembling culture. There's a bookstore at the small college where Mom teaches, but the fiction section is less avant-garde than the menu in the town's roach-ridden Dairy Queen; there's a movie theater, but the likelihood of a foreign film ever gracing Oakland is about the same as a choir of castrated goatherds yodeling Verdi's *Requiem* at the elementary school.

Thirdly, there's Mom herself: the great Virginia York, Pulitzer prize winner, current New Hampshire Poet Laureate, and standard bearer for all things literary and/or hoity-toity. Of course I love her, but that's beside the point. She's arrogant, moody, and a major pain in the ass, and never more so than when she's in her own fiefdom; we end up fighting within milliseconds of me stepping through the front door. When she visits me in Providence, we get along ten times better; she doesn't seem to feel the need to treat me like a kid, so I don't feel the need to act like one.

And last but not least, there's Mom's beautiful, brooding, Victorian monster of a house. I know every square inch of the place, having basically rebuilt it from scratch nineteen years ago, when I was a senior in high school, after Mom had a psychotic meltdown and morphed into a giant, bipedal termite, chewing the walls apart faster than I could repair them. She's fine now, thank God, and the house looks better than ever, but there are a thousand stray memories in every room, floating around like dust motes and making it hard to breathe. Oddly enough, the majority of these memories—aside from Mom's illness, and a few other nightmarish moments—are good, even great, but therein lies the problem: I hate being reminded how much I fucked up my life.

The only place the bus stops in Oakland is at the corner of Main and Linden, next to Bridge's Pharmacy, and I'm the sole passenger getting off, right before sunset. The pharmacy is already closed for the day, and since my only luggage is my backpack the driver just opens the door and tells me to have a good night. I wince as I step into the late summer heat and watch the Greyhound pull away from the curb, on its way to the next zombified town, twenty miles down the road. My ex-seatmate Brenda now waves at me through the window as I hitch up my backpack and wave back, heaving a sigh of relief to escape her clutches.

Downtown Oakland is just two blocks long, and it's deserted this time of day. Oakland has a couple thousand people, give or take, but only when Cassidy College is in session, so less than half that number are currently in town. I turn west on Main Street—an uneven, beat-to-hell brick road—and start down the sidewalk to Mom's house, about a mile away, also on Main. I could call Mom to come get me, but I like walking, and I want to clear my head before I see her. I'm dressed lightly, in sneakers, shorts, and a T-shirt, yet I'm already sweating; the setting sun is brutal and the air is so wet I feel like I'm trudging through a Louisiana swamp. I hear a vehicle approaching from behind and I glance over as a green, mud-spattered pickup passes by. The beefy, sunburned driver has his window down; he's wearing a sleeveless shirt, and his muscled shoulder and arm are slick with sweat. He slows his truck to a crawl, then a full stop.

"That you, Noah?" he calls out, as I draw even with him.

I come to a halt as well, not having a clue who he is. I've only come back to town a handful of times since I left for college, and I've forgotten most of the people I used to know.

"Yep, sure is," I say, searching his face. He's got a thick red beard, and it's hard to make out his features—but he looks to be about my age, and his voice is oddly familiar.

"You don't recognize me, do you? I'm Perry. Perry White."

My stomach muscles clench. Jesus Christ, what are the odds of meeting *this* dick-wad, two minutes after getting to town? Perry White and some of his ape-men cronies once beat the living shit out of my ex-boyfriend and me. They got arrested for it, too, but a troglodyte judge let them off with just a slap on the wrist. I haven't seen White since my high school graduation, but I have no doubt he's the same award-winning prick he always was. I eye him warily, praying he's not in the mood to risk another run-in with the police. His biceps are bigger than my thighs, and even though he's not threatening me at the moment, God only knows what's going through that cinderblock of a head.

"Hey, Perry," I say, forcing myself to sound casual. "Long time no see."

"You ain't aged at all," he says. "I recognized you right away, second I saw you." He pauses for a second, looking uncomfortable. "You visiting your mom?"

I nod, wondering why he's bothering with small talk. I know for a fact he's got some nasty scars under that beard, courtesy of me; I damn near tore off his cheek when he and his friends jumped J.D. and me.

"Yeah, I just got here," I tell him.

"Bet she'll be glad to have you home." He pauses, then grimaces. "That lady sure hates me. Every time I see her around town she tells me to go to hell, even when I got my kids along."

I don't know what surprises me more: the rue in his voice, or the way he keeps avoiding my eyes. I shrug. "Yeah, well, she takes a dim view of people who beat up her son." It's unwise to provoke him, but my mouth has a mind of its own. "She's funny that way."

He flushes a little, but otherwise doesn't react. "Can't say as I blame her none." He finally looks at me directly. "I know you hate my guts, Noah, and you got reason. I been wanting to say sorry for a long time, but I ain't seen you till just now, or J.D., neither."

I blink, having no clue how to respond. I haven't thought about this asshole in years, but now that he's right here in front of me, all my old anger and helplessness are waking from a long coma. He and his friends put J.D. and me in the hospital; I came close to losing an eye. Does he really think it fixes anything to say "sorry"? It's all I can do to not flip him off and start chucking rocks at his truck; I'd be more than happy to tear off his other goddamn cheek. I don't trust myself to answer, so I just nod, acknowledging that I heard him. He watches me for a minute before he figures out no forgiveness is forthcoming, then he sighs a little and nods back.

"Okay, guess I best be going," he says, popping his truck in gear again. "Welcome home."

I watch him drive away, irritated at myself for feeling guilty about how sheepish and sad he looks. It's his own damn fault if he feels bad, and there's no reason on earth for me to accept his apology. I'm not his father confessor.

I kick a tuft of grass at the edge of the sidewalk, staring after the green truck until it disappears. "Yeah, fine, whatever, numb-nuts," I mumble.

I'd be lying if I said there's nothing I miss about rural New Hampshire. I miss all the old oak and maple trees, for instance, and the stone fences lining the street; I miss watching kids playing touch football and tripping all over themselves on their lawns at dusk, and the smell of salmon being smoked on a charcoal grill, and the bawdy chorus of birds, singing their horny lungs out to attract a mate. I miss how easy it is to get around everywhere on foot; I miss the freshness of the air, and the huge green spaces between the houses, and the lack of car horns and sirens; I miss having the sidewalk to myself, and not having to dodge around people yapping on their cell phones; I miss the red and yellow glory of an unobstructed sunset, and the quiet, steady cadence of my sneakers on the concrete, and the heady, distinctive scents of mint, goldenrod, and New England asters, growing wild in an abandoned lot. It may sound like a Norman Rockwell picture come to life, but it's real, and the peacefulness here goes soul-deep. It's the sweet flip side to the small-town dullness I was just bitching about a few minutes ago.

What can I say? A lot of things worth hating are also worth loving.

I'm a block from home when I see Mom, sitting on the steps of our front porch. The sun is a bare sliver on the horizon now, but there's still enough light to see her clearly. She hasn't noticed me because she's staring down at her bare feet; she's wearing a bright blue summer dress, and her long hair—once raven black, now streaked with white—is tied in a ponytail she's always messing with, draping it over her shoulder and worrying at the strands with her fingers while she thinks about whatever weird shit poets think about. She's sixty-eight, but she could easily pass for fifty, save for the wrinkles around her eyes that you can only see up close. She's waiting for me, of course, but even if she didn't know I was due to show up, she'd still be outside right about now, watching the sunset.

Virginia York: the most complicated person I know, running the gamut from holy woman to gargoyle, depending on the day.

Before Mom's psychotic break, she was already a well-respected poet, but not many people outside of academia knew who she was. I miss those days, to tell the truth, when she was more anonymous, even though I hated her poems back then—she went out of her way to be unintelligible to anybody who didn't have a thesaurus wedged up their butt. After she came unglued and put herself back together, however, her style gradually changed, and her audience has grown exponentially. She's not yet in the same ballpark as people like Maya Angelou or Seamus Heaney, but it's not just scholarly geeks who love her these days, and I run into strangers all the time who freak out when they learn I'm her son.

I'm not the one who tells them this, by the way; I don't have to. Anybody who's ever read her stuff knows the goddamn poem she wrote about me dropping out of art school when I was twenty. Considering that only a tiny portion of the world's population actually reads poetry, you might think I'd be safe from meeting so many people who do, but since I mostly hang around places like bookstores, art galleries, museums, and coffee shops, it's a rare week that goes by without someone wanting to know what it's like to be "The Lost Soul" in the poem's title.

Just peachy fucking keen, I always tell them.

She claims, in the poem, that I stopped painting, but I never did; I just dropped out of the Rhode Island School of Design. Mom acted like this was the end of the world, though—Jesus, she was pissed—so she told the whole damn *universe* about me "breaking faith" with myself, and wasting my talent. Granted, it's a lyrical, masterfully crafted sestina, about a lot of things outside the scope of my personal life: parents and children, heartbreak and expectations, innocence and mortality—but all these high-minded, philosophical musings are a little hard for me to appreciate, given that they came at the expense of my privacy.

Anyway, suffice it to say that being Virginia York's offspring has been, is, and always will be something of a mixed blessing.

She finally looks up just as I reach the edge of our property. She tosses her ponytail back over her shoulder and gets nimbly to her feet, smiling, as I cut across the lawn. We haven't seen each other in almost eight months.

"You made it," she says. Oddly enough, her fondness for stating the obvious is kind of endearing.

"Just barely." I shrug my backpack off at the bottom of the porch steps. "My seatmate's salivary glands came close to flooding the bus." She leans down to kiss my cheek, and I lift her off the steps and spin her around in a circle, her feet resting on mine. "You've lost weight," I tell her. "Do you have a parasite or something?"

"Not since you were in my womb," she says, making me laugh. She hugs me hard, then grimaces at my sweaty shirt. "You're soaking wet. Why didn't you call me to come get you?"

"I wanted to stretch my legs." I set her down again and we step back a little to study each other. We look alike, but she's a whole lot prettier. We both have olive-colored skin (her mother was Portuguese), and we're skinny and short, with the same narrow shoulders, small noses, thin lips, and black hair—

I'm starting to get some white in my hair, too—but Mom could wrap herself in a burlap sack and shave her head without losing any of her natural beauty; her cheekbones alone are enough to make people stop and gawp at her on the street. That being said, the first thing most people notice about her is her intense green eyes. When she looks at you, really looks at you, it's like stepping in one of those airport scanners that sees you right down to your pubes.

"What's wrong?" she asks me.

"Nothing. I'm just a little tired. It was a long week." I retrieve my backpack. "Have you had supper yet?"

"Nope. What are you hungry for?" She leads me in the house. "The pantry's full, so take your pick."

She's always glad to have me home—at least for the initial few minutes—but she seems abnormally pleased tonight, glancing over her shoulder and beaming at me as I stop for a second in the entry hall to kick off my shoes.

"Anything's fine," I tell her. "I'll help cook, but I need a shower first. I feel slimy."

"Take your time. I'll make drinks while you're de-sliming."

She goes in the kitchen and I head upstairs. It's hot and stuffy up here; Mom hates air-conditioning, and the ceiling fans and open windows are no match for the summer heat, at least until the temperature falls at night. My old room still looks pretty much the same—window seat, huge walk-in closet, lots of bookshelves—but most of my old stuff is in Providence, or boxed up in Mom's basement. My bed is still here, though, and my dresser, which still has some of my clothes from high school; in the corner is my old easel, along with paper, canvas, and a much-abused set of brushes and paints. I left the clothes and my spare art stuff here on purpose, so I wouldn't have to pack a lot when I visit. The sight of my bed, with its threadbare blue spread, makes me smile; J.D. and I had a lot of fun in that bed.

I drop my backpack on the mattress and wander down the

hall to the bathroom, past Mom's room and the two unused guest rooms. This house is way too big for just Mom—it was too big for three of us, when J.D. and I also lived here—but she'll never sell it, and I'm glad. It's easy for her to keep clean, because all the floors are wood, and she doesn't have a lot of stuff; I'm pretty sure she was a Spartan warrior in one of her past lives, and clutter makes her homicidal. The only exception to her no-clutter rule—and it's a huge freaking exception—is books. She's probably got five or six thousand of the things, overflowing shelves, tables, and chairs in every damn room save the kitchen and bathroom. To be fair, quite a few were Dad's that we brought with us from Chicago after he died, but he's been gone for twenty years, and every time I come home Mom has added at least two or three new bookshelves to the house, sprouting up here and there like creeper vines on a wall. I inherited my parents' genes for book-hoarding; I can barely take a step in my apartment in Providence without stubbing my toe on a goddamn novel or short story anthology.

The shower is an old clawfoot bathtub with a curtain around it. I strip off my clothes and climb in, turning on the faucet as cold as I can stand it. I gasp a little as the cool water cascades over me, but it feels great to rinse the sweat from my body and hair. I close my eyes to wash my face, and the memory parade starts up in my head, just like it does every time I come home.

How many times did J.D. and I shower together in this tub? A few hundred? He'd usually stand behind me, resting his chin on my shoulder and clasping me around the waist; I loved the feel of his body against mine, and the sound of his voice in my ear as we talked. He liked to sing in the shower, too, and he had a great voice, but sometimes he'd purposely mess up songs I loved, just to rile me. One time, for instance, he sang Tom Waits's "Romeo Is Bleeding," but he did it in an eerily accurate Bee Gees falsetto; I sprained my thumb trying to cover his mouth and shut him up. Another time, he—

"Oh, for Christ's sake," I mutter, opening my eyes. I crank the water to freezing, in punishment for letting my mind wander. "Give it a rest, loser."

I fish out an old pair of soccer shorts and a tank top from the dresser, then head downstairs, barefoot. Mom's back is to me as she chops vegetables at the counter, and there's a big, ice-filled pitcher of what appears to be rum and ginger ale—a summer staple in the York household—on the island in the middle of the room. Our kitchen is gigantic, with a breakfast nook in the corner and a huge window over the sink; Mom is listening to piano music on the radio as she works.

"What can I do?" I ask.

Startled, she glances over her shoulder. "I didn't hear you coming. Pour us both a drink, will you?"

I obey, bringing her a full glass, and she tells me we're having burritos. We toast each other, and I lean against the counter and watch her mince an onion. She usually chops stuff so fast that the knife blade is a blur, but tonight she's going at a more leisurely pace, humming to the music and looking out the window. The sun is down now but Mom never turns on lights until it's full dark, so she can still see outside.

"New neighbors moved in last week," she says, nodding at the house across the lawn. "A middle-aged couple, with horrifying taste in furniture. I haven't met either of them yet, but I've been spying on them ever since they moved in."

"That's very neighborly of you." I wander to the refrigerator and find a block of cheddar cheese to grate, knowing she'll want some. "So what's the verdict? Friends or foes?"

"The jury's still out, but I'm not optimistic. The man threw a hissy fit at the movers for tracking dirt in the house, and the woman wears more makeup than a geisha." She steps back from the counter, allowing me to get the cheese grater from a drawer. "They have a nice dog, though—a cocker spaniel who comes

over to visit every time I sit on the porch. It has a severe underbite that reminds me of one of my old boyfriends."

She's being so chatty and cheerful that she's actually starting
to weird me out. The last time I came home, we barely greeted
each other before she started in on me about my lack of a serious job (I teach art classes, part-time, at the community center,
to supplement the spotty income I make from sales of my
paintings); she then moved on to everything else I'm missing in
my life: close friends, a positive attitude, ambition, common
sense, proper nutrition, etc. I can't help but wonder why she's
being so nice tonight. It's not that she's never good company—
she can be really charming and funny, if you catch her at the
right moment—but I tend to bring out the worst in her. Nothing has changed in my world since the last time, so obviously
something is going on with her.

"Speaking of old boyfriends, how's Walter?" I ask. Walter
Danvers is also on the faculty at Cassidy College. He was
Mom's first real boyfriend after Dad died, and they've had an
on-again, off-again relationship for years.

She shrugs. "Same as always. Terribly sweet, terribly earnest,
terribly boring. He keeps asking me to marry him, and it's driving me crazy. Thank God he's out of town this week."

I actually like Walter, as opposed to some of the other bone-
heads she's been involved with. "You could do a whole lot
worse," I tell her. "At least he doesn't have an underbite."

She snorts. "That's setting the bar rather low, don't you
think?"

I throw together a salad while she browns the meat, onions,
and garlic in a skillet; she asks me about my own love life.

"Same as always," I tell her. "No one to write home about."

I'm standing at the island and she turns to look at me. "But
you've been dating?"

My turn to shrug. "Occasionally."

"Please tell me you're being careful, and not having sex with
random strangers."

I grin at her. "Uh, define random."

"Don't be cute, Noah."

"Does someone count as a stranger if I know his first name?"

"Noah."

"Relax, Mom. You know how much I hate hookups." This is true enough, as far as it goes: I *do* hate hookups. They're highly unsatisfying, meaningless, and forgettable, but sometimes my tyrannical penis is too stupid to care. "What's the music we're listening to?"

"I didn't catch the title, but the composer is Ignacio Cervantes." She points the spatula at me. "Why are you changing the subject?"

"I'm not. Who's Ignacio Cervantes?"

She sighs. "A Cuban composer from the late nineteenth century, but that's all I know about him." She turns back to the stove. "Fine, keep your secrets. What kind of beans do you want in your burritos?"

I raise my eyebrows. It's not like her at all to let me get away with being less than forthcoming: I was sure she was gearing up for a heated interrogation.

"Black beans would be great," I tell her, staring at the back of her head. "Who are you, woman, and what have you done with my mother?"

She actually laughs, disconcerting me even more.

"I'm serious," I say. "What's gotten into you?"

She looks over her shoulder again, and the love I see in her face makes my throat close a little. "Dinner first, okay?" she says. "We can talk afterwards."

So, there are a few things you should know about why Mom cracked up when I was a kid. I don't really like talking about it much, even now, because it's a long, convoluted, unbelievably fucked-up story, but the gist of it is that when we bought this house and moved in, there was a ton of remodeling to do, and we started finding stuff the previous owner—an elderly crackpot named Carlisle—had hidden around the place, in glass jars and metal tins. There was a necklace, and a marriage license, and some old pictures, and at first it was kind of fun trying to piece together why all this crap was in our walls and floors. It ended up being a lot less fun, however, after Mom, J.D., and I discovered the skeleton of Carlisle's infant daughter one night, under the furnace in the basement. It was a grisly, awful time for all three of us, but for Mom it was catastrophic, because it triggered some equally awful, long-repressed memories of her own childhood, and how she'd been raped and impregnated by her own father when she was only twelve. As if that weren't bad enough, after she gave birth to the baby it was taken away from her, against her will.

Anyway, once all this traumatic crap from her past reared up, Mom went haywire and had to be put in a psych ward. She eventually recovered—she's one of the toughest, most resilient human beings I've ever met—but I know it was absolute hell for her to climb out of the deep, dark pit in her head. I would probably have gone nuts myself while she was in the hospital, if it weren't for J.D. He was living with us by then, since his parents had thrown him out for being gay. He kept me grounded, and helped me feel safe and loved, and gave me hope that things would eventually get better.

Mom misses him almost as much as I do.

The best part of our house is the massive wraparound porch, looking out on both Main and Silver Streets. There's a porch swing, but Mom and I prefer sitting on the front steps, like she was doing when I first got home tonight. We return there after dinner and plop down on the top step, side by side. Mom has switched to iced tea, but I'm still drinking rum. It's full dark now, and the mosquitos are out, but we've slathered ourselves with repellent to confound the little bastards.

For a while we don't talk much. I know she's got something

on her mind, yet she seems content at the moment to just watch the stars with me. As always, every time I look up at the night sky I think of my father, who introduced me to most of the constellations in the Northern Hemisphere. When I was little, I used to sit on his lap, both of us tilting our heads back as he pointed out whatever caught his eye. He didn't just know the constellations; he knew the myths behind them, too. He was a gifted storyteller, and I still remember everything he taught me—but what I remember most is leaning against him, enfolded in his arms, and the smell of pipe smoke in his sweater. I was a weird little kid: one time I fell asleep while we were sitting like that, and dreamed of Castor and Pollux sitting by a fire with Orion and Dad, all four of them smoking a pipe.

A jingle of metal tags by our feet draws my attention down to Earth again, and a small dog trots up the steps, panting and snuffling. It must have black hair because I can barely see it.

"Hello there, Sadie," Mom says. "I was wondering if you were going to put in an appearance tonight."

A wet nose probes my shin and I reach down to scratch the dog's ears. "How do you know her name is Sadie?" I ask.

"I've heard our new neighbors calling for her. They keep her on a chain in the backyard, but she's apparently figured out how to free herself."

"Good for you, Sadie," I say. "Flee your oppressors."

The dog sprawls out on the step in front of our feet, making herself at home. I rub her belly with my toes, and she huffs in contentment.

"I keep thinking about getting a dog of my own," Mom says. "It might be nice to have an uncomplicated relationship, for once in my life."

I snort. "The poor thing would starve to death within a week. You don't even remember to feed yourself when you're writing."

"I never starved you, did I?" She threads her arm through

mine, in the darkness, and squeezes my bicep. "Listen, honey, I've got something I need to tell you."

I turn toward her; her face looks pale in the starlight. "That's not a particularly reassuring way to begin a conversation."

"Sorry. I don't mean to be melodramatic." She rests her head on my shoulder. "This last spring, I started getting cramps in my right thigh. I didn't think much about it at first, but then it started happening in my left leg, too, so I went to see a doctor. It turns out I've got ALS."

I stare blankly into the night. I open my mouth to say something, then close it again. I don't know what I thought she was going to tell me, but that wasn't it. I'm vaguely aware that all the air has left my lungs, and that I can't seem to refill them.

I know next to nothing about ALS, except that it's always terminal. And horrific.

"Are you sure?" I ask hoarsely.

"I'm afraid so."

"Jesus." My brain isn't working any better than my lungs. I can feel Sadie's rapid heartbeat beneath my foot, and I'm vaguely aware that my pulse is almost as fast as hers. I clear my throat. "How come you didn't say something before?"

"I didn't want to tell you over the phone, and you couldn't get here until your summer teaching was done." She hesitates. "I also needed a little time to come to terms with this, on my own. No one knows but you. I haven't even told Walter."

"How bad has it gotten?" I swallow convulsively. "I mean, what can we expect, in terms of—"

I can't finish the sentence.

"Most people live from three to five years, once the first symptoms appear," she says. "Sometimes more, sometimes less. I may get lucky, because my symptoms started in my legs. If things had started in my upper body, the disease would likely be progressing a lot faster."

"Jesus," I say again. I know she's speaking so calmly to help me digest what she's telling me, but I'm about two seconds from screaming my goddamn head off, and her matter-of-factness is just adding to my sense of unreality. "Did you get a second opinion?" I demand. My voice is quivering. "You look just fine to me. Are you absolutely *positive* you have it? Doctors screw up all the time."

She sighs. "I've lost track of how many doctors I've seen, and how many tests I've gone through. I didn't want to believe it at first, either—I still don't want to—but I'm afraid there's no longer any doubt." She lifts her head off my shoulder and runs a hand through my hair. "I still feel fine, mostly, but I tire quickly, and my leg muscles twitch a lot, especially in bed." She rests her fingers on my cheek. "I'm sorry, son. I know this is a lot to take in."

The gentleness in her tone undoes me. I start to cry, leaning into her touch. "So what happens now?" I ask. "There must be something we can do besides just sit around and wait for you to . . . to get sick. Have you talked to anybody about alternative therapies, or experimental drugs? What do Chinese doctors use, for instance? Those guys know all sorts of crazy shit that American doctors have never even heard of."

"I've talked to some Eastern medicine specialists, and they don't have any solutions, either. The best anyone can do is to maybe slow things down somewhat. My muscles are atrophying, and nothing can stop the progression. It's relentless, or so I'm told, and the end won't be very pretty. Feeding tubes, ventilators, etc." Unbelievably, she smiles: I can see the flash of her teeth in the darkness. "On the plus side, my doctor said that I may soon become prone to fits of inappropriate laughter. I told her that my son has the most inappropriate sense of humor on the planet, so maybe I'll finally think you're funny."

I try to smile back at her, but my face crumbles. She takes me in her arms, and holds me like she hasn't held me since I was a little boy. "It's okay, sweetie," she murmurs.

"The hell it is," I sob.

"I mean it," she says. She's crying, too, but more quietly. "It's not the way I would've chosen to go, of course, but I'm not done yet, and I'm hoping to last a good long while." She kisses my forehead. "Whatever happens, though, I'll be okay. I've had a damn good run. I married a kind, passionate, fascinating man, and we raised a beautiful, talented, one-of-a-kind son, and I've done work that I love, and I've accomplished more than I ever dreamed possible. I swear to you, Noah, that even if I keel over tomorrow, I'll die happy."

I should be comforting her instead of the other way around, but I'm too broken. I can't remember anything ever hurting like this, not even Dad's death, or when J.D. and I said goodbye for the last time. It's not as if I didn't know Mom was going to die someday, but part of me never really believed it. God knows, I've often felt like strangling her myself, but the thought of her being gone from the world, truly gone, is so awful that I can't wrap my head around it. Deep in my infantile psyche, even now, Virginia York is an immortal being, like Artemis or Apollo; I've always believed that time simply couldn't touch her. How stupid is that?

She clears her throat when we're both a little calmer, and leans back. "There are a couple of other things we should talk about tonight, before I get too tired," she says, wiping her face.

My throat is so raw that I can't speak, but I grunt in protest; I'm not sure how much else I can take.

"The hardest part is done, I promise," she tells me. "I just have a couple of favors to ask."

I don't know how late it is now, but Mom said good night hours ago. I should probably head to bed, too, but I'm still on the porch. Sadie, the neighbor's cocker spaniel, got called home about the same time Mom went upstairs, so I'm completely alone. Night owls (of the human variety) are a rare bird in Oakland; there's only one other house in the neighborhood, besides ours, with lights on—I left a wall sconce on in the kitchen so that I could find my way in to refill my glass, as necessary—and the lights in the other house go out one by one, even as I sit here, watching. No one is out on the roads at this hour, either; only three cars have passed by all evening. Oakland is dead tonight, dead as a chunk of petrified wood. Deader, even. Dead as disco; dead as chivalry; dead as the moon. I lie back on the porch with my drink on my chest, and listen to the crickets.

I'm stupendously drunk, in case you were wondering.

I typically don't drink much, but tonight is a special occasion. It's not every night, after all, that I discover my mother has a fatal illness. Nor is that my only reason to debauch; no, indeed.

A couple of favors, Mom said.

She didn't call them dying wishes, but that's what they are, of course. One came as a complete surprise to me and one didn't, but both are utterly ridiculous, and impossible to grant. She wouldn't let me answer her, tonight, but told me to sleep on it.

Sleep, my ass. I may never sleep again.

The first thing she asked—the predictable one—is that she wants me to move home. She said she knew it was selfish of her, but she wants to spend as much time with me as possible, before she dies. She said she wouldn't expect me to take care of her physically when she's no longer able to fend for herself; she plans to hire a full-time nurse to wipe her butt and sponge-mop her vagina, hence sparing me years of therapy. (Okay, she didn't phrase it quite like that, but those were the visuals that I couldn't prevent from popping into my head.) She reminded me that even though sales of my paintings have been gradually improving I'm still barely managing to pay my bills in Providence, and that I can live here for free, and paint as much as I want to. She said she bet that I could also get hired as adjunct faculty for the art department at Cassidy College, or, if that doesn't pan out, I could definitely find some private painting students in town who would be *absolutely thrilled* to learn from me.

Christ have mercy.

I don't even know where to start with how shitty all this makes me feel. I didn't say anything at the time—mostly because I was still reeling from finding out she was sick, but also because I didn't want to spew my supper all over the sidewalk at the thought of moving back to Oakland. True enough, I have trouble making ends meet in Providence, but I love the city, and my friends, and my easygoing teaching gig at the community center, and I'm actually starting to get a toehold in the art world there. I can also get laid anytime I feel like it, which is nothing to sneeze at. There's nothing in Oakland for me, and living with Mom would be a nightmare even if she were healthy, let alone when her body starts falling apart. I'll come visit her as much as possible, of course—hell, I can come home once a month, if I have to—but I'm NOT going to live in this medieval little shithole ever again. Period. End of discussion.

The second favor—the surprising one—is less vomit-inducing, but just as absurd.

She wants me to help find her daughter. Carolyn. The baby she had when she was twelve, after getting knocked up by my may-he-rot-in-hell-for-all-eternity grandfather. Carolyn, my older sister (half sister, technically) whom I've never met, and who would now be fifty-six, if she's still alive. The very same older sister, by the way, that I was led to believe was gone forever, lost in time, as impossible to find as a brontosaurus turd on the floor of the Grand Canyon.

Apparently I was wrong.

Mom never told me, until tonight, that she knows the name of the adoption agency in Illinois—she grew up just outside Chicago—where she and her father took their baby after it was born, back in 1966. She doesn't yet know the name of the family who adopted Carolyn, or where she is now, but she filled

out some paperwork a couple of months ago to get the bureau-
cratic ball rolling, even though (A) record keeping for adop-
tions in Illinois was, at best, pretty laughable in 1966, and (B)
her father shoveled a mountain of horseshit all over the adoption agency, lying about his and Mom's names, who the baby's
father was, where they lived, and why there was no birth cer-
tificate. Mom still remembers all the phony names her dad used,
however, and she says she's been told that's possibly enough to
track Carolyn down, assuming the relevant information hasn't
been lost or destroyed in the ensuing years.

I think her ALS is making her delusional.

I'm not opposed, at least in theory, to the idea of tracking
down my half sister—it might even be kind of cool to meet her.
The coolness quotient starts breaking down, though, when you
think about how messed up things could get if we *do* find her. I
can't imagine Carolyn would be too pleased to learn that her
biological father is also her *grandfather*, which means that
Mom and I will have to lie to her—thus starting off our acquaintance in the middle of a goddamn psychological mine-
field. When I asked Mom why she hadn't tried to find Carolyn
before, she told me she'd put it off until now for exactly that
reason. She said she's also been scared that Carolyn might look
like her/their father, and she wasn't sure if that was something
she could bear to see. Now that she's dying, though, she's decided it's finally time to find out if she still has a daughter
somewhere in the world, and if there's a possibility for them to
get to know one another.

I need another drink.

An owl hoots somewhere nearby, probably in the oak tree
behind the house. I listen to it for a couple of minutes, as condensation on my glass soaks through my shirt and chills my
chest. I think about going upstairs for my cell phone, to see if
anybody has tried to reach me tonight, but then I realize I don't
care. There's no one I want to talk to right now, not even J.D.

He loves Mom, too, and has a right to know what's going on, but hearing his voice tonight might kill me, especially after all the time that's gone by since we last spoke. I briefly toy with the idea of distracting myself for an hour or two by going on the sex apps and looking for someone pretty to hump, but the last thing I want to do right now is go skinny-dipping in Oakland's tiny gay gene pool. I want to be held tonight, yes, but not by a stranger; I want to be touched, not mauled; I want to be loved, not fetishized.

I'm hurting, and I have no idea what to do about it, or where to turn for help.

I want to feel safe again, and be told that everything is fine. That's a monstrous lie, of course, but I'm okay with dishonesty tonight. Honesty may be a virtue, but it's also a coldhearted son of a bitch, capable of flaying the skin off your soul. Sometimes the only way to survive a too-close encounter with the truth is to be held by someone who loves you, and tells you what you want to hear, and makes you believe that tomorrow will be better, even though it won't be.

My mother is dying.

Someone lie to me.

CHAPTER 2

I don't remember coming to bed last night, but I guess I must have, since the first thing I see when I open my eyes is my pale blue bedroom ceiling, in dire need of a fresh coat of paint. I stare up at it stupidly for a while, fixated on the hesitant progress of a spider as it crawls over the popcorn landscape, pausing every few inches to rest. It's still early morning but the sun is up; there's a cool breeze coming through the open windows and the birds are flipping out like they always do around sunrise, screeching like little kids on a playground.

Maybe that spider over my head isn't resting. Maybe it's meditating on the futility of existence.

I close my eyes again and sigh, not wanting to face this day.

My head hurts, but not as badly as it should, considering I drank enough rum last night to impress Ernest Hemingway. I roll on my side and watch the breeze ruffle the red and white curtains above the window seat. The clothes I was wearing before bed are strung across the floor in a crooked, telltale line; I apparently wrestled my shirt off by the door, then stumbled sideways a few steps before ridding myself of my soccer shorts, then lurched to the bed to yank off my boxers, now knotted in a dissolute ball by the foot of the nightstand. Following this stupefied striptease, I must've kicked off most of my bedding, too, because the only thing left on the mattress is two pillows and a fitted sheet—and myself, of course, in all my hungover glory: nude, nauseated, and reeking like an Elizabethan armpit.

I pull a pillow over my head, wishing I had the willpower to smother myself.

The sun may be bright and shiny, but everything else sucks just as much as it did last night. Mom still has ALS, and I still have to tell her that (A) I'm not moving home, and (B) trying to find her daughter is an epically stupid idea. Once I break the bad news, we'll no doubt get into a big, ugly brawl, with both of us saying things we shouldn't, because neither of us has any impulse control. She'll cry, and I'll cry, and then I'll hate myself for (A) making a dying woman feel like shit, and (B) not being smart enough to convince her that *she's* the one who's being unreasonable. It doesn't really matter if I'm right or wrong, however, because I'm screwed either way: from here on in, her illness is the ultimate trump card.

Jesus. We haven't even had the damn fight yet, and I already hate myself.

My bladder feels like a turgid water balloon, so I lift the pillow off my head and force myself to get up, pulling on my boxers and grabbing my phone from the dresser on my way out the door. I stumble to the bathroom, past Mom's room. Her door is open, but her bed is rumpled and empty; she's apparently already downstairs, girding herself for combat. I hope to God she doesn't drink too much coffee before I join her. She's hypersensitive to caffeine, and the last thing I need when we talk is for her to be hanging from the goddamn ceiling fan and chattering like a magpie.

After I pee, I turn on the shower and let the water get hot while I check my phone messages. A few guys on Grindr and

Scruff have hit on me since yesterday; I scroll through their messages with a jaded eye. One guy tells me that I look like an "angle"—I assume he means "angel," but maybe he's into trigonometry—and that he wants me to shoot a big "lode" (sic) down his throat; another guy says that he really likes my face pic, but could I please send him a close-up of my cock; another guy thinks it's cool that I'm "into art," but also wants to know if I happen to like giving rim jobs. I delete all three messages—not because I've got anything against vulgar language, oral sex, or displaying my genitalia to complete strangers, but because the first guy is clearly a halfwit, the second guy's profile says that his favorite things are "powerlifting, reality TV, and country line dancing," and the third guy is old enough to have slept with Walt Whitman. A fourth guy, however, looks more promising. He's thirty-one and calls himself "Ajax," and he's got curly blond hair, blue eyes, and a sweet, self conscious smile. He says he loves to read, and he prefers meeting for coffee or drinks before getting in the sack, and he's completely fine with not having sex if "the vibe" isn't right. His profile isn't particularly original, but at least he can spell, and it appears he's right here in Oakland.

I don't respond, but I save his message, just in case I need a distraction later today.

After a long, mindless shower, I wipe the steam from the mirror and look at myself. My eyes are bloodshot and puffy, and my skin is three shades whiter than usual, but I don't feel as bad as I look, thankfully. I open the medicine cabinet and go hunting for the razor I left here the last time I came home. My beard is light and I don't actually need to shave this morning, but I'm stalling for time before heading downstairs. There are a couple of prescription pill bottles in the cabinet, next to the ibuprofen and the dental floss. I assume they're for Mom's ALS, and I pop the lid off one and stare with morbid fascination at the innocuous-looking white pills—Gablofen is the drug name on the label—wondering what the hell they do, and if they'll actually help her. Confronted by this evidence of the new reality in the York household, I put the bottle back where I found it, feeling sick to my stomach.

If Mom was diagnosed in early May, like she said, then she's been dealing with this shit for three months, all on her own. I should probably be pissed that she didn't tell me until now, but to be honest, I doubt I'd tell anybody, either, if it were me. What's more personal than a walk to the gallows? I'm kind of grateful, actually, that she didn't drop the ALS bomb on my head sooner, and let me remain in ignorant bliss for most of the summer. As badly as I handled the news last night, I would've been ten times worse if she'd told me before she was ready to talk. I'm pretty sure one of the main reasons she held off saying anything was that she needed time to figure out the best way to cope with her drama queen of a son.

My throat closes as I think about all the long weeks she sat on this information, working everything through. She must've been lonely and sad beyond belief—not to mention scared shit-less—but I didn't have a clue what she was going through, even though I talked to her at least a dozen times during her solo trip through hell. I lather my cheeks and neck, and avoid looking in my eyes, for fear of the judgment I might find there.

When I walk in the kitchen, Mom is sitting at the island, cradling a cup of coffee in one hand and scribbling in a note-book with the other. She looks up and smiles.

"Morning," she says. "You look a little rough."

"Morning," I mutter, heading for the coffee pot. Mom has already set out my favorite coffee mug—a hideous ceramic thing with a monkey's head painted on it, and a handle that's supposed to be the monkey's arm, curved up to scratch its ear. It's as ugly as an anal wart, but it can hold almost half the damn pot.

"What are you writing?" I ask, looking over my shoulder. "I know it's not a poem."

She jots down something else before answering me. "What makes you say that?"

"Because you didn't close your notebook the second I came in the room." I sit kitty-corner from her at the island. "J.D. once told me he accidentally walked in on you when you were working on a poem, and you completely spazzed, like he'd caught you paging through a dildo catalog."

She snorts. "J.D. would never say something so infantile: That appalling simile is pure you. And for the record, I didn't 'spaz' at J.D. He just startled me, that's all."

I ignore this. "So you are writing a poem?"

"As a matter of fact, no. I've started keeping a journal. It helps my brain to focus in the mornings, before I start working."

"Maybe I should try that." I'm relieved that she's not immediately diving into the hard stuff we need to talk about. "I just doodle on a sketch pad until I'm awake enough to start painting."

"Same thing, really." She studies my face. "Speaking of painting, what are you working on these days? You haven't posted anything on your website in a while."

I shrug. "Nothing, really."

She raises an eyebrow, knowing me too well to believe me. I'm always working on something.

I sigh. "Just some kid I saw on Thayer Street last week, riding his skateboard."

"And?"

"And what?"

"Don't be difficult, Noah. Why did you paint him?"

I know I should be glad that she's genuinely curious about my work—a lot of successful artists couldn't care less about what their kids are up to, even when those kids are fellow artists—but it's hard for me to talk to her about it. Half the time I don't have a clue why I paint what I do, and every time I try to put it in words I sound like a moron.

"The way he moved, I guess," I say, watching the steam rise from my coffee mug. "He was on the sidewalk, weaving around pedestrians like a lunatic, and he was about fifteen, with bright red pants and no shirt. He looked like an ordinary kid, mostly, except ten times more graceful than any kid that age has a right to be. I took a video with my phone so I could paint him when I got home." I look up at her and grimace. "But what I've done so far is crap. I've got most of the details right, but the grace is missing, and it's pissing me off. I left it in Providence because I needed a break from the goddamn thing."

"You'll figure it out eventually. You always do." She gives me a wry grin. "I'd tell you to be patient, but you'd just mock me."

I return the grin. "Damn right." Over the years, I've rescued several of Mom's manuscripts from literally going up our chimney in smoke: she can be breathtakingly childish when she feels her writing isn't going well. "Thank God I didn't inherit your penchant for setting fire to my own creations," I tell her. "I can't afford the canvas."

"I haven't burned a single word all summer long," she says, putting her pen down and stretching her back. "Having my expiration date bumped up a bit must've mellowed me."

Our smiles linger a moment, then fade in tandem, harnessed to the big goddamn elephant she just turned loose in the room. I sip at my coffee and sigh, knowing that if I don't grow a pair of balls now, I probably never will. "Uh, Mom, look—"

"Nope," she interrupts. "Let's not have that conversation yet, okay? I realized last night after we spoke that it was unfair to ask you to reach a decision so quickly."

I'm not surprised that she predicted what I was going to say, but I can't believe she's actually shying away from a confrontation. The temporary truce she's offering is tempting, but I shake my head, wanting to get this over with. "I don't think more time will change anything."

"Maybe not," she says quietly, "but hear me out." She waits for my reluctant nod. "I'm aware that you were planning to go back to Providence in a few days, but since you don't start teaching until mid-September, how about just staying here until after Labor Day? That way—regardless of what you decide to do in the long term—we'll have more time together, and at least we can start looking into finding Carolyn. How does that sound?"

I scowl. "Labor Day is more than two weeks away. Remember what happened the last time we spent that much time together?"

Right after finishing college—I eventually returned to RISD to complete my degree, after a three-year hiatus—I'd been between apartments in Providence, so I came home for the month of July. Before our mother-and-child reunion was even half over, the house was a war zone, complete with daily explosions, flanking maneuvers, and terrifying forays into enemy-held territory. She hated everything I was doing, or not doing, with my life. She raged at me for not considering grad school and turning down a couple of apprenticeships that came my way; she said it was like I was deliberately sabotaging my career. I told her I wanted to create art at my own pace, on my own terms, and I accused her of being a hypocrite, since she'd always gone her own way as a writer and never done a degree or taken a job she didn't love. She shouted that all I was doing was avoiding reality, screwing my brains out, and sulking like a child because my paintings weren't selling and things weren't going exactly the way I thought they should; I shouted back that she'd been lucky enough to get married to somebody a hell of a lot more stable than she was, both financially and psychologically, and had supported her whenever she got a wild hair up her butt. She acidly reminded me that I'd had someone like that, too, but I'd opted for a life alone, to which I reminded her, with equal acidity, that she was obviously opting for a life alone, too, since even back then she was playing with Walter's heart like it was a goddamn yo-yo. She called me a smart-mouthed little prick; I called her a stage mother on steroids, etc. etc.

Lather, rinse, repeat; day after day, for a month. It was a wonder either of us survived.

"That was years ago," she says now. "We're different people than we were then, and the circumstances have completely changed." She gets up and moves to the refrigerator. "How about an omelette for breakfast?"

"Who says we're different people?" I protest, squirming as the invisible noose tightens around my neck. "I mean, granted, you've been way cooler so far this time than you've ever been, but what happens when your old buddy Satan decides it's time to repossess you?"

Yeah, okay, I'm trying to yank her chain, which isn't very mature, but it's necessary.

"Nice try," she says, smiling. "I'm sorry if you were spoiling for a fight this morning, but I'm not in the mood. Just consider staying until Labor Day, okay? I don't believe that's a lot to ask for."

I gawk at her as she calmly raids the refrigerator for eggs and cheese, humming to herself as if she hasn't got a goddamn care in the universe. How am I supposed to win an argument she isn't interested in having?

"Jesus Christ," I mumble. "I liked you better when you were a psychopath."

After breakfast, Mom says she needs a nap, so I pour myself another vat of coffee, snag a dog-eared copy of Patrick O'Brian's *Post Captain* from one of the bookshelves in the entryway, and head out to the front porch. As much as I love O'Brian's writing, I doubt I'll be able to concentrate enough to read this morning, but it's worth a shot.

I sit down on the top step again, in the same spot where I drank myself blind last night, and look listlessly around the neighborhood. The breeze that blew through my bedroom window earlier is gone, and the sun is starting to bake the earth. I roll up the sleeves of my T-shirt and watch two gray squirrels skitter up and down the trunk of a maple tree across the street. Further down the block is the house where J.D.'s family lived when we first met; it's changed ownership half a dozen times since then, and the newest residents have painted it bright blue.

Sadie, our next-door neighbor's cocker spaniel, suddenly darts across our front lawn, hellbent on catching a chipmunk. It escapes by darting down a hole by the sidewalk, and Sadie claws at the earth, sending clumps of grass and dirt flying. I clap my hands to stop her from destroying Mom's lawn and she jumps, startled, then trots up our front steps and apologizes, bathing my feet with drool. I reach down to scratch her ears.

"Sadie! You get back over here right now!"

A bald guy with a potbelly and skinny legs is standing on the boundary between his property and ours. He's dressed in sandals, gray socks, green shorts, and a pink polo shirt, and he looks upset.

"Don't pet her," he orders. "You'll just encourage her to keep running away."

He clearly isn't concerned with making a good first impression, and I eye him warily. His tone is abrasive, and I'm half tempted to tell him I'd run away, too, if I had an owner who wore pastels. He calls Sadie again, snapping his fingers, and I give her a farewell pat.

"You better scoot on home, girl," I tell her. She returns to him reluctantly, head lowered like a penitent in a confession booth.

"She keeps getting off her chain," the guy says, bending down and sternly shaking the rough of Sadie's neck. His eyes meet mine briefly, and then skitter away. "I think somebody is sneaking in our yard and letting her go on purpose, because there's nothing wrong with the chain."

I blink, wondering if he's joking. If he's not, Mom's new neighbor is a paranoid schizophrenic.

"I see," I say neutrally. "That's too bad."

"I'll catch them sooner or later, I promise you that." He picks up Sadie and stalks off without another word.

"Nice to meet you," I mutter.

He stops and glares over his shoulder. "What?"

I'm impressed he heard me say anything at all; he must have the ears of a bat. I smile sweetly at him. "I was just welcoming you to the neighborhood."

"Oh." He gives me a suspicious look, then nods curtly and turns away again. Before he gets home, the screen door of their house bangs opens and a woman—his wife, presumably—steps outside. She's short and anorexic-looking, and dressed in a pink and white paisley dress. Mom wasn't kidding about her wearing too much makeup; even from fifty feet away her garish red lipstick and purple eyeshadow is alarming.

"Shame on you, Sadie," she scolds as her husband draws near. "You need to stop running away, you naughty thing."

"She's only running away because some delinquent is setting her free." He lowers his voice, but just barely. "The neighbors are encouraging her, too, by pampering her every time she gets loose. I wish they'd stop doing that."

Oh, good. He's crazy, *and* he's passive-aggressive.

I stare across the lawn, amazed by his rudeness, but he refuses to make eye contact. His wife at least has the decency to glance at me and look a little embarrassed, so I give her a friendly wave.

"Hi, I'm Noah," I call out. "I have a dog-petting fetish. Sorry about that."

She frowns. "I have neuritis in my knee," she calls back. "I can't chase after Sadie, so poor Freddie has to do all the dirty work. Please don't pet her anymore."

I'm going to go out on a limb here and say that I don't believe Freddie and his wife are angling to be my new best friends.

"Sure," I say. "I'll just pretend she's invisible the next time she comes over." The sour look on Freddie's face tickles me. "And if that doesn't work, I'll slip into my hyena costume and scare the bejesus out of her."

"Noah." Mom is standing at our screen door, likely having heard everything through her bedroom window while she was trying to nap. "Don't."

Freddie is finally looking directly at me. "I don't appreciate your sarcasm, buddy."

"Yeah, well, I don't appreciate your wardrobe, Freddie, so I guess we're even."

"Noah!" Mom snaps, coming out on the porch and resting a warning finger on my shoulder. "Please excuse my son's incredibly bad manners," she calls out. "I'm Virginia York, and I'm sorry we haven't met until now. Noah and I will do our best to discourage Sadie from coming to visit us, if it's causing problems for you."

Freddie is still too busy glaring at me to respond, but the woman takes a couple of steps toward us. "I'm Faith Overton, and this is my husband, Freddie. We'd appreciate that very much, thank you." Freddie looks like he wants to add something less conciliatory but Faith takes him by the elbow and leads him back in their house before he can manage it.

"Wow," I say, glancing up at Mom. "What a cute couple. How about we invite them for dinner?"

She sighs. "I don't suppose it's ever occurred to you that picking fights with everyone who annoys you isn't always the wisest course?"

I laugh. "You're one to talk. How are you and Don Levinson doing these days?"

She sniffs and looks away. "We're getting along fine lately, thank you."

"Uh huh. That's not what Walter told me at Christmas."

Don Levinson is a pompous jackass on the faculty with Mom at Cassidy College. He has a hair-trigger temper and no sense of humor, and Walter told me that Mom loves to provoke him during faculty meetings.

"Walter exaggerates," she says.

"So you didn't actually call Levinson 'a priggish little pedant' in front of your whole department?"

The corners of her mouth twitch and she quickly turns away to hide her face. "Stop antagonizing the neighbors."

After lunch, I toy with the idea of doing some work while Mom is upstairs writing, but I'm too restless and unsettled to paint right now. I sign on Grindr again to see if "Ajax" wants to meet up. He does, it turns out, but he says he's cooking something and can't leave his house for a while, so he invites me over for a drink. I tell him I can't handle alcohol today— I'm still in rough shape—and he offers to make me a root beer float.

Deal, I text back, getting his address. **Seeya in a few.**

He lives on the other side of town and I don't feel like walking in the heat, so I knock on Mom's bedroom door and ask to borrow her car. She doesn't answer for a minute—I can't see through the door, of course, but I'd bet my left nut that she's sitting at her desk, chewing on her pencil and scowling at this interruption—then she asks where I'm going. I'm glad she can't see me either when I tell her I want to take a drive in the country, to look for landscapes I'd like to paint.

"Fine," she says. "The keys are on the table by the back door."

I say I'll be home in a couple of hours but she doesn't answer; I know from long experience that she's already forgotten I'm there. I brush my teeth and hurry downstairs, slipping my feet into a pair of shabby flip-flops before scooting out the back door. I wince as I climb into her car and touch the scalding steering wheel. She bought this ancient, white Toyota Corolla used a few years back, but I'm pretty sure the only time she ever drives it for anything besides grocery shopping or work is when she comes to visit me in Providence.

I feel kind of bad about lying. She wouldn't care that I have a date, but she'd lose her shit if she knew I was going to a stranger's house for a first encounter. I ordinarily agree that it's wiser to meet people in the no-man's-land of public space—in case they turn out to be serial killers or something—but the emotional turmoil in my head at the moment makes for truly crappy company, and the only thing that stands a chance at diverting me is sex, or at least the possibility of it. If I don't like the guy I won't fuck him, of course, but at this point—provided he speaks in complete sentences and makes a decent root beer float—I'm predisposed to give him the benefit of the doubt.

Anyway, Mom doesn't need to know everything about my love life, and I can always salve my conscience later by taking that drive in the country I said I was going to, once I leave Ajax's place.

His house is small and blue, with a big patio on one side, enclosed by a trellis swarming with honeysuckle vines. He opens his front door as soon as I ring the bell. He's an inch or so taller than me, and he's dressed in cut off chinos and a plain white T-shirt. I'm relieved to see that he looks just like his picture on Grindr, except that his curly blond hair is a little longer. He's clean-shaven, clear-skinned, and boyishly handsome—he even has dimples—and his body is lean and attractive.

"Hey, Noah, thanks for coming," he says. "Come on in."

Neither of us proffers a hand to shake or a cheek to kiss, which I'm glad about since we haven't yet clarified if this is just a meet-and-greet, or if we're going to get naked. Some guys reach for your zipper the instant you step in the goddamn door, and that always turns me off; I require at least a couple minutes of civil interaction, even if I'm horny, like now. I kick off my flip-flops and he leads me through a narrow, cluttered living room with a leather couch, two beanbag chairs, and a large screen television, not currently turned on; we pass by the open door of a small bedroom with an unmade bed, and then we're in the kitchen. He's got air-conditioning but it's still pretty hot in here from the oven: a good sign, as he apparently wasn't lying when he told me he was cooking something.

He smiles nervously, making me wonder how often he does this sort of thing. "Is vanilla ice cream okay in your float?"

"Sure. Can I help?"

"Nah, it's okay. It'll just take a minute."

The kitchen is cramped but clean, with a single window by the table and a fridge that looks like a prop from a 1950s TV show, with a curved top and a cobalt-blue exterior. I lean against the counter and ask him what he's cooking, and he tells me he's roasting tomatoes from his garden. He digs ice cream out of the freezer and root beer from the fridge; I watch him scoop the ice cream into two mugs, fussing to make sure he gives us each the same amount. While he pours the root beer over the ice cream, I stare with frank appreciation at his slender waist, firm ass, and bare legs and feet. I figure it's not rude to ogle him so openly, since he's also checking me out, as the foam settles in the mugs. His eyes linger on my face for a second, then drift over the rest of me, too, before coming back up to meet my gaze.

"Hi," I say. "Nice to meet you."

He laughs, blushing, and hands me one of the floats, his fingers brushing mine. He's standing pretty close. "You're really cute," he says shyly. "Can I kiss you?"

I should probably slow things down a little, but he seems sweet, normal, and clean, and I can't seem to think of a good reason to keep my distance. "Sure."

He leans forward and our lips meet; after a minute our tongues get acquainted, too. His free hand—the other one is still holding his own float—attaches itself to my right hip, then sneaks around my back and under my shirt. His fingers are cool on my spine, and my breath catches in my throat.

"Is this okay?" he asks.

"Depends," I say. "Is your name really Ajax?"

He laughs again. "No. It's Jessie."

"Good." I hook the index finger of my free hand on the tack button of his cut offs, under the hemline of his T-shirt; I can feel his navel with my knuckle. "Ajax is a really dorky name, but I like Jessie just fine," I tell him.

He kisses my Adam's apple. "I didn't want my real name on Grindr, but I couldn't think of a good fake one."

It's hard to concentrate with his lips on my throat. "How'd you come up with Ajax?"

"I was watching a dumb movie about the Trojan War." He sets his glass down on the counter and pulls me up against him with both hands; our erections collide enthusiastically through the fabric of our shorts. "Is Noah your real name?" he asks.

"Nope." I set my glass down, too. "It's Ulysses."

So much for conversation.

I park Mom's car on the shoulder of a soporific county highway, about ten miles outside of Oakland. J.D. and I used to come here a lot whenever we wanted some time alone, because this part of the road overlooks a small, isolated valley, with a lot of pine trees and a creek running through it, and it's peaceful and pretty. We'd sit on the hood of the car and chat for hours, sometimes about nothing at all, sometimes about weighty adult stuff, like what we were going to do with our lives, and where we wanted to end up when we got old and crusty. Back then, we were sure we'd be together forever. We were in love, and best friends, and we couldn't imagine the world without each other in it.

Jesus, we were so full of shit.

I get out of the car—grimacing as the mid afternoon heat engulfs me—and wander off the shoulder of the sticky asphalt highway into the welcoming shade of the nearest pine tree. I showered at Jessie's place after we were done fooling around, but my skin is already slick with sweat.

Jessie was fun, but I don't want to hook up with him again. He was a decent lover, and kind, but we don't really have anything in common but a fondness for dick, and sex is never as much fun the second time around, if that's all you've got going for you. I'm happy he lives in Oakland and was on the prowl today, too—God knows I needed the diversion—and I'm also pleased that STIs aren't likely to be an issue: I'm on PrEP, and we used condoms, like good boys. He asked for my phone number as I was leaving, but I told him I wouldn't be in town for long, and quickly said goodbye. I hope he takes the hint and doesn't stalk me on Grindr; I'd rather not hurt his feelings by blocking him.

Mom thinks I have a problem with intimacy because I haven't had a close relationship with anybody since J.D., but I disagree. Granted, I seldom make it to a second date with anybody, but I'm more than willing to get serious with the first guy who happens to look, act, smell, talk, sing, smile, laugh, think, kiss, and fuck like J.D.

Yeah, I know. Pathetic.

The only reason we broke up is because I'm an asshole. We never stopped loving each other, or enjoying each other's company. After our first year together—the year from hell, when Mom was in the psych ward and J.D.'s parents disowned him— our second year was easy, probably the best of my life, because Mom was back to normal, and J.D. was living with us. I took classes at Cassidy and waited for him to finish high school, and our plan was to move to a big city somewhere and attend the same university. He needed a great music school, though, and I needed a great art school, and none of the places who wanted him also wanted me, or vice versa. We had to give up on the idea of living in the same town, so I ended up at RISD in Providence, and he went to the New England Conservatory, in Boston. At first we made things work, getting together whenever we could, but after another year went by I got my head firmly lodged up my ass, depriving my brain of oxygen. Feel free to laugh uproariously, but I was convinced I could be the next Picasso, if I only had more time to paint. I decided I could no longer pursue both my art and a long-distance relationship, so I told J.D. I needed some time off. That goddamn conversation still haunts me.

He came to Providence to see me for the first time in over a month, having no idea that I'd made up my mind to break up with him that weekend. (I knew I had to do it in person, not by phone, or worse, in a Dear John letter.) But when I opened my apartment door to him that night, his goofy, crooked smile lit up the whole room like a Roman candle, per usual, wreaking havoc with my intention to have " the talk " right away. I put things off until the following morning, when he was getting ready to leave. I took his hand and sat on the couch; I choked out my pathetic prepared speech and I started to cry as the trust and sweetness in his eyes gave way to baffled pain and anger.

"Help me understand," he said, barely able to speak through his own tears. "We haven't even seen each other for the past five weeks. Just how am I 'getting in the way' of your painting?"

I tried to explain, but everything I said came out garbled, like I was babbling in Klingon. When I reminded him that we spoke on the phone daily, sometimes for hours, I made it sound like he'd been holding me hostage on the other end of the line every time we talked; when I told him I loved him more than anything in the world but found myself with no time to paint, it came across like I thought of him as an annoying distraction. I knew I was making an unholy mess with every word I uttered, and I tried again to clarify what I really meant, but by then he'd had more than enough of my shit.

"You think I'm not *distracted* just as much by you, Noah?" He suddenly yanked his fingers from my grip. "It's called love, dumbass! We're *supposed* to be distracted."

"Please don't be mad," I pleaded. "I just don't know what else to do. Whole weeks go by when I can't paint at all because I miss you so much. How am I supposed to work when I'm thinking about you every damn second?"

He threw up his hands. "So your genius solution is to just boot me out of your life?"

"No! Of course I'm not booting you out of my life. But everybody keeps telling me I can be a great painter if I'll just get serious, and I don't know how to do that while we're still together."

All these years later, I still want to knock my teeth out with a rock when I remember my self-centeredness, but what stings even more is the memory of J.D.'s kindness. He was beside himself that day, yet he didn't poke fun at my grotesquely overinflated assessment of my talent, no matter how much I was begging for it. Even when he was devastated he wouldn't let himself stoop to cruelty.

"Who says you can't be a great artist and still have love in your life?" he asked. "Can't we at least try to figure something out?"

I didn't have an answer for him, of course, especially considering that almost every dead painter I worshipped—Dalí, Klee, Manet, et al.—had been successfully partnered in life, but I honestly didn't think I could manage such a feat. It's a complete mystery where I'd picked up the fatuous notion that going it alone was necessary to make anything of myself, but I couldn't shake it.

Anyway, since the only "reason" I had for breaking up was half-assed, at best, of course I dug in my heels harder than ever, no doubt because a significant part of me was terrified I might be wrong. I hadn't been making sense from the start of the conversation, and the longer we talked the more frustrated and hurt J.D. became. Our argument grew heated, and as the minutes passed I could feel our relationship dissolving like sugar in water, but I was too stubborn to do anything about it. Somewhere along the way he stopped making sense, too, and after a lot of crying and yelling between us, he finally stormed out of the apartment, telling me to go fuck myself before slamming the door behind him.

Pride and stupidity overrode my common sense for too long, so by the time I got down to the street, chasing after him, he was gone. I cried for most of the next month, but my inner idiot-child was too busy wallowing in self-inflicted misery to pick up the damn phone and attempt to repair the damage I'd done, at least a little bit. I told myself we'd patch things up eventually, and the break would be good for both of us; I reassured myself that hard choices like this were part of having a successful career in the arts. He didn't call, either—who could blame him?—so I told myself he obviously didn't want to talk to me.

I was such a fool.

It was another couple of years before I finally admitted to myself that I'd made a colossal mistake, and by then it was too late. He'd fallen in love with someone else, and they ended up getting married.

Jesus. If there's an award for douchebaggery, no one deserves it more than me.

I kick at some pine needles at the base of the tree, frightening a rabbit from a nearby thicket. A hot breeze ruffles the tree branches above my head, and the play of shadow and sunlight on the ground around me is mesmerizing, making me wish I'd brought my sketchbook along. I'd like to try to capture the chaotic, rippling beauty of this bucolic quarrel between darkness and light. Such squabbles are always prettier in nature than they are in the human soul.

Cell phone reception out here is crappy, so when my phone buzzes in my pocket it startles me.

"I just finished writing for the day," Mom says, forgetting, as usual, to say hello. "Are you coming home for happy hour, or shall I start without you?"

"Are you trying to kill me?" I ask. "My head still hurts from last night."

"Then don't drink so much tonight. Where are you?"

I tell her, then ask if she wants me to pick up anything on my way home.

"Only if you'd like something besides prosecco with our appetizers. I've got some decent prosciutto, and an amazing cantaloupe." She pauses. "I just finished speaking with your aunt Cindy. It looks as if she and Janelle are flying in for a visit tomorrow."

I almost drop the phone. Neither Mom nor I have seen her younger sister, Cindy, since I was nine years old. They never had a big falling out or anything, but they haven't been close since they were children, and now they only talk on the phone once a year or so, saying things they don't mean, like "We should get together soon, it's been much too long." Janelle is Cindy's adopted daughter, and Cindy didn't have her yet when I was nine, so she's a total stranger. Mom and I have seen pictures of her, but all we really know about her is that she's Korean by birth, and somewhere in her mid twenties.

"Wow," I say. "Did hell freeze over or something?"

"Just about. I decided I should tell Cindy about the ALS, and it shocked her enough that she offered to come see me. I said there was no hurry, and you were here visiting, but she still insisted on flying out immediately. She's acting like I'm on my deathbed."

I ask if she's sure that having them come is a good idea, and she says probably not, but she couldn't say no after all these years, especially since Cindy was crying the whole time they were talking.

"Oh, good," I say drily. "Another bawl-baby in the family. That's all we need."

She snorts and says she's opening the prosecco; I tell her I'm on my way, and hang up.

I guess it might be cool to see Aunt Cindy again. The last time I spoke with her was when Mom was going loony tunes; she was the one who told me about Mom's sexual abuse at the hands of their father. She offered to fly out to help me deal with everything, but I turned her down, mainly because there was really nothing she could do. She was nice to talk to, though, and I remember thinking that maybe I should get to know her better. Meeting Janelle might be interesting, too—she's my only cousin, because Dad didn't have siblings and Mom only had Cindy—but with my luck she'll probably turn out to be a devil worshipper.

I look around at the valley for a minute, then stare down at my feet in their raggedy-ass flip-flops. I really need to call J.D. soon and tell him about Mom, but I can't handle that conversation yet. Knowing I might catch him when he's with his doofus of a husband makes me want to puke.

CHAPTER 3

After I got back yesterday from my postcoital drive in the country, Mom and I had a subdued dinner, then watched TV for a while, flipping channels without really noticing what was on. We spoke a bit about Cindy and Janelle's impending visit—they're staying for a week—but we had the attention span of two not-very-bright squirrels; I think our porch talk the previous night took more out of us than we'd realized. Mom went to bed around nine, and I only made it another hour or so before calling it quits. Once I was in bed, though, I couldn't sleep, so I googled ALS on my phone.

Yeah, I know. I'm a moron.

I was aware that ALS is a death sentence, but even though Mom warned me things were going to get ugly, I didn't realize what a gross understatement that was. Even an ax murderer on death row in Texas has the comfort of knowing his final moments will be quick, but with ALS there's no such nod to mercy—just a long, insanely cruel death by paralysis and suffocation. My brilliant, fierce, and beautiful mother will almost certainly go out gasping for air—blue in the face, literally—

since assisted suicide (yes, I researched *that* fun topic, too) is illegal in Live-Free-Or-Die New Hampshire. What's the point of living *free*, for Christ's sake, if your life is a living hell, and you have no legal option for ending it?

If I know Mom, she's already got a contingency plan for moving someplace she can die without unnecessarily suffering, like Vermont or Maine. She has a high pain tolerance—I once saw her catch two fingers in a car door, and she didn't even cry out—but the slow asphyxiation she'll experience when her lungs begin to collapse will no doubt generate a whole different level of misery. After she gets to the point where she no longer wants to stick around, she won't put up with someone else telling her she has to.

Jesus. I'm already obsessing about this shit when she's still more or less okay: What the hell am I going to do when she starts to unravel?

Anyway, in spite of my abysmally stupid choice for bedtime reading, I somehow managed to pass out around midnight, and when I got up this morning—not hungover like yesterday, praise be, but still drained and headachy—Mom and I cleaned the guest rooms for Cindy and Janelle. They're flying into Boston today, then driving here in a rental car. It's early afternoon now, and we're expecting them around suppertime.

"So, will you take a break from writing while they're here?" I ask Mom.

We're washing the lunch dishes, and she raises an eyebrow, as if she's never heard such a stupid question.

"Why would I do that?"

"Oh, gosh, I don't know, let's think." I'm washing and she's drying, since she's the world's crappiest dish washer; if I didn't come home every now and then, there'd be crusty globs of food on every pan, plate, and piece of cutlery in the house. "Maybe because our guests might not understand why you're disappearing every day for three or four hours."

"They're big girls. They don't need to be entertained." She takes a skillet from me and inspects it for cleanliness, which is hilarious. "Besides, I already told Cindy that I'd have to write while they're here."

It's oddly reassuring that she can still be a selfish dick, at least when it comes to her poetry. "Fine by me," I say, "but don't expect me to babysit them while you're cozied up in your room."

"I don't expect anything of the sort, so long as you're painting, or drawing," she says. "But if all you're doing is taking long drives in the country—like yesterday—you may as well ask them to join you." She pauses. "That is, unless you intend to go someplace that might prove awkward for everyone involved."

Shit. She somehow knows I lied to her yesterday.

"I don't know what you're talking about," I mumble. "I just went up to that valley north of town, where J.D. and I used to go all the time."

"I see." Another pause. "And you were there all afternoon?"

I blush like a kid caught playing pocket pool. "Most of it."

"Noah."

"Okay, fine." I wash the last plate and hand it to her, then pull the plug on the dish water. "I went on a date. It was no big deal."

"So why didn't you just say that?"

I shrug. "I'm thirty-seven, remember? I'm too old to tell my mommy everything."

"You're also too old to be lying about something you claim was no big deal."

She's got a point, but if I admit that I'll never hear the end of it. "For the record, I didn't lie to you," I say feebly. "I just didn't mention the non-driving part of my afternoon. There's a difference."

She makes a face; she detests equivocation. "Can you tell me his name, at least?"

"Friedrich von Uberpenis," I say. "Why does it matter? I won't be seeing him again."

"That's exactly what bothers me. I don't understand why you waste your time on men you don't even want to admit you're seeing. It clearly isn't making you happy."

My temper flares; I hate it when she plays psychiatrist. "I need the exercise," I snap, "and it burns more calories than beating off."

"Now you're just being juvenile." She hangs up the dish towel to dry. "I wish I could find a way to talk to you about this, without making you mad."

The sadness in her voice silences me and I mutter an apology. A strand of white hair has escaped from her ponytail, and almost involuntarily I reach out to tuck it behind her ear. "It's just sex, Mom. I'll let you know if it ever turns into anything more."

We look at each other for a minute without speaking; I don't know what else to say, and she probably doesn't either.

"Does J.D. know about my ALS yet?" she asks quietly.

It doesn't take a genius to figure out why she's thinking about J.D. right now, but I refrain from giving her crap about it. "Not yet."

"Better tell him soon, okay? He's dear to me, and I want him to know." She turns to the coffee pot and pours herself a fresh mug. "I'd call him myself, but I think you should be the one to tell him."

When I was a kid, I was deeply in love with the sound of my own voice. I'd get up on my high horse and ride the pretentious nag for hours on end, ranting about anything and everything that pissed me off. Sometimes I had good reason to be pissed, but more often than not I was just being an oversensitive, intolerant prick, in the way that only a cocksure, naive, hyperverbal teenager can be. Mind you, I'm still capable of a damn fine sanctimonious rant now and again, but I fizzle out fast; it's hard to hold on to so much passion and certainty when I know for a fact that I'm just as full of shit as everybody else.

I often wonder what my seventeen-year-old self would think of me these days. I'm pretty sure I'd be a disappointment to him, mainly because he had such high hopes for me. He'd probably tell me that I've become a cesspool of moral relativism, and a coward when it comes to love, and a lazy bastard for not painting every damn minute of every damn day, like he used to do.

And if I saw him, I'd probably throttle the little turd before he could get a word out.

"They're here," Mom says, looking out the back screen door.

I told her I'd cook tonight while she plays hostess, so I'm currently at the stove, simmering a batch of Cuban black bean soup. Mom has been buzzing around the kitchen for the last half hour like a fly on meth, setting the table in the breakfast nook and bullying me about all the ways she thinks I'm fucking up the soup. I now join her at the door as a blue Chrysler parks behind Mom's car in the driveway.

Mom covers her mouth in a curiously girlish gesture as the passenger door of the Chrysler opens and Cindy climbs out, smiling and waving. "Oh, my God," Mom whispers. "My baby sister got old."

Twenty-eight years is a long time to go without seeing someone, and those years haven't been kind to Cindy. The last time Mom and I saw her, she was in her thirties—a thin, energetic, pretty woman with auburn hair, who looked younger than Mom. But now, anyone would think she was the older sister, by far. She's gained at least fifty pounds, her short hair is solid white, and she's hobbling toward us like a senior citizen, with a curved spine and two bad knees.

The driver's door pops open, and Janelle hops out, a complete contrast to her adoptive mother. Her birthparents were Korean, and in the last picture I saw of her she had long, coal-black hair that reached almost to her waist, but now it's dyed bright red and trimmed to shoulder-length. She's wiry and small, with a mischievous smile and huge eyes. She hurries to catch up with Cindy, then looks a bit impatient when she has to slow down again to match Cindy's pace.

"Wow, until right this second I didn't actually believe this family reunion was going to happen," I say. "Maybe we should wear name tags."

Mom lowers her hand and smiles, but her eyes are wet. She opens the screen door and runs, barefoot, toward her sister and niece. I put on my flip-flops and follow more slowly, not sure of the protocol here.

Having an extended family is an alien concept to me. Not only did Dad have no siblings, but his parents died before I was born. Mom's dad was alive when I was little, but I barely remember the guy since Mom didn't want much to do with him. (Until I learned what a sick fuck he was, I didn't understand, but I was so young when he died that it didn't take long to forget about him.) Anyway, seeing these two strangers in our drive-way, and knowing they're my aunt and cousin, is oddly moving, as is seeing Mom hurrying toward them.

Mom and Cindy are locked in a bear hug by the time I get close, and they're both crying. "Life is so unfair," Cindy says. "You haven't aged a day."

"You look pretty damn good yourself," Mom says, lying.

Janelle and I approach each other a little warily, but when I smile and say hello she steps up and gives me a hug. I'm no giant myself, but her head only comes up to my chin.

"Hey, cuz," she says, as we step back. "You're a lot less scary-looking in person than on Facebook. Your profile pic-ture is super serious."

Mom snorts. "Noah hates cameras," she says, finally releasing Cindy to hug Janelle. "Every time somebody tells him to smile, his mouth droops at the corners like he's had a stroke."

"Hi, Aunt Virginia," Janelle says. "I love your poems so much. Especially the one about Noah."

Mom thanks her, smirking at me over her shoulder: She knows full well what a sore spot that goddamn poem is. I scowl at her, but before I can say anything Cindy grabs me and plants a wet kiss on my cheek, squeezing me hard enough to crack my spine. She smells like peppermint gum.

"Hi, Noah," she says. "I can't believe how much you look like your mom. You sure turned out good."

I tell her hi and pull back to study her. Up close, I can still see the woman she was when I was nine, even with all the white hair and added weight. Her blue eyes are just the same, as is the way she bites her lip; the sweetness of her smile hasn't changed, either, nor has she lost her odd habit of cocking her head a little to the left—a quirk I'd completely forgotten about.

Something cold and wet brushes my shins and I look down in surprise; it's Sadie, apparently free from her chain again.

"Oh, look at the cute little doggie," Cindy says, bending down to pet her. "Is he yours?"

"Nope, that's Sadie. She belongs to our neighbors."

Right on cue, the Overtons' back door flies open and Freddie emerges, wearing a canary-yellow polo shirt and orange shorts; he hurries over, clapping his hands to get the dog's attention. "Sadie, get over here right now!" he calls, stopping about ten feet away.

"Better not pet her, Cindy," Mom warns.

Cindy looks up, perplexed, as Freddie claps his hands again. Sadie licks Cindy's fingers once in farewell, then trots back to her owner.

"I've asked you not to pet her when she gets off her chain!" Freddie snaps, rubbing his bald head and declining to look directly at any of us.

"My sister and niece just arrived, Freddie, and didn't know

that was a no-no," Mom says. Her tone is cool; I'm pleased to notice she's getting tired of the jackass, too. Cindy and Janelle are gaping at him.

"Well, perhaps you should've told them," he declares, scooping up Sadie and stalking back toward his house.

"Oh, for Christ's sake, Freddie," I call after him. "Why don't you just buy a new dog chain?"

"The chain works just fine!" he bellows over his shoulder.

"Okey-dokey." I lower my voice. "But you might want to ask your doctor if anti-hallucinogens are right for you."

"Noah," Mom warns, as Janelle giggles.

"What did you just say to me?" Freddie demands, spinning around. I forgot about his bat ears.

"I said it's always good to see you," I tell him.

"No, you didn't! You said something insulting, and I won't stand for it!"

"Is this guy for real?" Cindy whispers, concerned.

"Sadly, yes," Mom mutters back. Her composure is impressive, given that we've now gained something of an audience: Two neighbors across the street are watching the show, as is a little boy, passing by on a scooter. "Let's get your things from the car and go inside, shall we?"

"I demand an apology!" Freddie cries.

"Fine!" I say cheerfully. "I'm sorry you're a fruitcake."

Mom shoves me toward the house. "Go inside, now, Noah, or I swear to God I'll rip out your tongue and feed it to Sadie." She turns to Overton again. "Noah shouldn't have said that, Freddie, but I do think you're overreacting."

Faith Overton scurries out of their house, frantically pulling on a bathrobe over a skimpy blouse and an equally skimpy skirt. "Freddie, come back home now, okay?" she pleads. "It's time for dinner."

"Not until I get an apology!" he insists. His face is redder than Janelle's hair.

Mom points a finger at me before I can respond. Freddie's

outburst isn't intimidating in the slightest, but Mom's finger could quell a mob of peasants with pitchforks. She doesn't even wait to see if I obey her before she faces Freddie again. Faith now has her husband by the elbow, and Sadie is nervously licking his hands, but neither of them seems capable of placating him.

"I suggest we all discuss this some other time, when you're calmer," Mom tells Freddie. "Enjoy your evening."

"I insist on an apology!" he cries again.

"It's unlikely you'll get one," Mom says, shrugging. "You are, however, more than welcome to stand here and scream your bloody head off, if it makes you feel better." She turns her back on him with regal disdain.

Oh, how I love her sometimes.

She shoos me toward the house and herds Cindy and Janelle to their car to get their things. Freddie is still standing there with Sadie in his arms, but he's too outraged to speak; Faith whispers something and tugs at his elbow again, and they're gone by the time we all get back inside.

"Cindy and Janelle," Mom says, setting down a suitcase, "I am so, *so* sorry you had to witness that absurd little soap opera, and I hope to God the rest of your stay will be drama-free. Our new neighbor is a very strange man."

I snort. "He's a penis in pastels."

Janelle laughs and even Cindy smiles a little, but Mom isn't amused. "Would it kill you to act your age for once in your life, Noah?" she asks. "You made that situation far worse than it needed to be."

I wander over to the stove to check on my soup. "Freddie would've been just as mad if I hadn't said a word. He's a crackpot."

"Maybe so, but did you really need to throw gas on the fire?"

She's not wrong, of course, but since she's no longer on the verge of an explosion I can't help needling her a little. "Wow, that's a really original metaphor," I say. "No wonder you won the Pulitzer."

She flushes purple, but when she sees that both Cindy and Janelle are trying not to laugh, her sense of humor, blessedly, gets the best of her temper. She laughs, too, albeit grudgingly, throwing up her hands in exasperation.

"You are such a shithead," she tells me.

"He's probably right, Virginia," Cindy says, surprising us. "About your neighbor, I mean. I'd bet anything the poor man has a personality disorder of some kind."

I forgot to mention that Cindy used to be a therapist. Mom told me she'd started out as a social worker, then went into private practice with a friend, who bought her out a couple of years ago when she retired.

"Wonderful," I grunt. "Can we get him committed?"

Cindy smiles again. "I doubt that's necessary. But you should be careful with him anyway, Noah, and be kinder, if you can. He's clearly not a happy soul."

Janelle rolls her eyes a little. "Mom can't stop counseling people," she says playfully, "even though no one is paying for it anymore."

Cindy raises her chin, just like Mom does when she's pissed. "I'm not counseling anybody, Janelle, I'm just—"

"It was a joke, Mom," Janelle interrupts. "Lighten up."

Mom gives them a tour of the house while I make a pitcher of sangria and tend to the food on the stove. I realize belatedly that we don't have any sherry vinegar—the finishing touch to my soup—so when Mom and our guests reappear I tell them I have to make a quick run to the store. Janelle asks to tag along, and I grab Mom's car keys as the two of us step out the back door, leaving Mom and Cindy to guzzle my sangria and do the long-lost-sister thing. I can hear them through the screen as we walk away from the house; they're both talking a gazillion miles a minute, trying their damnedest to cram the last three decades of their lives into three minutes of conversation.

Our house has a circular driveway, so Janelle doesn't have to move their car; we climb into Mom's sauna-like Corolla, both of us gasping in the heat as I roll down the windows and get on the road as fast as possible. The air-conditioner works, sort of, but we'll be at the store before it kicks in.

"God, it's way hotter here than in Petaluma," Janelle says, lifting her neon red hair off her neck and poking her head out the window to catch the breeze. "I thought New Hampshire was supposed to be cold."

"Not in August," I tell her. "At least not in this part of the state. It wasn't this hot when I was a kid, but the last few summers have been brutal."

"Fucking oil companies," she says vehemently. "Those greedy pricks are turning the whole planet into a giant toaster oven."

I don't disagree, but the change in her demeanor surprises me; she seemed so sunny and soft-spoken before. " Uh-oh," I say. "Looks like I'm not the only potty mouth in this family."

She grins. "Don't tell Mom. She hates it when I swear." She peers around, checking out the neighborhood. "So what do you do for fun around here?"

I point at a young mother and two little girls, splashing around in a kiddie pool in their yard. "We play in kiddie pools, like that one, and pick fights with bald neighbors."

"No, seriously. You must at least have a bar, right?"

"Sort of, if you like crappy beer and greasy food, and don't mind being stared at by everyone when you walk through the door." I glance at her. "People around here wouldn't know what to make of a real-live Korean. Especially one with bright red hair."

I like her laugh; it's an uninhibited cackle. "In that case, can we go there sometime while I'm here? I love stirring up trouble."

I tell her sure, if she wants, and she looks happy. A second later, we pull into the grocery store parking lot—Edgerton's, owned by the same family for a hundred years or more—and climb out of the car. My shirt is sticking to my back, making me wish I was a kid again, when I could get away with wearing nothing but shorts all summer long.

"I'm really sorry about Aunt Virginia getting sick," Janelle says out of the blue. "Mom feels terrible about not coming to visit her all these years."

I shrug. "My mom feels guilty, too. We could've visited you guys just as easily, but we only went once, before you were even in the picture."

"I wonder why they've never made plans to get together until now." Janelle falls into step beside me as we saunter across the hot asphalt to the store entrance. "You can tell they still love each other a lot, from the way they were crying today when we got here. I've never seen my mom cry like that before."

I'm pretty sure the main reason Mom and Cindy have avoided each other all this time is because their childhood was hell on Earth, but I don't know if Janelle knows about our pedophile granddad, and I'm sure as hell not going to be the one to break the news if she doesn't. The old bastard died long before she was born, so for all I know Cindy may have chosen to keep her in the dark. It suddenly occurs to me that I have no clue if Cindy was abused by Grandpa as well; Mom never said, and I never asked. If I had to guess I'd say it's more likely than not.

Jesus. It's hard enough being a kid without having to worry about a deranged predator stalking you in your own house.

Bill Edgerton—the oldest grandson of the original grocery store owner—is fussing with a display of canned tomatoes near the front door when we walk in. His wife, Melinda, is at the cash register, assisted by a pimply high school boy bagging a young woman's groceries. Bill is a short, round, rough-spoken guy in his sixties. J.D.'s first job was here at Edgerton's, when he was in high school, and Bill treated him well, so I've always liked him.

"Well, now, look what the cat drug in," he calls out when he sees me. "Noah York, as I live and breathe."

"Hi, Bill." I pause to chat and Janelle wanders off to poke around the small but surprisingly well-stocked store. There are only four aisles, but the shelves are jam-packed from floor to ceiling.

"You still living that bohemian dream of yours down in Providence?" Bill asks me, shaking my hand. He's craning his head to look after Janelle, wondering who she is. I decline to enlighten him.

"Yeah, but I'm not too good at it," I say. "I came home to get pointers from my mom."

"Lucky her, having a son who actually listens to her. My idiot kids never hear a word I say unless I shout it in their goddamn ears."

"Maybe they've just gone deaf," I say.

Melinda snorts at the cash register and Bill grins. "Smartass," he says. "Dammit, Carl, how many times do I have to tell you not to put the bread in the bottom of the bag? You think this nice lady here wants her bread smashed to smithereens?" He turns away from the blushing bag boy and looks at me again. "You and J.D. still in touch these days?"

I don't mind the question, coming from him. Bill was one of the few people in town who never gave a crap that J.D. and I were a couple. "Not very often," I say. "Last I heard, though, he's doing fine."

"He was the best damn worker I ever had. Tell him I said hi, next time you get a chance." He lowers his voice in a rare moment of tact. "That poor boy over there has less brains than a goddamn grapefruit."

A large mirror in the upper corner of the store allows Bill to keep an eye on the parts of the store not in his direct line of sight; he's using it now to check out Janelle as she rummages through the wine and beer section at the back of the store. I take pity on his curiosity.

"Her name is Janelle," I say. "She's my cousin, from California."

"Cousin, huh?" He blinks as he digests this, then he grins again. "Not much resemblance, which makes her one lucky young lady." The grin abruptly disappears as he glances in the mirror again. "Uh, Noah, your cousin just stuck something in her skirt pocket that doesn't belong to her."

I look in the mirror, shocked; Janelle is casually inspecting the label on a bottle of wine, seemingly oblivious to our scrutiny. I turn back to Bill, wondering if he's joking, but he's dead serious. "Are you sure?" I ask quietly.

"Yep. I think she took a church key, but it might be a corkscrew."

I can't believe Janelle would do something so stupid; she doesn't seem the type. "Jesus, Bill. Any chance you're wrong?"

"Afraid not. How do you want to handle this?"

I'm impressed that he's staying calm and speaking so softly that only I can hear him. I'm also grateful that he's bothering to ask my opinion. If I weren't there, I'm pretty sure he'd already be calling the cops.

"I don't have a clue," I mutter. "I only met her half an hour ago." I think fast, hating the idea of having to tell Mom about this. "How about I go talk to her, just to make sure there's not some mistake? If she took something I'll get it back from her, of course, but I'd really appreciate it if we can avoid involving the police."

Bill looks like he's already regretting his self-restraint, but he nods. "Okay, but make it fast, Noah, and get her out of my store. Shoplifters piss me off royally."

I take a deep breath and walk down the aisle to the other end. Janelle gives me a warm smile when I walk up to her. She's wearing a sleeveless white blouse and a pretty green skirt; I covertly glance at the skirt pocket, but the fabric is too loose to see if there's something in it.

"What kind of wine does Aunt Virginia like?" she asks. "I want to get her a gift."

"She likes pretty much everything, as long as it's not sweet." I hesitate. "Uh, this is awkward as hell, Janelle, but the store owner just told me he saw you take something off the shelf and put it in your pocket."

She freezes, her smile turning brittle. "Seriously?" She looks around me and sees Bill, watching us in the mirror. Her eyes narrow. "He's full of shit, Noah. I bet he just doesn't like people with my complexion coming into his stupid store."

I consider this for a second. "I don't think that's what's going on," I tell her, reluctantly. "Bill's not really like that."

"Are you saying you believe him instead of me?" The hurt on her face makes me feel like crap; she's either completely innocent, or a terrific actress.

"I'm saying we don't have much choice except to prove him wrong." I glance down again at the pocket in question. "If he's made a mistake, he'll feel terrible about it, and probably give us a whole case of wine to apologize."

She glares at me. "I don't have to prove a fucking thing to him, Noah! I didn't take anything!"

Something about her indignation suddenly seems a little phony to me—as does the fact that she could easily put an end to this, right now, by letting me see in her pocket. "You don't have to show him," I tell her, "but he'll call the police if you don't, and then you'll get searched, anyway." I pause, wishing I weren't growing more certain by the second that she's lying. "If you *did* happen to take something, Janelle—and I'm not saying you did—it's still not too late to give it back, okay? Bill won't call the cops, and we can just go home."

She actually stomps her feet in rage; her face is nearly as red as her hair. "Fine!" she cries. She yanks something from her pocket and slams it down on the shelf. "It's just a cheap piece of shit anyway!"

She storms from the store, sobbing, and as she passes Bill at the front door she shouts something incomprehensible—another profanity, probably. I pick up the corkscrew she tried to steal, figuring the least I can do for Bill is to buy the damn thing. I slowly return to the front, somehow remembering to snag a bottle of sherry vinegar on the way, and when I reach the cash register, Melinda and her customer are looking highly stimulated, though they're polite enough not to stare. The bag boy, on the other hand, is openly gawking at me, his mouth hanging open. This is probably the most excitement he's had since his first boner. Bill is gazing out the window after Janelle.

"Sorry, Bill," I tell him. "I really don't know what to say."

"Me either." He looks over his shoulder and shakes his head. "Good luck with your family visit."

Janelle is already in the passenger seat when I get back to the car. She's still crying and doesn't look at me, and when I climb behind the wheel and hand her the paper grocery bag she sets it on the floor by her feet. I start the engine and pull out of the parking lot.

"Uh, are you out of your mind?" I ask her as gently as I can. "I mean, seriously. Are you out of your freaking mind?"

She sniffles but doesn't answer.

"It's a five-dollar corkscrew, Janelle. Why not just buy the damn thing, if you wanted it?"

Still no answer. It's easy to forget she's an adult; she has snot on her upper lip and is sulking like I just took away her Juno My Baby Elephant doll. The chatty, self-sufficient young woman I first met today is nowhere in sight, and I find myself recalling, somewhat wistfully, my thoughts from yesterday, when I was fretting she'd turn out to be a devil worshipper—at least that would've been entertaining, not just childish and inexplicable.

I give up trying to make her talk, and the silence seems to calm her because by the time we get back to the house she's at least stopped bawling. We stay in the car as she wipes her face, then she picks up the bag from the floor and sets it in her lap before finally looking at me.

"Please, please, *please* don't tell Mom," she says. Her lips tremble as she glances in the bag and notices the corkscrew. "I promise it won't happen again while I'm here, okay?"

What the hell am I supposed to say to that?

I clear my throat. "I'd really like to know why it happened in the first place."

She looks away. "I have a problem with stealing stuff. My shrink says I'm a borderline kleptomaniac, but most of the time I can control it. I didn't mean to take anything in that store, Noah. I just couldn't help it."

She may still be bullshitting me, but for now I'll play along. "Does your mom know?"

She snorts sourly. "Of course. She's the one who sent me to a shrink, because she couldn't deal with me anymore. I've been stealing since I was twelve. Until today, though, I haven't taken anything in almost a year. Mom will be so pissed if she finds out." She brushes sweat off her forehead and scowls. "She'll pretend it's okay, and she'll say all the right things about how it's an illness, and not my fault, but she'll still be pissed. She always is."

The car is stifling. I open the door to get more air, but I don't step out yet; we need to resolve this before we go inside. I search her eyes and she looks back at me fearfully, like she's just stuck her head in the guillotine.

I sigh. "Fine. I'm not exactly in a hurry to mess up the big family reunion, so I'll keep my mouth shut. Just don't go in any other stores while you're here, okay?"

She takes my hand and squeezes it; her hand is as sweaty as mine. "Thanks, cuz. I owe you, big-time." A hint of her former playful smile returns. "Can we please go drink sangria, now?"

When we walk in the back door, Mom and Cindy are deep in conversation, but they break off when they see us. Two-thirds of the sangria pitcher is empty, so at least they've kept themselves well hydrated during our absence.

"Sheesh," I say, pouring a full glass for Janelle and the dregs for me. "What a couple of lushes you old dames are."

"Just make another batch, barkeep, and never mind the wisecracks," Mom says, reaching for the grocery bag Janelle is carrying. "I'll put the vinegar in the soup. You always add too much."

A twitch of anxiety crosses Janelle's face as she surrenders the bag, and I want to kick myself for not leaving the corkscrew in the car, because of course Mom immediately finds it and asks why I bought it. We've already got half a dozen of the damn things in the house.

"I don't know, I just liked it," I say lamely. "You can never have enough corkscrews."

She raises her eyebrows. "Actually, I'm pretty sure you can."

Cindy is watching Janelle—her bullshit detector has clearly been triggered—and Janelle gives herself away by breaking eye contact. Cindy's face darkens and she starts to say something, but Janelle bursts into tears and rushes from the room.

For once, Mom is at a complete loss. She just stares after Janelle, then at Cindy, and finally at me. "What did you do now?" she demands.

CHAPTER 4

Joy may cometh with the morning, but sometimes the morning cometh too goddamn early.

I wake up right before sunrise. The house is preternaturally quiet, and I'm pretty sure everyone else is still in bed. I want more sleep but I know I won't get any; once my mind reboots, it stays online for the rest of the day. After a few minutes of picking grit from my eyes and yawning, I crawl out of bed, tug on a pair of shorts, stumble to the john to pee, then tiptoe downstairs in semi darkness, enjoying the feel of the smooth wooden steps beneath my feet. It's been a long time since I've been awake before Mom; I can't even remember the last time I beat her to the kitchen before breakfast. I turn on the light over the sink, wincing at the brightness, and get the coffee brewing, hoping no one else shows up and starts yapping at me before I'm in the mood to talk.

I have a lot to think about.

Last night was surprisingly fun, once Cindy and Janelle made peace about the corkscrew incident, and an embarrassed Janelle could be persuaded to stop hiding in her room. My soup was kick-ass, the sangria flowed freely, and I finally had the chance to get better acquainted with my aunt and cousin.

Cindy seems to be a good soul, and she's nowhere near as intense, prickly, and complicated as Mom. I'm sure that's a healthy thing, from a psychological perspective, but it also makes me feel a little sad for her, oddly enough. She told us last night that she volunteers for hospice, and the Salvation Army; she reads a lot of mystery novels, likes to cook Italian food, and is learning to speak Spanish; she listens to indie pop and folk music, likes watching pro tennis on TV, and goes to a lot of movies and plays. But when she was telling us about herself, there was no true fire in her voice, not even once, and it made me wonder if anything she's doing ever really trips her trigger. Her life sounds full, I guess, and she's probably way happier than I'll ever be, but I found myself missing the passion that's so much a part of Mom. Whenever Mom talked last night, she was, as usual, like a big pot of spaghetti sauce simmering on the stove, suddenly getting too hot in this or that spot and splattering all over everything. She may have mellowed a lot since her diagnosis, but if she's speaking about something she loves—like poetry, or teaching, or dark chocolate, or Chopin's nocturnes—or something she hates—like Senator Douchebag, or climate science deniers, or mansplainers, or overcooked asparagus—she's a woman on fire, just like she's always been.

For instance, she went off on an epic tangent for at least ten minutes because Janelle made the mistake of asking about an international poetry class Mom is going to teach in the fall. Mom's face lit up like she'd just been given a pony for Christmas, and she rattled off a couple of poems that she was going to use for the class, one by some Japanese guy and the other by a Croatian lady. Both poems were pretty long and intricate, and I could see how impressed Cindy and Janelle were that she knew them by heart. They would've been even more impressed if they'd known she probably has at least five hundred other poems that she can access just as easily, all stuffed in her cranium like Styrofoam peanuts in a shipping crate. It used to drive me insane when she'd trot one out like that, because I thought she was showing off, but I finally figured out that she only does it because she can't help herself. She loves poetry so much that she wants everyone else to love it, too.

Anyway, personality differences aside, the two sisters share a lot of the same gestures and facial expressions. Both of them twist their hair in ratty knots, and neither of them can keep their hands to themselves, always touching stuff as they talk—their plates, the candle in the center of the table, their own chins, their wineglasses. Most of their conversation wasn't about their childhood, but Cindy occasionally alluded to it, like when she mentioned a high school boyfriend of Mom's, or told Janelle and me how Mom's laugh sounded exactly like *their* mother's laugh. (My grandma died when they were teenagers, and Mom never talks about her, so even that tiny morsel of information intrigued me.) Mom changed the subject, however, whenever Cindy veered into territory like this, deftly keeping the focus on adulthood, and Cindy eventually caught on and stopped doling out nostalgic tidbits.

Janelle didn't talk much at first and just watched our mothers, as fascinated as I was by the novelty of seeing them side by side. I'm sure she was also still smarting from being outed as a klepto, but once we all had a snootful of sangria she loosened up, telling us about her job—she's a graphic designer for one of the vineyards in Sonoma—and about her current boyfriend, Alan, who she described as "really sweet, and super hot, but kinda dumb." From the offhand way she talked about him, I get the feeling that her sex life may be almost as casual as mine, but obviously I didn't think it would be a good idea to compare notes with our mothers in the room.

The weirdest part of the whole night for me was when Mom told Cindy and Janelle about wanting to find Carolyn.

First off, Mom just brought the subject up out of the blue,

like she was talking about the price of cherry tomatoes at a local farm stand. Secondly, Janelle didn't even bat an eye when Mom told them, so I guess that means she *does* know about our sicko grandpa. Thirdly, Cindy batted both eyes so damn hard it's a wonder her pupils didn't get sanded off; she simply couldn't believe that Mom intends to track Carolyn down after all these years. She asked Mom point-blank if she thought that was a good idea, considering that the first question out of Carolyn's mouth, if we find her, is likely going to be "So where's my dad?"

And me? I just sat there, trying to figure out how my cozy little family unit had somehow gone from two members to four—all discussing a potential fifth—during the time it took to eat a bowl of soup.

It's been years since I've seen Mom so relaxed with anyone but me, and honestly, I felt a little jealous that she was showing her home face to people I barely even know, family or not. But then I caught myself doing out-of-character things, too, like not minding when Cindy rested her hand on my forearm several times during the evening—I'm not usually a touchy-feely kind of guy—and sharing a bowl of ice cream with Janelle, when I normally get grossed out by the whole communal-food-trough thing.

I don't understand why intimacy is so easy with these people. It's clearly not just a DNA quirk, because Janelle's chromosomes and mine are as different as toenails and kielbasa, and it's not a love thing, either, because I honestly don't yet know Cindy and Janelle well enough to love them. But maybe between the four of us there's enough goodwill floating around to somehow glue us together as a unit, regardless of the fact that a close bond isn't really logical.

Either that, or I accidentally added Ecstasy to the sangria.

The coffeemaker finishes brewing and spits out its last few drops in the pot, and I fill my ridiculous monkey mug and lean my shoulder against the open doorway to the dining room, watching through the windows as the sun rises. A bar of sunlight on the skin of my stomach is already warm to the touch; it's going to be another scorcher of a day. The house is still quiet, save for the whirr of the ceiling fans and the hum of the refrigerator motor, and I sip my coffee and let my mind wander again.

Before bed last night, I borrowed Mom's laptop and started poking around on sites that specialize in helping birth parents find kids they put up for adoption. Mom told me she's already signed up with the national adoption reunion registry, but she's not the savviest person in the world when it comes to googling shit, and I'm sure there's a ton of stuff she hasn't checked out that can help us track down Carolyn. Mom told me all the relevant details she has—the date she gave Carolyn up, and the phony names her dad used at the adoption agency—and I added this info to several different websites before I fell asleep.

Toby and Nan Thatcher, by the way: the names my grandfather made up for the parents of baby Carolyn. Dear old Grandpa was a scuzzball, but at least he did us the favor of fabricating something more original than Jones or Smith, which might help us find Carolyn more easily.

"Morning, sexy."

I jump, splashing coffee on my hand, and turn around to find Janelle leaning on the kitchen island, smiling at me. She's wearing an oversized Led Zeppelin T-shirt that covers her to mid thigh, but her legs and feet are bare.

"Jesus," I say. "How long have you been standing there?"

"Just a minute. I said good morning but you were a million miles away."

"It takes me a while to reenter this dimension after I wake up." I wipe my hand on my shorts, then point at the coffeepot. "Want some nectar of the gods?"

"I'd love some."

I pour her a mug and she earns my approval by taking it black; we wander over to the breakfast nook and sit across from each other at the table, yawning and scratching ourselves awake. She doesn't seem inclined to talk much, which suits me fine, but as the coffee starts coursing through her veins she visibly perks up, looking out the window for a while and then at me.

"You're in pretty good shape for a middle-aged American dude," she says. "What's your secret? Do you run or something?"

"Nope. I just can't afford to eat. I'm a starving artist."

"Ah, the poverty diet. I can relate. The main reason I moved back home with Mom last year was because I got sick of ramen noodles." She picks up the salt shaker and fiddles with it. "But as soon as I save up some money, I'm getting the hell out."

"I don't blame you. It sucks not having your own place." I hesitate for a minute, not sure how much I feel like telling her. "My mom just asked me to move back home," I say. "She wants us to spend more time together before she dies."

Janelle's eyes are disconcertingly empathetic. "Is that what you want?"

"God, no. I mean, I'm fine with spending more time with her, but I'd rather overdose on hemlock than live here again."

She laughs. "That's maybe a little extreme. So what did you say when she asked you?"

"I tried to tell her no, but she refused to talk about it until I've had more time to think."

We fall silent again, but it's an oddly comfortable silence. We're not exactly strangers anymore, but it still seems funny how normal it feels for the two of us to be sitting here together, half-naked and frowzy, like a couple of little kids waiting for the adults in the house to wake up and feed us. Janelle rouses herself after a while to refill our mugs, but after she brings mine back to me, she starts circling the kitchen restlessly, studying some of my artwork that Mom has tacked on the walls over the years. Most of it is crap I painted before I had any clue what I was doing, but there's one portrait of Mom and J.D. that turned out okay, and my ego is gratified when Janelle pauses to admire it.

"You have so much talent it's sickening," she says. "Who's the cute blond kid sitting next to your mom?"

"My first boyfriend. He lived with us for a while when we were in high school."

"Are you shitting me?" She gapes at me over her shoulder. "Your mom actually let your boyfriend shack up with you when you were just kids?"

"Long story, but it was kind of a weird time."

"You can say that again," Mom says, startling us both as she walks into the kitchen. She's wearing a tank top and what looks like a pair of my old soccer shorts, and her hair is sticking up all over her head, like Medusa's snakes.

"Is everybody in this house a ninja, or am I just going deaf?" I demand. "Stop sneaking up on me."

Mom makes a beeline for the coffee, sighing when she realizes there's not enough left for a mug. "Oh, the humanity," she says, reaching for a new filter to make a fresh batch. Her fingers fumble a little bit and she drops the filter on the floor. "God is punishing me for oversleeping."

"You feeling all right?" I ask. "You haven't missed a sunrise in decades."

"I'm fine. Just a little sluggish today."

I watch her closely as she bends down to retrieve the filter, knowing that fatigue and clumsiness go hand in hand with ALS. She catches me spying on her. "I'm fine, Noah," she says again, smiling reassuringly as she straightens. "I just didn't sleep well. Too much on my mind, I guess."

She starts poking around in the fridge and cabinets, asking what we want for breakfast, and Janelle offers to help. I get up to help, too, but Mom tells me to go wake Cindy first. On the way to the stairs I retrieve my phone on the coffee table in the living room, where I forgot it last night. There's the usual bullshit notifications from Grindr and a couple of texts from a friend in Providence; I ignore those for now and thumb through my email. As always, there's a trillion spam messages, but as I'm wading through all the shit I come across an email from one of the birth-family reunification websites that I signed up on just last night. The subject line says "Your Search Results," and the email tells me that a positive match has been located in their records; it also says I need to sign on to confirm the details and pay a "finder's fee" before they'll release the information to me.

"Yeah, like that's not a huge, steaming pile of crap," I mutter, knowing it's way too soon for any kind of results. I read yesterday that searches like this can often take weeks, months, or even years to turn anything up, and scams happen all the time. I send the email to trash and start walking for the stairs again, but my feet stop moving before I get out of the living room.

By itself, the finder's fee isn't necessarily a scam; nearly all the reunification sites charge money, either up front or once a match has been found. Sometimes it's a buttload of money, too, depending on how hard it is to find the people you're looking for, but I also read that if the search is easy—as is sometimes the case, particularly if it turns out that the person you're looking for happens to be looking for *you*, too—then the cost is often minimal. Sighing at my own gullibility, I recover the email and run a quick fraud check on the company, expecting to see red flags popping up all over the place.

It appears legit.

My phone is too slow, so I plop down on the couch and grab Mom's laptop, logging on with her password. I'm still highly suspicious that finding Carolyn could be this simple, but I can at least see what their fee is, and make damn sure I'm not being punked. I click on the embedded link in the email.

"Noah?" Mom pokes her head in the living room doorway. "Quit dawdling, would you? Breakfast will be ready soon, and I'm sure Cindy will want to join us."

I'm glad she can't see the computer screen from where she's standing, because I'd rather not get her hopes up until I know more. "Just a sec," I say. "I'm answering an email from work."

"Make it quick, please. Unless Cindy has changed dramatically since we were girls, she sleeps like the dead. She'll need time to resurrect."

Janelle says something I don't hear and Mom disappears back into the kitchen. The website tells me that my search for Carolyn has been successful, and for seventy-five bucks I can see what they know about her. I skim over a few glowing testimonials from people who've found their own biological family members using FamilyByBlood.com; I google everything I can think of to convince myself that it's horseshit, but everything keeps coming up clean.

"Sometime this century, Noah," Mom says, reappearing in the doorway.

I make a face. "Yeah, yeah, okay, I'm on my way." I close the computer reluctantly, warning myself that I need to do more research before I take this any further, but who am I kidding? I already know I'm going to spend the goddamn money as soon as breakfast is over.

* * *

Birth name: Carolyn Anne Thatcher. Birthdate: Oct. 7, 1966. Birthplace: Chicago, Illinois. Biological parents: Toby A. and Nan M. Thatcher, 107 East 3rd Street, Warrenville, Illinois. Adopted Nov. 3, 1966, by Kenneth F. and Frances L. Kaine, 55 Compton Avenue, Apt. 4, Peoria, Illinois."

The good news is I now have the names of Carolyn's adoptive parents. The bad news is their address is fifty-six years old, and everything about the "Thatchers" is total bullshit that I already knew.

But at least it's a start.

I'm sitting on the window seat in my bedroom, with the door closed for privacy. Mom is letting me use her computer for a while, because I told her I had to write a recommendation for a friend who wants to work at the community center where I teach. It was a feeble lie, but it gave me enough time to dig out my credit card and fork over seventy-five bucks, to see what the adoption website could tell me about Carolyn. Part of me wants to run downstairs right now and show Mom what I've found, but another part is stomping on the brakes, telling me to keep my bony little ass on the window seat until I've thought this through.

I google Carolyn's name in various combinations—Carolyn Anne Kaine, Carolyn Anne Thatcher, etc.—but I'm not surprised when no one pops up who seems likely to be her. By this point in her life, it's a good bet she's married and has a different last name; I guess it's even possible that her first name is no longer Carolyn, as the Kaines could have changed it after adopting her. A search for the Kaines themselves is equally unfruitful: After sorting through white page listings and other useless crap—for instance, the address of their old apartment building is now a parking lot—I finally dig up a two-line, 2007 obituary notice in a Peoria newspaper for Kenneth F. Kaine, but it doesn't even list any surviving family members. I hope that doesn't mean Carolyn and Frances are dead, too, but of course they could be.

So now what?

Frances's name produces even fewer hits than Carolyn's. If either woman is still alive, it's quite an achievement these days to leave no digital trace whatsoever; I didn't think that kind of anonymity was even possible anymore. Maybe they're frontier-hermits, and are currently huddling around a fireplace in a cabin somewhere in rural Alaska, swilling gin from the bottle and skinning rabbits for soup while fifteen feral cats piss on their rug and shred their curtains.

Cindy knocks on my door, startling me, and sticks her head in the room. "How's your recommendation letter going?"

I'd almost forgotten that's what I said I was doing. "Slow. I'm not very good at this sort of thing."

"Want to take a break? I feel like going for a walk before it gets too hot. Any interest in joining me?"

I glance at the time on the laptop and wince when I realize

I've been at this for an hour and a half, with next to nothing to show for it. I stretch my back and smile at her.

"Sure," I say. "Just give me a sec to finish this sentence, okay?"

She beams at me, like she was expecting a refusal. "Take your time, I'm not in any rush."

After she closes the door again, I chew on my lip, thinking hard. I email myself a couple of web links that might be worth pursuing, then erase my search history on Mom's laptop, not wanting her to stumble across anything I don't want to share yet. Even the little information I've found so far would throw her in a tizzy. I want to find Carolyn, too, but I'll be damned if I'm going to put up with Mom pestering me every goddamn step of the way.

"I'm sorry I'm so slow, Noah," Cindy says, taking my arm to steady herself on a patch of crumbling sidewalk. "My doctor tells me I need to get more exercise, and I'm trying, but I'm not in very good shape these days."

Unfortunately, that's an understatement: We've only gone a couple of blocks and she's already red-faced and winded.

"I like walking slow," I tell her. "I'm a natural-born ambler."

Janelle and Mom both chose to stay home. Mom has a deadline to finish a poem she was asked to write for *Harper's*, and Janelle begged off because she said she didn't sleep well last night and needed a nap.

Cindy squeezes my bicep. "It's good of you to be so patient with an old lady. When I walk with Janelle she's always at least five steps ahead. I keep threatening to put her on a leash with a choke collar but she doesn't pay any attention."

I grin, but I'm only listening with half an ear. Now that I've actually begun the search for Carolyn, I can't stop thinking about her. I assumed, naively, that learning the names of her adopted parents would be all I'd need to track her down, but now I'm not so sure. I'll keep googling them today in hopes that something else turns up, but if my luck doesn't change I may need a different strategy. I guess I could call the agency in Chicago that handled her adoption, but I'm pretty damn certain it's illegal for them to release any info, and even if someone took pity on me and broke the rules, I doubt they'd have anything more recent than what I've already learned. It's possible some of the other birth-family websites I registered on last night will produce something useful, but I'm not counting on that, either.

Maybe I should tell Mom to hire a private detective and let me go back to wasting my free time on Grindr.

"This is a charming little town," Cindy says, admiring a ring of blue and cinnamon hibiscuses circling a nearby patio. "But I'm still surprised Virginia chose to move here. She always used to talk about how much she loved Chicago."

I nod. "She did, but we needed a serious change of scenery after Dad died, so she took the first job offer that came her way." I sigh. "It was a good move at the time, but I couldn't wait to get out of here when I left for college. I expected Mom to leave eventually, too, but she caught the small-town bug in a way I never did."

She studies my face. "Too quiet for you?"

I grimace. "The only difference between this place and a morgue is the toe tags."

She laughs. "I remember your mom telling me once that you were—let's see, what was her exact phrasing? Oh, yes, she said that you were 'prone to macabre hyperbole.' I guess I'm starting to see what she means."

I snort. "Jesus. 'Prone to macabre hyperbole.' Has she always talked like that, or was she less of a freak when she was a kid?"

"Let's just say she was always unique," Cindy says tactfully, pausing to rest in the shade of a spectacular old sycamore. "Virginia was reading at a high school level when she was seven, and had a better vocabulary than most adults, let alone the other kids in her class. She spent her entire childhood correcting everyone else's grammar."

"I'm guessing she didn't get invited to very many birthday parties," I say, shaking my head.

Cindy smiles. "Not often, no. That was fine by me, though, because I loved having her to myself. We played in our yard every day, after school. She had a wonderful silly side to her personality, but she never showed it to anyone but me."

It's hard to imagine Mom ever being silly on purpose; I'd always assumed that what she did for fun as a girl was teach herself Sanskrit, or something equally torturous.

"What do you mean?" I ask, intrigued.

"Oh, she went out of her way to make me laugh by doing ridiculous things. She used to fill her cheeks with marbles and sing the alphabet, or she'd tie her ankles together with a belt and try to waltz—you know, anything she could come up with. My favorite was the time she pretended to be a fish out of water, flopping on the grass. I laughed so hard I'm surprised I didn't rupture my appendix."

I stare at her in disbelief. "You're kidding. The great Virginia York imitated a fish?"

"She could imitate people, too. God, she was funny. She did an absolutely fantastic impersonation of our next-door neighbor." Cindy hesitates, and her smile abruptly fades. "Of course, all of that was before our dad . . . did what he did. That pretty much put an end to Virginia's childhood."

I flinch, suddenly sick to my stomach, and she takes my hand. "I'm sorry, Noah. I know it must be hard to hear about that part of her life."

I nod. "It is, but I'm actually glad to know that the two of you had some good times beforehand. She's never said a word to me about when she was a little girl."

"Believe it or not, she was mostly a happy-go-lucky kid back then. Dad was never much of a father, of course—he was always a bully to us and Mom, and he had an awful temper—but at least he didn't start to force himself on Virginia, until she hit puberty." She pauses. "After that, he never left her alone, and she became a different person."

We resume walking, and I ask about her mother, and why she didn't intervene.

"She had a gift for looking the other way," Cindy says. "She was terrified of Dad, and even after Virginia got pregnant, Mom managed to act as if it happened by magic." Her voice grows bitter. "I know she was almost as powerless in that house as Virginia and me, but to this day I've never understood why she didn't even try to step in. If anyone ever did something like that to Janelle, I'd rip off his testicles, or at least die trying."

Her unexpected fierceness reminds me of Mom, and makes me wonder again if my granddad also abused her. I still don't feel like it's my place to ask, even now that we're talking about this. I suppose it's possible that after Mom got pregnant, Grandpa had an epiphany about the consequences of fucking your own daughter, and managed to control himself with Cindy.

Or maybe he doubled down.

I ask what I feel I can: "Did Grandpa still molest Mom after she had Carolyn?"

She purses her lips. "He tried to get in her bed again about a month after the baby was born, but Virginia was ready for him. She stabbed him in the arm with a pocket knife. He wasn't hurt badly but he bled all over everything while he was trying to get the knife away from her. He beat her senseless to punish her, but after that night he never had the guts to try a repeat performance. I think he finally realized the only way he'd get near her again was over her dead body." Cindy chokes up. "I guess we should be grateful he wasn't a necrophiliac, in addition to everything else."

I put my arm around her shoulders, both of us too upset to say anything for a while. No wonder Mom has never wanted to talk about this stuff. How could it ever be anything less than agonizing to relive it? She must've had an enormous amount of courage to defy her own father like that, when she was only twelve; God only knows where she found the strength.

I only wish she'd managed to stab the son of a bitch in the jugular instead of the arm.

As we round the corner of Mom's block on our way back home, we see Freddie and Faith Overton in their yard, on their hands and knees in a riotous patch of peonies. They're absorbed in whatever they're doing and don't see us; I can hear them speaking in relaxed voices, though I can't make out what they're saying. I didn't think Freddie was capable of relaxation, and I'm even more surprised when he reaches out and gently brushes something from Faith's chin. It's a loving gesture, and makes me reevaluate him, at least a little bit. Maybe he's not a complete dick-ear; maybe he's just aggressively unfriendly with strangers, and eventually mellows out. I guess I could dial back my own tendency to be an asshole and see what happens.

Unfortunately, that's a hell of a lot harder than it sounds.

Mom has reclaimed her laptop when we get back, so I resume the search for Carolyn on my phone. I still haven't found anything by lunchtime, though, so after we eat I take a break to do something less frustrating. I feel the urge to paint, so I ask Cindy and Janelle if they'll sit for a portrait, and I'm pleased when they say yes. It's too hot to stay inside, so they sit together on the porch swing and sip mimosas while I set up my easel a few feet away.

There are a lot of reasons I love painting. One of the main ones is because I get to stare at people as long as I want, without getting bitch-slapped for rudeness. Another is that I have an excuse to not talk unless I feel like it, and there's a real freedom in studying someone intently with no expectation of conversation. I love the smell of the paint, and the feel of the brush in my hand; I love how my mind slows down, focusing on my fingers and the canvas for hours at a time. I love watching the painting evolve from nothing at all to something beautiful—if I don't screw it up, that is—and I love the little moments of revelation, when I see colors and details with an almost painful clarity.

Cindy is self-conscious at first—sitting stiffly and forcing a smile, until the mimosa kicks in and she gets used to my beady little eyes watching her so closely—but Janelle seems to enjoy the attention. She has amazing skin and an elfin, almost ethereal face, but I'm more fascinated by her imperfections, like the small mole near her left ear, and a slight, half-moon scar at one corner of her mouth. Ditto for Cindy's crooked nose, and the three distinct, vertical wrinkles between her eyebrows. I seldom notice these sorts of things until I'm painting someone, but once I spot them it usually means I'm on the right track to making a decent portrait. I don't emphasize the flaws, but I don't whitewash them, either—I just try to see the truth about the person, warts and all.

"How's it going, Noah?" Cindy asks after a while.

I stand back from the canvas and study it. I've still got a lot to do before I'm satisfied, but so far it's not bad. I especially love how I've caught the contrast between Cindy's right knee and Janelle's left one, side by side on the swing: white vs. tan, thick vs. thin, old vs. young—yet both very human, and vulnerable.

"It's getting there," I say. "Do you guys need a break?"

They say yes please, and stand up to stretch, then they both come around the easel to look at themselves. Neither says anything for a minute, but I can tell they like it by the expressions on their faces.

"Oh, my," Cindy murmurs at last. "Bravo, Noah."

"Yeah," Janelle says. "You're amazing, cuz."

"I'm glad you like it," I say. "I can make it better, though, if you don't mind sitting for another hour or two."

"Of course we don't mind," Cindy says, then hesitates. "Can I please have it when you're finished? I mean if you're willing to sell it, of course."

"It's yours, for free," I tell her. "But you have to make me a mimosa, before we start again."

"Done. Just let me use the bathroom first."

She kisses me on the cheek, making me blush, then disappears inside. Janelle stays with me a minute longer, head cocked to one side as she looks at the painting.

"Am I really that tiny?" she asks. "I look like a Korean version of Tinker Bell."

I grin. "No comment."

She pokes me in the stomach. "Well, at least you made me look pretty. Thanks for that."

"I just paint what I see," I tell her, and she beams at me over her shoulder as she walks to the door, almost bumping into Mom, coming out. They dance around each other, eventually switching places.

"Cindy insisted I come take a look at your painting," Mom says, standing beside me. She studies it for a long time without saying a word, then finally nods her head once, like she's greeting someone she respects on the street, and it makes me feel ridiculously proud.

"That's my boy," she says, heading back inside.

Finally.

The obituary notice for Frances Lynn Kaine says she died on May 30, 2011, in Madison, Wisconsin, and that she's survived by her daughter and son-in-law, Carolyn and Ben Fortier, their son Oliver Fortier, and two grandchildren, Leo and Michael Fortier, all from Fall River, Massachusetts.

Holy shit. I found her.

It's the middle of the night and I'm bleary-eyed with screen fatigue from the past four hours in my bed, staring at this freaking laptop, so all I can do now is gape at the screen, dumbfounded. The big sister I've never met apparently lives half an hour away from my apartment in Providence. I find several Carolyn Fortiers immediately on Facebook; only one is from Fall River, though, and she sort of looks like Mom and me, but with fairer skin, short blond hair, and bigger shoulders. She has a husband, a son, and a couple of grandkids. She's a dental hygienist.

I can't believe she's real.

I know that's a dumb thing to say, but until right this very second she was always just a possibility—the once-upon-a-time baby girl from Mom's intensely awful past, who may or may not have survived this long. But here she is, in living digital color: a real, smiling, breathing, adult human being, with a full name, a job, and a family of her own. I not only have a sister, I have a brother-in-law, a nephew, and a couple of grandnephews. I skim through some of her recent posts; she apparently likes cute cat memes and quasi-sappy, new-agey quotes about never giving up, being your own light in dark places, etc. It's kind of insipid stuff, but at least she's not posting scary shit about Trump being the second coming of Christ, so I guess I should be grateful for small favors.

I resist the urge to drag Mom's butt out of bed and show her everything. It's past three in the morning, and I know I'm not thinking clearly. I can't afford to mess this up, and once I open my mouth, there's no going back.

No one but me knows anything, at the moment. Of course I'll tell Mom soon, but what if Carolyn wants nothing to do with her? Maybe she resents being given up for adoption; maybe she had a childhood from hell, too, and blames her birth parents for everything bad that's ever happened to her. I want at least an inkling of the kind of reception Mom will get when they finally connect, so I can soften the blow if it's hostile. As tough as Mom is, it would wreck her if Carolyn doesn't want to meet. There must be a way to make things easier for both of them, but I'll be damned if I know how.

I close the lid of the laptop and put it on the floor, then turn off my light. I'm going to try to sleep for a few hours, and hope I wake up with a clearer head and some kind of plan. I shut my eyes, but I doubt very much I'll get any rest tonight; the pictures I saw of Carolyn and her family seem to be imprinted on the inside of my eyelids.

Jesus. I have a sister.

I need to talk to someone who can help me figure all this out, but the list of people in my life who might actually have something useful to contribute in this situation is pretty damn limited.

In point of fact, there's only one.

"Uh, Mom, what's your car doing today?" I ask, walking into the kitchen. Mom, Cindy, and Janelle are still chatting in the breakfast nook, where I left them forty minutes ago after we all ate this morning; I'm surprised Mom hasn't already barricaded herself in her bedroom to write.

"Depends," she says, giving me a warning look that plainly means "There's no way in hell you're using my car to go get laid again."

I sigh, knowing I have to tread lightly. "I think it's time to tell J.D. about your ALS, but I can't do it over the phone. He's not going to take the news any better than I did, and I should be with him when he hears it."

She blinks. "I don't want it to be any harder for either of you than it needs to be," she says, clearing her throat. "But are you sure talking face-to-face is a good idea? The last time you got together it didn't go so well."

Bruce—J.D.'s vacuous, controlling, jealous dipshit of a husband—pitched a fit a few years back when I visited them, and I ended up saying things I probably shouldn't have. I also ended up with a fat lip.

"Telling him on the phone just feels wrong," I say, sidestepping her question. "You didn't want me to get the news that way."

She frowns, looking down at the counter. "Fair point."

I'm not lying about needing to tell J.D. in person about Mom's ALS, but once I'm in Wellesley, Massachusetts, where he lives, it's just another hour to Fall River, and Carolyn. I haven't decided if I'm actually going to try to hunt down my sister today, but my plan is to talk to J.D., tell him about Mom, and get his advice. If he agrees it's not a terrible idea to check out Carolyn on my own, I'll already be nearby.

Mom turns to Cindy and Janelle and explains who J.D. is, then faces me again. "It's up to you how you tell him, but you should wait until after Cindy and Janelle's visit. They're only here for the rest of the week, and if you go to Wellesley you'll miss an entire day with them."

I figured she'd say this. "Yeah, I know, my timing is crappy." I face Cindy and Janelle. "I feel terrible about doing this while you guys are here, but J.D. is family, too, and I don't think it's right to keep him in the dark. He'll already be hurt that we waited this long."

Point scored: From the corner of my eye, I see Mom chewing on her lip. She knows we should've reached out to J.D. sooner; he loves her far more than he loves his own mother. I'm hoping she feels guilty enough to send me on my way, because of course I can't tell her why else I'm in such a rush: I'm worried she'll somehow find out about Carolyn before I can do some reconnaissance.

Yeah, I'm being a manipulative sleazeball, but it's for a good cause.

"I completely understand how you feel, Noah," Cindy says, before Mom can respond. "If you think you should talk to J.D. in person, you should go. Janelle and I will miss your company today, but we'll be just fine."

Bless her supportive, trusting, therapist's heart.

Janelle doesn't look as if she agrees, but she doesn't say anything. I truly do feel shitty for ditching her and Cindy, but it's necessary. When I came up with this half-assed plan, I toyed with inviting Janelle to come along for the ride—thereby eliminating Mom's main objection to me splitting town—but I don't know Janelle well enough to tell her what's going on.

"I'm really sorry," I tell her and Cindy. "I'll be home tonight." I look back at Mom. "I won't stay a second longer than I have to, I promise. You know how much Bruce hates me."

She snorts, but she's still tugging indecisively at a lock of her hair. "How do you even know J.D.'s home? Maybe he's on vacation."

"No, he's home. He's been bitching on Facebook every day this week about his marching band rehearsals." J.D.'s a high school band director, so he's always in town in August, herding a bunch of sweaty, hormonal kids with musical instruments around a football field and screaming himself hoarse to keep them from tripping over their own feet. "I'm hoping to catch him at the school, instead of his house."

From the way Mom is eyeing me I can tell she suspects I'm holding something back—she's not an idiot—but she also knows I'm not completely bullshitting her. I endure her scrutiny quietly, trying to look innocent, and she finally sighs.

"If you really think it will help J.D., I guess you better go," she says. "Give him my love, and have him call me as soon as you're done talking."

It's a three-hour drive from Oakland to Wellesley, and the road is quiet this morning, so I've got plenty of time to question my sanity. For distraction, I listen to a schizophrenic playlist I put on my phone, singing along with Janis Joplin, James Taylor, Radiohead, Lui Collins, Crash Test Dummies, Ella Fitzgerald, Edith Piaf, and Bonnie Raitt. I stare through the windshield at the lush fields and stone walls of New Hampshire and try to enjoy myself, even though I haven't been this nervous since I was a teenager.

Today could be a disaster.

Even if I'm lucky enough to catch J.D. at his school—thereby avoiding limpdick Bruce—I doubt he'll be overjoyed that I'm showing up uninvited. We've stayed in touch fairly regularly since we broke up sixteen years ago, but we've only seen each other three times, and two of those were soon after our breakup. The last time was six years ago, and to explain why it's been so long, here's a helpful, annotated timeline:

2005: We split up, and didn't talk for more than a year. Not even by text or email. My finger hovered over his name in my phone more times than I could count, wishing I had the balls to just push the damn button, but I was too afraid he wouldn't answer, or that he might've blocked me—or worse yet, that he'd answer, but his voice would be polite, impersonal. Or maybe just bored. I could've handled his anger if he was still mad at me, but I couldn't bear to find out he'd become indifferent.

2006: We met by accident in Boston. I was visiting the Museum of Fine Arts, and I bumped into him on the street. He was halfway through his junior year at the New England Conservatory, and was on his way home from a rehearsal; he had his trumpet in a gig bag on his back. We went to his apartment for a drink, and two hours later we were in his bed, humping like bonobos. The next morning, we talked about getting back together, but I was still too much caught up in the "I can't be a great artist if I'm in a relationship" bullshit I'd been telling myself, so we said goodbye again. We both cried a lot—it hurt almost as much as our initial split—but at least we resumed calling and texting after that, so it didn't feel so final. Even then, I think I knew I was being an idiot; I'm pretty sure part of me always believed it was just a matter of time before we'd find our way back to each other.

Here's a text exchange from what I like to refer to as "Noah York's Dumbshit Period":

Me: **Hey, am I waking you up? I know it's late.**

J.D: **Nah. I'm writing a term paper for Music History. It's due tomorrow, so I'll be up all night. What are you doing?**

Me: **Painting a portrait of some lady I saw in the subway this week. It sucks, though. It looks like I painted it with the brush handle stuck up my butt.**

J.D.: **Lol. You should try that technique and see what happens. You could squat over the canvas and wiggle your hips like a belly dancer.**

Me: **I'm afraid I'd enjoy it too much and wouldn't be able to stop. Anyway, I was just thinking of you and wanted to say hi.**

J.D.: **Ahh. Hi, sweet man. I miss you.**

Me: **Hi.**

J.D.: **Everything okay with you?**

Me: **I'm good, just tired. You okay, too?**

J.D.: **Yeah, I'm good. Hey, I dreamed about you last night.**

Me: **Really? What was I wearing?**

J.D.: **Wooden clogs and a pith helmet.**

Me: **You're making that up.**

J.D.: Ok, you only had the pith helmet. Other than that you were naked.

Me: Don't make me horny. I don't have time to jerk off tonight.

J.D.: It only takes you like thirty seconds.

Me: Okay, so maybe I do have time.

J.D.: Just don't make a mess in your pith helmet. So do you miss me, too?

Me Duh.

J.D.: I'll take that as a yes?

Me: I gotta go. I need to finish this stupid painting before I go to bed.

J.D.: Careful with the paintbrush. You might rupture something.

Me: Haha. Good luck with your paper.

J.D.: Thanks. Talk to you soon.

Me: Yep. Oh, and J.D.?

J.D.: What?

Me: I do miss you.

J.D.: Good.

2007: He came to see me in Providence, in June, to tell me he was dating a guy he liked a lot, but before things got too serious he needed to know where things stood with us. He said the guy's name was Bruce, and he was in law school, but at first he wouldn't tell me anything more, saying he didn't want me to think he was trying to make me jealous.

"I just wanted you to know there's someone else in the picture now," he said, gazing out the window as we sat at my kitchen table. "I love you, Noah, but I can't wait around forever for you to change your mind about getting back together. If you don't want to be with me, I need to move on with my life."

My breath got a little shaky. Since he'd arrived, we'd been playing footsie under the table while we ate mac and cheese straight from the pan, and I'd been looking forward, extremely, to having sex with him again. His sudden earnestness startled me, as did the mention of rebooting our relationship. Ever since we'd hooked up in Boston the previous year and resumed regular phone contact, I'd been questioning myself about just how committed I was to remaining single. But now that he was actually there with me—and essentially drawing a line in the sand—I felt more conflicted than ever.

"Of course I want to be with you," I said. "But I still don't know how to make things work between us, with my career. I mean, we don't have to decide right this second, right?" He looked at me again, and the sadness on his face made me feel uneasy. "I mean, we've both had sex with other people since we split up. What makes this Bruce guy so special?"

J.D. bit his lip. "He's really smart, and kind, and generous, and he always makes me feel good about myself. He comes to all my concerts, and he says he's in love with me, and he wants us to date exclusively, and see what happens." His eyes welled up. "I'm not trying to make you feel shitty, Noah, but it's just nice being with someone who goes out of his way to be with me, and doesn't think his career is the single most important thing in the world."

The pain in his voice stung me, as did the highly unpleasant realization that someone else might actually be a better fit for him than I was.

"I guess I can understand why you like him," I muttered, trying to be fair, but a wave of jealousy immediately swamped my attempt at decency. "Please tell me he's ugly, at least."

He laughed through his tears. "You wish."

We talked all night—both with and without clothes—but by the time he had to go back to Boston in the morning I still had no idea what to do, so I told him I needed more time to think about it. He said he'd already given me three years, and was sick of waiting, but he relented a little at the pathetic look on my face.

"Okay, you've got until the end of the month," he said. "But then that's it, okay?" He hugged and kissed me. "I really mean it, Noah. Shit or get off the pot."

I knew he was serious, but I still hadn't made up my mind by June 30th, so I put it off a little longer, figuring another week or two wouldn't matter in the greater scheme of things.

It did.

By the time I finally called him in mid-July (to beg for yet a little *more* time) he said no, of course, because it was too late; he was already in an exclusive relationship with Bruce. He said he still wanted to be friends with me, but we couldn't have sex anymore; he also said we should probably not have much contact for a while, either, just to be safe.

It hurt like hell, but God help me, I still didn't believe, even then, that the two of them would last.

2008: J.D. and Bruce got hitched. Mom and I were invited to the wedding but didn't attend; me because I couldn't bear it, her because she thought J.D. would feel he needed to take care of her, if she went by herself.

2009–2015: J.D. and I touched base probably once or twice a year, but never in person. Whenever he mentioned Bruce I pretended it didn't bother me; he always asked if I was dating any-body, but changed the subject quickly if I said yes.

2016: He told me Bruce kept suggesting I should come for a visit, because he wanted to meet me. J.D. and I talked it over and decided there was no longer any danger of old feelings resurfacing if we saw each other. The second he opened the door of his house, though, I knew we'd been dead wrong. When he hugged me, the clean, familiar smell of his skin over-whelmed me; my knees almost buckled from the weight of all the memories. His body against mine was as warm and com-fortable as the fleece blanket we used to share on our bed; his earlobe touching mine brought tears to my eyes, and when we let go of each other and stepped back, his eyes were wet, too.

And that's when I saw Bruce, standing behind him, not looking one bit happy.

Everything went downhill really damn fast. I was supposed to stay for the whole weekend, but we didn't even make it through dinner. Whenever J.D. or I brought up something from our past, Bruce would sigh, pout, or quietly radiate spite from his seat at the table; J.D. and I did everything we could to draw him into the conversation, but it didn't help. J.D. got embarrassed and frustrated, and I tried not to let Bruce's overt hostility bug me. Eventually, though, my mouth overrode my brain, and—after one particularly annoying eye roll from Bruce—I asked if he was always so pleasant, or if I was just lucky enough to be there when he was in good form. He got really pissy then, and accused me of "coming on" to J.D. I opened my mouth to re-spond, and J.D. seized my wrist.

"Don't, Noah," he begged. "Please, *please*, just let me handle this, okay?" He waited for my nod before releasing me and turning to Bruce. "You know how much I love you, sweetie, but you're way out of line. Noah's not coming on to me, we're just talking."

"Bullshit," Bruce insisted. "He can't take his big puppy-dog eyes off you. It's pathetic."

I swear I hadn't been hitting on J.D. Granted, my thoughts about him were far from platonic, but I was pretty certain there was nothing in my behavior to merit Bruce's anger.

"I don't have puppy-dog eyes," I protested mildly, though my patience was wearing thin. "They're more like a lemur's."

"Don't, Noah," J.D. repeated, exasperated, but I could tell he was fighting a smile.

"Cute," Bruce snapped at me. "You think you're funny, but you're not."

"Sorry," I said. "It's hard to be funny when there's a jealous little bitch in the room."

I overestimated his self-control: He launched himself across the table and punched me in the mouth. J.D. had to wrestle him to the floor to stop him from hitting me again, and we quickly agreed it might be a good idea to cut our visit short.

2022: It's now six years later, and I'm not anticipating another invitation anytime soon.

Anyway, that's just one of many reasons today could be a disaster. My unannounced presence at Carolyn's house in Fall River, if I go there, may be just about as welcome as the Black Plague; Mom could somehow find out what I'm doing behind her back; Bruce could come after me with a machete: the list is endless.

Why the fuck am I doing this?

If you're not familiar with Wellesley, Massachusetts, it's a picturesque New England town near Boston, with an absurd amount of money, ginormous houses, private schools and colleges, landscaped lawns, etc. If J.D. weren't married, he couldn't afford to live here, but Bruce is a contract lawyer for some heavy-duty tech company. I pull into town in the early afternoon, snarf a ham sandwich at a little deli, then find my way to the high school, praying J.D. is there instead of at home. The school parking lot is mostly empty since classes don't start again until after Labor Day, but the instant I get out of Mom's car I hear the marching band rehearsing nearby, but out of sight: the football field must be behind the building.

Like a kid chasing the Pied Piper, I follow the bastardized strains of something only vaguely recognizable as "Defying Gravity" from *Wicked*, around the corner of the building. My armpits are already sweating from nerves, and the instant I see the field, surrounded by bleachers and a fence, my heart starts to race. It's a couple hundred yards to the bleachers and I can't see J.D., but the din from the band echoes off the bricks of the building behind me, growing more deafening with each step.

It was stupid to come here. Even if he wants to see me, he won't be able to talk until he's done rehearsing, which might be hours. Did I think he'd just drop everything the second I showed up? As usual, my brain doesn't function well when he's in the picture; I just wanted to see him, and I didn't think things through. I should turn around and leave, but my feet have a mind of their own, carrying me up a concrete ramp and into the middle of the bleachers.

The band is spread out before me, weaving a shape unknown to geometry. J.D. is directing from an elevated platform on my side of the field, at the fifty-yard line, with his back to me.

I'd know that ass anywhere.

The rest of his body is equally recognizable; he hasn't changed much at all, at least not from where I'm standing. He still looks enviably young and fit in shorts and a T-shirt.

The band comes to a standstill at the end of the song, and the drum majors run around like sheepdogs, herding stray kids into position as J.D. bellows through a megaphone. There are several other spectators in the bleachers, so the kids don't take any interest in me as I sit to watch. J.D. rehearses the same song again and again; it's only at the end of the fourth repetition that he happens to glance over his shoulder at the bleachers, and spots me.

He fumbles the megaphone, nearly dropping it.

We stare at each other for a few long seconds, and he finally gives me a strained smile and a wave. I start breathing again as he turns back to the band, telling them to take a ten-minute water break. He climbs down from the platform and I meet him at the foot of the bleachers. He looks as slim and strong as ever, but his face is more lined than I remember, and his hair — what I can see of it, since he's wearing a baseball cap — isn't as blond as it used to be.

"Noah Freaking York," he says, but he doesn't look mad as much as incredulous. He hugs me hard, but releases me almost at once; some of the kids are watching us. "What the hell are you doing here?"

"Ah, well, you know how much I love marching bands." I'm grinning like an idiot, in spite of everything. It's so damn good to see him. "By the way, if you make them play that fucking song again I'll slit my wrists."

He scratches his sunburned nose and grins back. "Don't tempt me. Seriously, man, why are you here?" He searches my face. "Not that I'm not happy to see you. I just wish you'd called first."

"I know, and I'm sorry. I've got a couple of things to tell you, and I didn't think Bruce would be overjoyed to see me. I know you're working now, but do you have any time later today, when we can talk?"

He hesitates, frowning. "What's so important you couldn't just call?" A foreboding seems to grip him, and he takes a sudden step forward. "Shit, Noah. Is your mom okay?"

I bite my lip and look away, not wanting to say anything else until we're someplace private. "She's okay," I lie. "But there's a lot to talk about."

His eyes — why do I always forget how blue they are? — are

waiting for mine when I look back at him, like he's trying to read my mind. He glances down at his watch impatiently, but his voice is gentler when he tells me that his rehearsal is supposed to be over at three thirty. "Come back then and we'll go get a beer," he says.

I'm at the football field at exactly 3:25, just in time to catch the band's appalling rendition of "Memory" from *Cats*. I wait at the foot of the bleachers again as J.D. dismisses the kids with a few hurried words of encouragement, then talks to his drum majors for a minute as everyone else wanders off the field. The kids pay closer attention to me this time as they walk by. I'm sure they're aware that J.D. is married, and they probably know Bruce by sight, so no doubt they're wondering who the hell I am, and what I'm doing here.

I'm wondering the same damn things.

J.D. joins me at last, still holding his megaphone and a clipboard. Neither of us says anything at first; we just stand there, looking at each other and waiting until all the kids are out of earshot.

"What the hell were you thinking when you picked the music for your show?" I ask, finally. "Have you no sense of decency, sir?"

He snorts, setting his stuff on a sideline bench. "The kids love it. Don't blame me."

Suddenly, we're hugging again, and this time he doesn't let go for a while. I rest my chin on his shoulder and hold him, not caring at all that his shirt is sweaty and he could use a shower. I also don't care that he's squeezing my ribs hard enough to make breathing problematic; he can keep right on squeezing until I pass out, as far as I'm concerned.

"So," he says at last, clearing his throat. "How about we go get that beer?"

I tell him it's better if we talk here, with no one else around, and he doesn't argue; he just leads me up to a shady spot in front of the announcer's booth, at the top of the bleachers. We sit side by side, and he takes off his baseball cap and wipes his forehead with his sleeve. His hair has receded a little at the temples, but there's no white in it.

"Mom's got ALS," I say quietly, before he can ask. "I just found out a few days ago."

He turns pale and reaches for my hand. I tell him what Mom told me about her condition, and we both cry, then he listens as I tell him about her wanting me to move home, and find Carolyn. I talk about Cindy and Janelle, too, and how I already found Carolyn, and what I'm thinking of doing after I leave here today. He doesn't say much while I'm talking, aside from asking a couple of questions; he just holds my hand and waits until I've caught him up on everything. He knows my whole family history, anyway, so it doesn't take long. When I run out of words, he stares down at our interlocked fingers for a while, and I wait for him to gather his thoughts.

"I don't know what to say about your mom." He leans against the announcer's booth. "I love her very much. I can't imagine what my life would've been like if she hadn't let me live with you guys back in high school." He turns his head toward me. "I'm guessing you know that she and I still talk on the phone every once in a while."

"Yeah, she told me." I lean against the booth, too, our linked hands resting between us on the bleacher seat. "I'm pretty sure she's plotting to disinherit me, and adopt you."

He grins. "Yep. The paperwork is already done." His grin fades. "Are you okay?"

I shrug. "Not really, no, but I've had a few days to get used to the idea. I'm sorry I didn't tell you sooner."

"Part of me almost wishes you'd never said anything at all." He squeezes my fingers. "But I would've kicked your ass if I'd heard the news somewhere else."

Voices are coming from the ramp in the bleachers below us, and three high school kids—a boy and two girls, dressed in running shorts, tank tops, and sneakers—emerge into the sunlight, chattering away. J.D. releases my hand before they spot us. I understand, of course; Wellesley may be a liberal town, but even so, I doubt very much that the school board would be pleased to hear a rumor about him cozying up to a man not his husband, on school grounds.

Not to mention how Bruce would react, if he found out.

"Sorry," J.D. says, looking embarrassed. "We're not doing anything wrong, but—"

"—but we'd have a hell of a time convincing anyone else of that," I finish. "I get it."

The kids notice us at last and J.D. waves at them; they wave back and one calls out, "Hey, Mr. Curtis." They make their way to the running track that circles the field and start doing warm-up stretches.

"Wow, they actually call you Mr. Curtis," I say. "I'm impressed."

"Don't be, that's an aberration. Most of the students here call me Jason."

His initials stand for Jason David, but he's always been J.D. "Since when do you go by Jason?"

He shrugs. "For a long time, actually." He smiles at my surprise. "You and your mom are the only ones left who still call me J.D. Even Bruce calls me Jason now."

"No shit?" I stare at him, wondering why he's never told me this before. "Why'd you change it?"

"I don't know really. It just happened. It feels more grown-up or something."

"Should Mom and I call you Jason, too?"

"Nope." He bends over to retie the lace on one of his sneakers. "I like being J.D. with you guys. It's a family nickname no one else is allowed to use."

That he still considers Mom and me as family, in spite of

everything, moves me immensely. I swallow past a lump in my throat and smile. "We have other names for you, too."

He laughs. "I bet."

"Mom's favorite is booger-muncher, but I prefer goat-fucker."

He laughs harder. "You are such an asshole."

We watch as the kids finish their stretches and begin running laps. I ask what he thinks about me going to meet Carolyn today, without telling Mom.

"I think you've got a death wish," he says. "I get that you want to protect your mom, but even if Carolyn turns out to be horrible, Virginia will still want to meet her, and I doubt there's anything you can do to make that easier." He glances at me. "Whatever you're going to do, though, your mom will kill you for not saying something to her right away, and the longer you wait—"

"—the more dead I'll be," I finish, sighing. "Yeah, I know. I should probably go home right now and start groveling." I swat a mosquito on my calf. "But what if Carolyn ends up being as touchy as Mom? I keep thinking maybe I can smooth things out before they meet."

"Right," he says, deadpan. "Because your diplomatic skills are so legendary."

I jab him in the side, making him yelp. "I came here for advice," I tell him. "Not abuse."

"That was your first mistake," he says, rubbing his ribs and sobering. "I don't have any advice, man. But I guess if it was me, I'd want to meet Carolyn, too, before telling your mom." He hesitates. "It may not be the right thing to do, but maybe it's not wrong, either."

I make a face. "Thanks. That's incredibly helpful."

"Shut up," he says, swatting my thigh.

Our eyes meet, and all the memories of being together—just like this, talking, touching, teasing each other—nearly overpower me, and I can see the same thing happening to him. I'm sure he remembers, as well as I do, what ensued nine times out of ten, after all the talking, touching, and teasing. We both glance instinctively at the kids, to make sure they aren't watching us, and then we look back at each other and smile ruefully, knowing we're playing with fire.

"Guess I better go," I say.

"Yeah." He chews on his lip, looking away. "You better."

He walks me back to the parking lot, both of us silent until we get there. With each step we take, his right hand nearly touches my left, and our feet—his in red sneakers, mine in sandals—are in perfect sync as we follow the sidewalk to Mom's car.

"Wow," he says. "Virginia still has her old Corolla."

"Yep. She likes to tell me it's the only reliable thing in her life." I dig my keys out of my pocket. "By the way, she ordered me to have you call her as soon as we're done talking today."

He nods. "I will."

"Tell her I had to run down to Providence, to pick something up at my apartment."

He raises an eyebrow. "But you're going to Fall River instead, right?"

"Yep."

"So you want me to lie to Virginia."

"Yep."

He shakes his head. "Nope."

"What do you mean, 'nope'? "

"I won't lie to your mom, Noah. I won't say what you're doing, but I won't lie to her."

I make a face. "Chickenshit. Okay, just tell her I said I have a couple of things to do before I head back to Oakland."

"That much I can do." He pulls me close and holds me tightly; his lips brush against my ear. "Love you," he says, his breath warm on my neck. "Good luck with everything."

"Love you, too." The intimacy is suddenly too much for me,

and I release him quickly, before my stupid, predictable erection announces itself. "And good luck to you as well."

His shit-eating grin tells me I should've let him go sooner. "What do I need luck for?" he asks archly.

"Your godawful marching band, for one thing," I say, blushing, but when I glance down surreptitiously at his shorts I'm gratified to note I'm not the only horny person here. "You also need luck disciplining *that* silly damn thing," I tell him. "I'd lend a hand, but I doubt Bruce would approve."

He blushes, too, laughing. "Go away," he says. "Stop complicating my life."

I get in the hot car, start the engine, and roll down my window. "Remember to call Mom, okay?"

"I'm doing it right now," he says, tugging his phone out of his pocket and waving goodbye. As I pull out of the parking lot and onto the street, he's still standing where I left him, looking after me.

CHAPTER 5

I've been to Fall River before, twice. It's a blue collar, predominantly Catholic town, with a plethora of abandoned and/or repurposed textile factories dating back to the area's heyday as a manufacturing mecca in the nineteenth century. Aside from great Portuguese food and wine, the city now has two remaining claims to fame: Battleship Cove and Lizzie Borden. At the risk of sounding like a lame-ass tour guide, Battleship Cove is a memorial park with some World War II ships and a submarine you can scamper around on, and the Lizzie Borden house is a bed-and-breakfast, where clinically insane people pay good money to sleep and/or have intercourse in the same rooms where Lizzie allegedly chopped up her parents with an ax.

The first time I came to Fall River, I went to Battleship Cove with a friend; the second time I came alone, to see a fado singer at a Portuguese restaurant. And no, of course I didn't go near Lizzie's freak show of a house, either time; just thinking about it makes my skin crawl. What the hell is *wrong* with people who want to do a sleepover in the same room where there was once a goddamn bloodbath?

I'm a bit on edge right now.

I'm in my car with the windows rolled down, sweating my balls off as I stake out Carolyn's house from across the street. It only took forty-five minutes to get to Fall River after I left J.D., and once I got here it just took another twenty minutes on my phone to find Carolyn. From start to finish, this search for my sister has been ludicrously simple. Even given that I nearly went blind from playing detective on the internet, it's preposterous that I just started looking for her a couple days ago. If I believed in fate, which I don't, I'd think that God was toying with me, setting me up as the butt of some twisted cosmic joke.

Anyway, here I am, feeling like a creepy stalker in front of a three-story, red brick house at the corner of Rock and Hannaford Streets. It's a stately, Victorian-era home, with half a dozen maple trees and one big-ass oak in a recently mowed yard, all surrounded by a wrought-iron fence. According to my creepy-stalker web search, 918 Rock Street is the current residence of Carolyn and Benjamin Fortier, their adult son Oliver, and Oliver's two kids, Leo, 16, and Michael, 11. What the internet isn't yet aware of, thank God (and what you may need a scorecard for), is that Carolyn is not just the half sister but *also* the aunt of your humble tour guide, which makes Benjamin said tour guide's brother-in-law *and* uncle; Oliver is therefore a nephew *and* cousin, which makes Oliver's kids—

Oh, for Christ's sake, Noah. Get a grip.

The reason I've been stewing in this car for an hour is because I'm paralyzed by cowardice. The Fortiers are home, or at least three of them are. One of the kids—Leo, the teenager, emerged from the house a little bit ago to toss some trash in the bin near the fence gate. The last picture of him that his mom posted on Facebook was at least a year or two old, so I was startled to see how much he now looks like me when I was his age, with the same skinny torso, long black hair, and olive skin. When he came outside tonight he was only wearing cutoff shorts, and he lingered by the gate for a few minutes, talking on his phone and sauntering around barefoot on the lawn until a woman's voice—Carolyn's, most likely—yelled from inside, telling him to come help Michael with the dishes.

That was twenty minutes ago, and yet here I cower, shitting in my drawers.

Apparently dinner is over, and the Family Fortier is now doing whatever it does on balmy August evenings. I'm fairly certain their plan for tonight doesn't include a visit from a mysterious, sweaty, middle-aged stranger, claiming to be kin. This being the case, there's nothing preventing me from aborting this suicide mission and hauling my craven ass back to New Hampshire, where I can then come clean with Mom. She'll be pissed I ventured this far without her, of course, but at least she won't be homicidal. Once I tell her what I know, we can figure out together how best to proceed, then I can go to bed with a clear conscience.

Fuck.

I force myself to open the car door and get out, pausing to unstick the back of my shirt and shorts from my skin. I should've thought to at least bring a clean shirt, but I wasn't counting on being pathetic for an entire hour once I got here. I slowly cross the street, my heart racing, and stop at the iron gate.

"Last chance, moron," I mutter. "Walk away while you still can."

I unlatch the squeaky gate and slither through.

Carolyn must dislike air-conditioning as much as Mom, because every window in the house is open; one on the second story has a box fan in it, going full blast. I climb the porch steps and rap on the flimsy screen door, painted dark green. The main door is open, so I can see the entry hall through the screen. I can also hear a TV in the front room on the left, where somebody's watching *Jeopardy*.

A kid's voice calls out "I'll get it" and two seconds later, Michael—I recognize him right away from Facebook—pops into the hall from the kitchen. He's a short, stocky kid with chipmunk cheeks, and he's dressed in blue shorts and a baggy white T-shirt.

"Hi," he says warily, stopping at the door and peering up at me through the screen. He probably thinks I'm a badly dressed Jehovah's Witness.

"Hi," I say. "Is Carolyn home?"

"Grandma!" he calls over his shoulder. "It's for you."

"Who is it, honey?" She's in the front room.

"Hi, Carolyn," I call back, before Michael can answer. "Sorry to bother you, but do you have a minute to talk?"

I hear a sigh, and the creak of a floorboard, then she's in the hallway, too.

"Yes?" Her tone is courteous, though not particularly welcoming as she joins Michael in the doorway. "What can I do for you?"

It's so surreal to see her up close. She has the same green eyes and sharp cheekbones as Mom and me, and our same smallish ears. Her bare feet, long and thin, look exactly like ours, too. If she didn't have blond hair and pale skin, she'd be instantly recognizable as Mom's daughter. As she studies me, her eyes narrow in puzzlement, as if I look familiar to her, too, but she can't quite place me.

I swallow hard, appalled to find myself near tears. "Hi," I say again. "My name is Noah York." I open and close my mouth a couple of times, a fish caught in a net. I don't want to just blurt out why I'm there, especially not in front of Michael, but I don't even know how to get her to let me in the door, let alone talk to me in private.

"Yes?" she says again, with a touch of impatience.

I clear my throat and get a hold of myself. "Uh, this is going to sound nuts, but we're, uh, kind of related."

She raises her eyebrows exactly the same way Mom does when she thinks she's hearing bullshit. "Related? What are you talking about?"

I glance at Michael, who seems intrigued, and then back at

Carolyn. "It might be better if we talk by ourselves first," I say. "It's nothing bad, it's just . . . weird. Can you maybe come out here on the porch, or something?"

She frowns. "I'm sorry, but I don't feel comfortable with that. Just go ahead and tell me what you mean."

I swallow again. I really should've thought about what to say before I got here; she's not going to believe me at all, and I'll be lucky if she doesn't end up calling the cops.

Inspiration hits. "Your birth name was Carolyn Thatcher," I say.

She puts a hand on her chest. "How on *earth* do you know that?" She looks at Michael, too, as if she's rethinking her decision to talk in front of him, and then she turns back to me. "I've never used that name in my life. I was adopted when I was just a baby."

"I know," I tell her. "By Kenneth and Frances Kaine."

Her surprise becomes alarm. "Who are you?" she demands. "How in *hell* do you know these things about me?" She looks over her shoulder. "Ben? Get out here, please!"

Oh, good. She's going to have her husband kick my ass.

"I found your adoption records on the internet," I say quickly. "I'm your half brother."

Her jaw drops and her eyes get huge.

"What's going on, Grandma?" Michael asks.

Ben steps into the hall. He's a tall, beefy guy with a bald eagle tattooed on his bicep, but he doesn't look threatening, just concerned. "What's wrong, sweetcakes?"

"What do you mean, you're my half brother?" Carolyn asks me. "That's . . . that's crazy."

I nod. "I know. But it's true."

"Who is this guy?" Ben asks.

There's a staircase by the door that leads to the second floor, and Leo suddenly appears at the top of the stairs, still just wearing cutoffs. As he trots down to join us, it's like seeing the ghost of my teenage self; his hair is a little bit longer than mine was, almost reaching his naked shoulders, but he looks every bit as cocky and curious as I used to be whenever anybody new showed up at our house.

"What's going on?" he asks, staring at me. "What did I miss?"

I turn back to Carolyn. "I know I sound like an escapee from a mental hospital," I tell her. "But please believe me. You're my half sister. We have the same mother."

She reaches for Ben's hand, but keeps her eyes on me. "I don't know where you got your information, but I find that hard to believe. I know next to nothing about my biological parents, but one of the few things I *do* know is that their last name was Thatcher. Didn't you just say your last name was York?"

"That was my dad's last name. And Thatcher was never really *anybody's* name. I mean, nobody related to you and me. Mom's maiden name was Thomas, and she never married anybody but my dad."

She clearly thinks I'm barking mad. "You've lost me," she says. "If your mom was never a Thatcher, how can I possibly be your half sister?"

I take a deep breath and start babbling like a meth-head. "I'm sorry, it's really complicated. Thatcher was just a made-up name that Mom's dad used when they gave you up for adoption. It wasn't Mom's fault, by the way. She didn't want to use phony names, or give you up, or any of it, but her dad made her. He was the one who invented the Thatchers, so there wouldn't be any way to trace them. Anyway, like I said, Mom's maiden name was Virginia Thomas, but now it's Virginia York. She's your mom, too. I mean, she's our mom." I know I should shut up now but my idiot tongue won't stop flapping. "I've got stuff I can show you on my phone about how I found you."

"This is crazy," she says again, shaking her head. "It has to be some kind of mistake."

A bearded, skinny guy about my age—it takes me a second

to recognize him from Facebook, but it's Oliver, Leo and Michael's dad—sticks his head out of the front room. "What the heck's going on out here?" he asks. "If you're not watching *Jeopardy*, can I change the channel?"

I grapple for a second with the weirdness of this man being my nephew, but then force myself to focus on my sister again. I glance at Leo, now standing behind his little brother at the foot of the stairs. "Just take a good look at your grandson, Leo, there," I tell Carolyn, somewhat desperately, because she's looking like she wants to close the door in my face. "If I were twenty years younger, you couldn't tell us apart, but even now you can see the close resemblance, right?" I take my phone out of my pocket. "I've got pictures of Mom, too. Do you want to see them?"

Glory, hallelujah: Carolyn may not believe me yet, but Ben is staring intently at both Leo and me, wonder dawning on his face.

"They do look a lot alike, Carolyn," he says. "I mean, maybe it's just a weird coincidence, but let's hear him out."

Carolyn frowns, but then turns to stare at Leo, too, as does Michael. Leo doesn't even seem to notice all the scrutiny; he's too busy studying me with frank fascination.

"Seriously, what's going on?" Oliver demands. "Who is this guy?"

I pull up a picture of Mom that I took a couple of years ago, around Halloween. It's one of my favorite photos of her; she's sitting on the front porch, reading a book, with her hair tucked behind her ears; she's got on a blue flannel shirt and jeans, and as usual her feet are bare. She didn't know I was taking her picture; I was home for a rare visit, and I got a bug up my ass to rake the leaves in the front yard. She came out to tell me I was doing it all wrong, but then stayed to read, and I happened to catch her just as she lifted her head from the book. She was completely unselfconscious, and clearly distracted, but the intelligence in her eyes was almost frightening, like she'd just figured out the meaning of life, or maybe God's secret nickname, or what the actual fuck happened to Amelia Earhart. She was also hauntingly beautiful; I caught her just when the autumn sun was at its gentlest, at twilight, making her hair and skin luminous.

"This is Mom," I tell Carolyn, holding my phone up to the screen door for her to see. "I took it a while back, but she hasn't changed much."

She seems almost reluctant to look, but after she stares at the picture for a while she opens the door, finally, and reaches for my phone, her hand trembling slightly. Ben and Leo lean in over her shoulders to see it, too.

"She looks like you, Grandma," Leo breathes, turning to gape at her. "Holy shit."

Ben flicks his grandson's head reflexively and murmurs "Language," but his heart isn't in it; he's too absorbed in the picture to focus on anything else.

"Let me see, Grandma," Michael begs, standing on tiptoe to get a better view. "She's really pretty. What's her name again?"

"Virginia York," I say. "Your great-grandmother."

I'm sure he's already figured this out, but he doesn't seem to mind the clarification.

"Slow down, please," Carolyn says. "We don't know that for sure, yet." She finally looks up from the phone and meets my eyes again. "But I suppose you better come inside."

"What's *your* name?" Leo asks me as I step in the door. "I didn't catch it."

"I'm Noah. Noah York."

"And you're my great-uncle?"

I nod, and he smiles shyly at me.

"We don't know that for sure," Carolyn repeats, with a touch more asperity. "Let's not jump to any conclusions, shall we?"

* * *

We end up sitting at a small round table in their kitchen, under a rickety ceiling fan that's useless in the heat. I'm wedged between Carolyn and Leo, with Michael on Leo's other side and Ben next to Carolyn; Oliver is directly across from me. I smell a little ripe from nerves—and from marinating too long in a hot car—but everybody else is sweating, too, and nobody's wrinkling their nose at me, so I guess it's fine. Ben offered me a Budweiser and I accepted, but now I wish I hadn't, since no one else is drinking anything. I feel awkward because they're all looking at me expectantly, and I don't have a clue what to say. Now that I've come this far, I'm finally waking up to how stupid it is to be here with no strategy for fielding Carolyn's inevitable questions.

Jesus, I'm such a moron.

Spending time with Cindy and Janelle this week has been strange enough, but this encounter with the Fortiers is even stranger, given that before a few days ago I didn't even know they existed, apart from Carolyn. My first impression is guardedly positive; I see amazement in their faces, and curiosity, but I also see kindness. The tightness in Carolyn's shoulders and the fidgeting of her hands on the table, though, makes her look brittle and nervous, and she seldom meets my eyes. Ben, on the other hand, is so still and calm that he might as well be a rock, and he gazes at me steadily, with no outward sign of mistrust. Oliver takes after Carolyn, physically, with a thin build and an inability to sit still, but when we make eye contact he smiles, and there's sweetness in it. Michael can barely contain his excitement at this unforeseen development—he's squirming like a puppy about to pee on the floor—and Leo is watching me so closely it's a little unnerving. Carolyn made him put on a shirt before we sat at the table, and he chose a DARK SIDE OF THE MOON tank top.

I take a deep breath and finally kick things off by showing Carolyn the email from the adoption website; she reads through it silently, then passes my phone to Ben. I explain how I used the info on the website to find the obituaries for her adoptive parents, which eventually led me here. She's shaken, I can tell, but if her stern face is any indication, she has no intention of letting go of her skepticism any time soon.

"Okay," she says, as Ben reads. "So is that all the information you have?"

"Pretty much." I take a swig of beer and wish it were something stronger—at this point, I'm tempted to ask for a shot of kerosene. "Mom gave me your date of birth, and the names her dad used at the adoption agency, but that's all she knew, besides when they left you there. I figured it would be a miracle if we ever found you, with so little to go on, but it just took a couple of days. It's crazy how fast it all came together."

"And your mother is sure that Thatcher is the name she and her father used? Toby and Nan Thatcher? It all happened an awfully long time ago."

I smile in spite of myself. "Mom's memory is crappy when it comes to normal stuff, like watering the plants, or paying her bills." I wipe off a puddle of condensation on the table from my beer can. "But if you ask her to name every single kid from her kindergarten class, she can do it in alphabetical order. She's a total freak."

Everybody smiles but Carolyn. "Even so," she says, " isn't it possible she may have made a mistake?"

I shake my head, sobering. "I don't think so. She told me she remembers everything about going to the adoption center, and leaving you there. She said it was one of the worst days of her life."

Carolyn's mouth tightens at the corners, and she asks to see the picture of Mom again. Oliver is reading the email on my phone, and objects to surrendering it, but Carolyn insists and he hands it back to me. I pull up the photo and pass it to Carolyn.

"How long ago did you take this?" she asks. "She doesn't look nearly old enough to be my mother." Her eyes flit across my face again. "And you don't look nearly old enough to be my brother, by the way."

I hesitate; this is dangerous territory. "Mom was pretty young when you were born."

"How young?"

I clear my throat. "Really young. She was twelve."

Everybody stirs, but Michael can't contain himself. "What?" he gasps. "That's only a year older than me!"

Leo rolls his eyes at his little brother. "No shit, Sherlock."

"Language, Leo," Oliver says.

Michael reddens. "You're a turd, Leo."

"Knock it off, both of you," Oliver says.

"Leo started it," Michael says, then looks at me again. "How come she had a baby when she was only twelve?"

I stall for time by sipping more beer, and Carolyn, watching me, unexpectedly steps in. "A lot of young girls get pregnant too early, Mike. It shouldn't happen, but sometimes it's . . . unavoidable." She eyes Mom's picture again. "So how old is she now?"

"Sixty-eight," I say, and watch everyone do the math in their heads. The numbers add up, of course; Carolyn is fifty-six. Ben and Oliver glance at Carolyn with raised eyebrows, and Leo and Michael grow visibly more excited. Carolyn, though, just chews on her lip, almost as if she's disappointed she can't just dismiss the whole thing out of hand.

She puts down my phone and fiddles with a salt-and-pepper shaker in the middle of the table. "So why didn't she come with you today, if you're both so sure I'm the one you're looking for?"

My face gets hot. "She doesn't know I found you." I grimace at their expressions. "I'm a dead man walking, by the way. She'll crucify me for doing this without her."

They're all thinking the same thing, no doubt, but it's Leo who asks. "So how come you didn't tell her?"

"I wanted to make sure she'd be welcome," I say carefully. "I know that sometimes people who've been adopted don't want anything to do with their birth family." I turn back to Carolyn. "I'm really sorry for just showing up like this, by the way."

My sister's face is a study in conflict. I thought her shock would be wearing off a little by now, but it's clear she's still reeling.

"Maybe it's for the best that you don't tell her, yet," she says. "Until we can absolutely confirm all of this, I mean."

"How do you suggest we do that, Mom?" Oliver asks, with a hint of impatience. "What else do you need?"

"I don't know," she says, frowning as she waves a hand at my phone, "but more than this." Her eyes slide from my face to Leo's, and she thaws slightly. "I'm not saying you're making this up, Noah. I just think we need to be really careful here."

"We can do a DNA test," I offer. "That would at least confirm we're family, right?"

"Makes sense," Ben says, and Oliver nods.

"I suppose so," Carolyn says. "But I need time to think, before we do anything like that." She touches my wrist briefly, as if to confirm I'm real; her fingers are warm. "Will you please tell me more about your mother?"

So far, so good: As long as she's not asking about her father, I don't have to lie. My introduction doesn't get very far, however, because once I tell them where Mom lives, and that she has a sister and niece, who happen to be visiting right now, Carolyn interrupts.

"She has a sister and a niece?" she asks, looking a little faint. "Just how big is your family?"

I can't blame her for her anxiety; for all she knows, she may have fifty half-siblings.

"That's all of us," I reassure her. "Mom and me, Aunt Cindy, and my cousin Janelle." I pause. "And now you guys, too, I guess."

Carolyn manages to refrain from telling me to hold my damn horses, but she changes the subject, asking what Mom does for a living, or if she's retired.

"Mom will never retire," I tell her. "She's a poet, by trade. She'll die with a pencil in her hand, trying to figure out what rhymes with aneurysm."

"Wait a minute!" Leo blurts. "I had to memorize a poem last year for my English class, called 'The Lost Soul,' by Virginia York. Your mom isn't *that* Virginia York, is she?"

I can't help wincing: Of course his English teacher would pick that goddamn poem and not any of a thousand others Mom has written. "Yep. That's her."

No one else at the table seems to know what we're talking about, which is a relief, but Leo's eyes are bugging out of his head. "Holy crap, that poem was *awesome*. It was about her messed-up son. That's *you*?"

"Yep," I say again, sighing. "She was exaggerating the messed-up part."

"Wow." He shakes his head and looks around the table. "I can't believe we're related to a famous writer."

I grimace, torn between aggravation and pride, per usual. "There are a lot of days when I wish I weren't." I can tell he doesn't know how to respond, and I grin. "She's a great lady, but she's also a royal pain in the butt."

Carolyn is listening closely, with a vulnerable, hungry expression she can't quite hide. Ben sees it, too, because when Oliver and the boys begin peppering me with questions he tells them all to pipe down and let me talk.

I figure I should steer clear of Mom's childhood, so I tell them about her job at Cassidy College, and how we used to live in Chicago until Dad died; I also tell them that she leads a quiet life, living alone and scribbling away in her room every day. I'm trying to not scare them off, so I don't talk about her moodiness or her temper; I say what a good cook she is, and how she knows everything because she reads so damn much, and I mention Walter, her sort-of boyfriend. I tell them about how she's always listening to the radio, and sometimes makes me dance with her if a song comes on that she likes. Carolyn abruptly stops me again.

"So why did you wait so long to try to find me?"

The change of subject catches me flat-footed, as does the fact that she's now looking at me straight on, unblinking. I suddenly wonder if she ever tried to find Mom. If she did, she would've hit a dead end, of course, thanks to Grandpa's lies, but it might explain why her own information was so readily available online.

"I'm not really sure how to answer that," I say slowly, fearful of stepping in shit. "Mom and I have always wanted to know what happened to you, but it's an unbelievably weird story, and I should probably let her tell it." Carolyn's face darkens a little, making me feel guilty; if I were in her shoes, I'd want to know everything right now, too. I touch her wrist, the same way she touched mine, and I'm relieved when she doesn't pull away from me. "What I *can* say, though, is that until just this week, Mom never told me about the adoption center, or the phony names. I knew I had a big sister someplace, but I had no idea where to look because Mom kept that stuff secret from me, my whole life."

"So why the sudden change of heart?" Carolyn demands, and there's an edge to her voice that wasn't there before. "Was there a 'Take-Your-Daughter-To-Work Day' coming up soon?"

I guess sarcasm is genetic.

I debate with myself for a minute, then tell them about Mom's

ALS. Carolyn flinches, and everybody is stricken silent, even Michael. I doubt he knows what it is, but he's smart enough to see it's not good. Ben eventually says that he's sorry to hear it, and Oliver and Leo murmur something similar. I thank them and wait for Carolyn's reaction, but she stays mute.

"I feel bad for dumping all this on you," I tell her. "You were probably having a perfectly nice, stress-free evening until I showed up on your doorstep."

She nods, not smiling. "It's a lot to take in." She considers my face again for a moment, then pushes away from the table. "Please excuse me, Noah," she says. Her voice is gentle, but firm. "I think my family and I need some time by ourselves, to talk things through. Would you mind leaving now, so we can do that?"

I probably shouldn't be taken aback by the dismissal, but I am. I look at her uncertainly for a second then tell her sure, that's fine, and I push away from the table, too, not knowing what else to do. Her family seems at a loss as well; Ben rests a hand on her shoulder and looks at her questioningly, and Leo goes so far as to tell her that I just got here. She silences him with the same don't-fuck-with-me look I've seen on Mom's face a thousand times.

"There'll be plenty of time to talk to Noah later, Leo, if we decide to pursue this," she says. "Noah, can you give Ben your phone number before you go? I imagine we'll be in touch soon."

She shakes my hand formally and then quickly leaves the room, but not before I see that her chin is trembling. Ben shakes my hand, too, but much more warmly; he tells me not to worry. "Carolyn's just thrown for a loop," he says. "I'm sure it'll all work out fine, once she chews things over."

The kindness in his voice moves me, especially because I'm not sure at all that he's right. It's pretty clear that Carolyn calls the shots here, and at the moment I'd say there's a fifty-fifty chance she'll decide to keep her distance from Mom and me forever.

"I really hope so," I say. "I'd like to get to know you guys better." Shaking hands with Oliver and the boys, too, I realize how true that is: Strangers or not, these people are family, and seem like a decent sort. Leo and Michael are openly disappointed, shuffling their feet and frowning.

I give Ben my contact info, thank him for the beer, and say goodnight, then just like that I'm outside again, walking to my car. I've been inside for such a short time that it's not yet full dark out; I can still make out the gothic details on the brickwork of a big Catholic church across the street. Just as I reach my car, someone softly calls my name, giving me a start. It's Leo, and he runs barefoot across the road to meet me.

"Sorry about Grandma making you leave like that," he says. "She's kind of annoying, sometimes."

I grin. "Wait until you meet your great grandmother."

"I'm going to come see you guys," he says, matter-of-factly. "I've got my own car, and she can't stop me."

His willingness to connect is endearing, but it's also worrisome; the last thing any of us need right now is a battle of wills between him and his grandmother. "You'd be more than welcome," I say. "But please wait until Carolyn makes up her mind about what she wants to do, okay? I don't want to get you in trouble."

"What's she gonna do, spank me?" he says disdainfully, but he darts a quick look over his shoulder at the house. "I'm not a little kid, and I'll be out of here soon, anyway."

Oh, God. He reminds me so much of me at his age that I don't know if should hug him or knee him in the balls.

"Fair enough," I say. "But even so, maybe you should wait at least a couple of days before you stir the pot. My mom is already going to disembowel me when I tell her about this, and if you show up without permission from your grandma, she'll do the same to you."

He laughs. "Okay, but I'm not waiting forever. I bet Dad and Michael will want to come, too." He sticks out his hand self-consciously, and we shake again; his hand is sweaty but his grip is firm. "Bye, Uncle Noah," he says, then trots back across the road.

I watch him until he vanishes into the house—he lingers for a second at the screen door, first, to wave at me—then I sigh and climb back into the car. It's going to be a long drive home, but that's just fine by me: With any luck at all, Mom will be in bed by the time I get there. I'd prefer a good night of sleep before I have to kiss my bowels goodbye.

CHAPTER 6

Well, fuck.

Even though I took my sweet time coming home—I stopped at a noisy, sticky little diner just north of Wellesley, and choked down a gut bomb of a cheeseburger—there are still lights on at Mom's house as I pull into the driveway. I roll up the windows and turn off the engine, then gather my courage to go inside. The lights don't necessarily mean Mom is still awake; she may have gone to bed and left Cindy and Janelle to their own devices. I'm fine with seeing them tonight, but if Mom's waiting to pounce when I walk through the door, I'm doomed. She'll want to know all about my visit with J.D., and why it took me so long to get home, and before you know it, I'll spill everything, and the jaws of Hell will open wide.

Yeah, okay, maybe that's a bit over-the-top, but you haven't seen Mom when she goes full-on, bugshit crazy.

"Calm down, loser," I mutter. "It's not like she's going to disown you."

I get out of the car and trudge wearily to the back door, but before I get there I hear the jingle of metal tags nearby on the lawn, then a small black shape appears at my feet and starts licking my toes.

"Hey, Sadie," I say, squatting to scratch under her collar. "How about we pack our bags right now and move to Siberia?" I don't dare pet her for long, in case Freddie comes looking for her. If I get in another brawl with that pastel buffoon before I even make it in the house, I'll never survive the Thunderdome portion of the evening with Mom. I give Sadie a farewell pat on the rear and stand up again, wincing at the stiffness in my knees.

The door is open—Mom always forgets to lock it—and I step inside and kick off my sandals. The kitchen is dark, but lights are on in the living room, and I sigh when I hear Mom and Cindy talking. I can't hear what they're saying, because there's music on the stereo: Rachmaninoff's second piano concerto, one of Mom's favorite pieces. She only listens to it when she's feeling sentimental, though, so she must be either a little drunk or a little blue.

I go to the sink and pound a glass of water, then pour myself a double shot of Scotch from Mom's liquor cabinet. I guess it's possible I could avoid telling her everything tonight, but I may as well get it over with. I sigh again, then head for the living room.

Mom and Cindy are on the couch, and Janelle is sitting cross-legged on the floor by the coffee table, facing them. Mom's feet are resting on Cindy's lap, which surprises me; it's odd they're still so comfortable together, when they've been apart so many years. I was quiet when I entered the house, but apparently they all heard me, anyway, because no one is surprised when I walk in.

"Hey, cuz," Janelle says. "Welcome back."

"Hi, sweetie," Cindy says. "Glad you made it home in one piece."

"There you are," Mom says. "I was hoping it was you in the kitchen, and not some urchin come to rob me blind."

I show her my glass. "This particular urchin stole some of your Scotch."

"Fine by me," she says. "That's the cheap stuff. I keep my Macallan well hidden." She studies me as I lower myself to the floor beside Janelle. "So how was your trip?"

I shrug, trying to look casual. "It was good to see J.D."

"He said that, too, when he called today. He said he couldn't believe it when he turned around and spotted you in the bleachers at the stadium."

"Yeah, he almost fell off his podium." I sip my drink and grimace; Mom was right about its lack of pedigree. "How did your phone call go?"

Her face softens, like it always does when she talks about J.D. "He was very sweet," she says. "Thanks for breaking the news to him. You did the right thing, going there."

"Your mom has been telling us about J.D. tonight," Cindy says. "He sounds like a wonderful person."

I nod, and with no warning the long day catches up with me. I must've been in a protective stupor on the way home this evening, but everything I've been repressing since I saw J.D. is now surfacing with a vengeance. It *was* good to see him again, but it was also painful. To hear him laugh, hold his hand, and cry with him was more than enough to short-circuit me for a month, but the hug he gave me when we said goodbye may leave a permanent scar. Then, of course, came Carolyn and her family—*our* family—and the memory of sitting with them all at their kitchen table is so strong right now that I swear I can still feel Carolyn's hand on my wrist, and smell Leo's deodorant—Old Spice, not Axe, thank God—and hear the gentle rumble of Ben's voice. I can't really handle much more tonight; I take a shaky breath and blink back tears.

"Oh, honey," Cindy says. "I'm sorry. I didn't mean to upset you."

"You didn't," I tell her. "It was just a really weird day."

"What's wrong, Noah?" Mom asks. She knows me well enough

to see that this isn't just about J.D. "Where did you go today, after you left Wellesley?"

In spite of my resolution to come clean, every instinct is telling me to lie my ass off.

"I found Carolyn," I say, meeting her gaze as best as I can. "She lives in Fall River, Massachusetts."

Mom sits up fast, and Cindy and Janelle both gape at me.

"She has a husband named Ben," I continue, "and a son named Oliver, and two grandsons, Leo and Michael."

Mom's eyes bore into mine. "You've already seen them?" she asks quietly. "You've already *talked* to them?"

I nod. "Yes. I'm so sorry I didn't tell you first, but I was worried that y—"

She raises a peremptory hand and I freeze, like Pavlov's dog. She tugs violently at her hair a few times and glances at Cindy, then back at me. Cindy starts to say that she's sure I had a good reason for not saying anything until now, but Mom cuts her off. I'd hoped curiosity about Carolyn would keep her anger in check, but no such luck: Her face is turning purple.

Hurricane Virginia has now been upgraded to a Category 5 storm.

"What were you thinking, Noah?" she demands. "How dare you not tell me about this until now? What gives you the right to keep this to yourself?" She leaps to her feet and starts yelling. "This isn't some goddamn game, Noah, this is my *daughter*! Do you know how long I've wanted to see her again, how hard it was for me to not start looking for her until recently? How can you not know what this means to me? What in God's name is *wrong* with you?"

I don't want to cry, but I can't help it. "I had to make sure she was a good person, before you met her," I say, my voice breaking. "I was worried about how she might treat you."

"That wasn't your decision to make! I'm your *mother*, Noah, I don't need to be babied!" She slaps the fireplace mantel in fury, sending a picture of Dad and me flying; Janelle miraculously catches it before it hits the floor.

My own temper stirs a little, in spite of my shame: She knows damn well my heart was in the right place, even if my brain was up my ass. "I wasn't babying you," I tell her. "I was just trying to help."

"Well, you damn well didn't!" she howls. "Christ, what have you done? What were you *thinking*?"

She looks around the room wildly, likely seeking more objects to destroy. Cindy touches Mom's arm, which is both brave and stupid; I'd rather stick my hand in a Cuisinart at the moment than go near my mother.

"What's done is done, Ginny," she says softly. "Maybe we should hear what Carolyn had to say to Noah?"

I've never heard anybody call Mom "Ginny" before, but for some reason it seems to reach her; she looks down at Cindy's hand on her arm and visibly fights to rein in her temper, breathing hard and chewing on her lip. I wipe my face on my sleeve, but I don't turn away when she glares at me for at least half a minute, and I'm rewarded when she eventually breaks eye contact. Janelle squeezes my shoulder, and I'm grateful for her support; I'm even more grateful to Cindy, for playing referee. I didn't think it was possible at this point to pull Mom back from the brink, but she somehow did it.

"You're right, Cindy," Mom mutters. "What's done is done." She faces me again. "But don't think for a minute that we're finished talking about this. I don't know how you can possibly justify your actions, and I'm going to have a hard time forgiving you."

Fresh tears course down my cheeks. "I never meant to hurt you," I say. "You know how much I love you."

She sits back down stiffly, but her eyes are no longer homicidal, just strained. "God only knows why I didn't strangle you in your crib, when I had the chance," she mutters. "Tell me everything that happened today. And I mean *everything*."

So I do.

I show her Carolyn's Facebook page on my phone, then I tell her how Carolyn reacted when I appeared on her doorstep. I describe the Fortier family in detail, and try to remember every word of the conversation we had; I talk about the expression on Carolyn's face when I showed her Mom's picture, and the tone of her voice when she asked me questions, and how Leo looks just like me. I tell her that Leo knew her name, and had memorized one of her poems for a class; I talk about Carolyn's skepticism, and her curiosity; I tell her how I avoided talking about Grandpa as much as possible, and how Carolyn abruptly sent me on my way after I told her about Mom's ALS, but also asked for my phone number, and said she'd probably be in touch soon. I describe how the rest of the family reacted, and how Leo followed me to the car and said he was going to come see us, regardless of Carolyn's wishes. I even describe their house, though by this point it's pretty obvious I'm over-compensating for my previous sins of omission. Mom listens to everything and doesn't interrupt me once; the naked vulnerability on her face is exactly the same expression I saw on Carolyn's face earlier that night, when I was describing Mom.

When I finally finish, no one says anything at all, which is fine by me. My throat is parched, and I don't know what else I can possibly tell them; I empty my Scotch in one gulp, almost gagging, and wait for somebody else to start talking. Mom opens her laptop and finds Carolyn's Facebook page again, to scrutinize her pictures; Cindy leans over to see, too, and Janelle joins them on the couch.

"So," Mom says at last. "Now what?"

I shrug helplessly. "We wait, I guess. They need time to figure stuff out."

"What about what *I* need?" Mom demands. "What if I call Carolyn right now, and tell her I'd like to see her?"

I hug my knees. "I think she might freak. She was kind of overloaded by all this."

"Which is exactly why I should've been with you today." She says this without heat, and because she's calm again I feel ten times worse than when she was yelling. "I may have been able to make things easier for her."

Cindy steps in again. "Or maybe it would've made things harder. There's no way to know, Ginny. It's completely valid for you to be upset with Noah, but it's also possible that he was the right person to initiate contact with the Fortiers."

Mom scowls at her. "Why do I suddenly feel like I'm in couples counseling?"

Janelle coughs to hide a laugh, and Cindy flushes a little, giving her daughter the evil eye. "I'm just suggesting it's more productive to focus on things as they are, instead of how they might've been," she says defensively. "But I apologize if I'm speaking out of turn."

"You aren't," Mom says. "I'm just not in a hurry to let Noah off the hook." She transfers her scowl to me. "It's immensely satisfying to watch him squirm."

Under the anger—way, way under, but still detectable—there's a trace of humor in her voice, and I breathe a little easier. It's kind of pathetic how much I hate having her so mad at me.

"Nice," I say, rising to my feet. "I'm going to get some more Scotch."

"Hurry up," Mom says. "I need you to go over everything again, to make sure you didn't leave anything out."

I nod, suppressing a groan, and head for the kitchen, but she stops me before I get there.

"You said Leo memorized one of my poems," she says, and glory be, there's a familiar twinkle in her goddamn eye. "But you didn't say which one."

I glower at her. "Which one do you think?"

"Good," she says shortly. "It serves you right. I hope he recited it to you, word for word."

*   *   *

It's almost one in the morning but I'm too wound up to sleep, so I'm reading Patrick O'Brian in bed when there's a soft knock on my door. It's another hot night and I'm naked; I grab a sheet and cover up before saying, "Come in."

The door opens, revealing a swath of red hair. Janelle steps in the room and closes the door behind her; she's wearing a white T-shirt and a pair of what looks like men's boxers. "I got up to pee and saw the light under your door," she says, perching at the end of my bed. "I can't believe you're still awake after all that drama tonight. I thought you'd be in a coma."

"My eyes won't shut," I say, adjusting my reading lamp so it's not blinding her. "Near-death experiences are a bit over-stimulating."

She laughs. "I'm glad you can joke about it. Your mom was seriously pissed. For a minute I really thought she was going to attack you or something."

"She might've, if your mom hadn't been there." I set my book aside. "Can't you sleep, either?"

She shakes her head. "Nope. But I always sleep badly. Too much monkey chatter going on in my stupid brain."

"I speak fluent monkey," I tell her. "Want me to tell them to shut the hell up?"

"Thanks, but it won't work," she says. "Nothing does."

I'm lying on my side, propped on an elbow, and I watch her as she looks around my room. There's not much to see, of course, but she takes her time, studying my old dresser and the window seat, and the walk-in closet. (There's a sticker on the closet door that I put there when I was in high school; it's a *Calvin and Hobbes* quote—*The surest sign that intelligent life exists elsewhere in the universe is that it has never tried to contact us.*)

"Do you ever miss being a kid?" she asks.

"Sometimes." I roll on my back and stare at the ceiling. "But it's not really the kid part I miss. I just miss people."

"Like J.D.?"

"Yeah. Him and my dad, mostly. What do you miss?"

"Sleeping." She pulls her knees up to her chest and hugs them. "Growing up sucks. When I was a kid, I slept like a baby. Now I can't sleep unless I'm stoned, and I couldn't bring any weed on the plane."

I tilt my head to see her better. "Sorry I don't have any. I've never been a big fan."

"That's okay. I don't imagine your mom has a secret stash, either?"

"Nah, her drug of choice is booze. Would a drink help?"

"Unfortunately not. The only time alcohol puts me to sleep is when I drink enough to black out, and then I wake up puking."

"How about some warm milk?" I tease. "A lullaby, maybe, or a bedtime story?"

"None of the above," she says. "Scooch over."

Without ceremony, she stretches out beside me, her back pressed to my side. In spite of the fact that I'm nude under the sheet, there's no flirtation to her intimacy; it's like having a cat curl up beside me, so I don't really mind. The only problem is that it's too hot to share a bed with another mammal tonight; I immediately start sweating.

"Sorry," I tell her, rolling away. "I'm burning up."

She sighs. "Yeah, me too. It was worth a try, though." She sits up and swings her legs over the side of the mattress, but she doesn't seem to be in any hurry to leave. "You know what else I miss about being a kid?" she asks.

I can't see her face, but her voice is wistful. "Nope. What?"

"Being forgiven for everything," she says. "The older I get, the less I get away with."

I hesitate. "With your mom, you mean? For stealing stuff?"

"Yeah, but not just that." She looks over her shoulder. "And not just with Mom, either. Everybody I know is getting sick of my shit."

"Be more specific, please," I say. "I love hearing about other people's failings."

She smiles. "Well, for one thing, I keep dating complete losers, who treat me like crap. And I'm a bitch to my friends, and I can't keep a job for more than a few weeks at a time, mostly because I can't get my ass out of bed in the mornings. I'm twenty-six, and I'm still living with my mom, and I don't do anything but watch TV, or go out partying with people I don't even like." She shrugs. "I'm basically just a fuck-up."

I grin back at her. "I know a lot of fuck-ups," I say. "It sounds to me like you're still an amateur." I reach up and tug gently at a strand of her red hair. "In fact, on a scale of one to ten—one being our insane next-door neighbor, ten being Hitler—you're maybe a three, tops."

She snorts. "Gee, what a relief. Where are you on this scale of yours?"

I lower my eyes modestly. "Well, I'm not one to brag, but Christ aspires to be like me."

"Uh-huh," she says, poking me in the stomach. "How about we ask your mom what she thinks about your saintliness? 'Open your eyes, child, and see the colorless world you've created . . .'"

"Gah!" I cry, sitting up at once and clamping a hand over her mouth. "You are mere seconds away from a horrible, painful death," I tell her. "That goddamn poem is strictly forbidden in my presence."

She giggles, peeling my hand from her face. "Your mom told me it was the quickest way to get you to shut up, if I ever needed to."

"What a vindictive, ruthless monster she's become," I say, then belatedly notice my bedsheet has slipped, leaving me indecent. I blush a little and readjust.

"Don't do that on my account," she says, unfazed. "Just because we're cousins doesn't mean I can't enjoy the scenery."

"Straight women are such harlots," I say, grimacing. "It's scandalous."

She laughs, leaning over to kiss my forehead. "I'll let you get back to your book," she says. "Thanks for the talk, cuz." She crosses the room, but she stops before opening the door to look back at me.

"You're lucky, you know," she says. "I mean, it sucks that your dad died, and that J.D. and you split up, but I never even knew my real parents, and I've never been in love with anybody." She bites her lip. "To be totally honest, I'm not sure I'm wired to love another person. Not even my mom, sometimes."

I have no idea what to say to that, but she doesn't seem to expect an answer. She steps out the door and closes it silently behind her, waving good night.

This family stuff is going to take some getting used to.

The chattering mind-monkeys that Janelle was complaining about must be contagious: I wake up a little after eight in the morning, and my idiot brain immediately starts regurgitating everything that happened yesterday. I need a lot more sleep, but I know there's no way I'll get any, so I sit up and groggily check my phone. There are emails and texts from friends and coworkers in Providence, but nothing pressing, so I go on Grindr instead to check out a couple of new messages. One is from Ajax/Jessie—the guy I hooked up with a couple days ago—telling me he wants a repeat performance. It's kind of a sweet note, but I write him a thanks-but-no-thanks response, saying I'm too busy. The second message is from a guy who calls himself The Boy Wonder. He says he's twenty-two, attends Cassidy College here in Oakland, and likes older men. He's cute, but too baby-faced for my taste—I doubt he even has to shave yet—and every sentence of his painfully vapid self-description has at least one emoji in it.

That being said, I wouldn't mind getting laid today, and he's got a hot little body.

I sigh. There's no way Warden Mom will let me out of her sight for the next millennium. I hit delete, pull on a pair of boxers, and head for the shower. If I get desperate later on I can always barricade myself in my room for a few minutes and whack off.

Cindy's bedroom door is closed as I pass by, and so is Janelle's, but Mom's is open and she's not in her room. She must've had a rough night because her bed is a wreck of twisted sheets and mangled pillows. I hope she's not as tired as me; if she is, we're likely to pull each other's hair out before noon. Her desktop is clean except for a pencil and a notebook. I'm tempted to sneak in and see if she's been writing anything offensive about me lately, but my nosiness has its limits. I'd be furious if I ever caught her looking at any of my paintings I wasn't ready for her to see, so I guess I should probably refrain from prying into her rough drafts, even though a little forewarning might be nice if she's gearing up to roast me in public again.

I pee, brush teeth, and shower, then throw on a T-shirt and clean shorts. When I get downstairs I find Mom sitting in the same spot as last night, on the couch in the living room, sipping coffee and looking at her laptop. All the windows are open, and for the first time since I came home this week there's a cool breeze blowing through the house. I sit beside her without saying anything, and she barely glances at me; she's studying Carolyn's Facebook page again.

"Do you think she'll call today?" she asks.

"Hard to say." I drop my head on her shoulder. "But I wouldn't be surprised at all if we hear from Leo. He doesn't strike me as the most patient kid in the world."

Her head rests against mine. "You're still not forgiven, you know."

"Understood," I tell her, yawning. "But you may want to reconsider your body language. I'm getting kind of a mixed message here."

"Shut up," she says. We look together at the pictures of the

Fortiers; there's a good one of Carolyn, Ben, and Oliver sitting on their front porch, eating watermelon and mugging for the camera. "What am I supposed to do if Leo wants to come see us before Carolyn is ready to talk to me?" Mom asks. "I have no intention of undermining her authority, but I also want Leo to know he's welcome here anytime."

I already told her last night, of course—in tedious detail—about my conversation with Leo, and how he agreed to wait a couple of days before coming to visit. "Maybe you should just flip a coin," I say. "Heads, you piss off your daughter. Tails, you piss off your great-grandson."

"Thanks a bunch," she says darkly. "Has anyone ever mentioned that you're an ass?"

I laugh. "Not since last night."

There's a loud knock on the front screen door, startling both of us. Nobody who knows Mom in the slightest would dare show up on her doorstep at this hour; she may be an early riser, but she guards her quiet mornings zealously.

"What the hell?" I mutter.

She shrugs, dislodging my head from her shoulder, and tells me to go see who it is. I roll off the couch, sighing, and when I get to the door I'm surprised to see a gray-haired, obese, uniformed cop on the other side of the screen. It takes a second to recognize him, because he's changed so much since the last time I saw him, but then he smiles and I realize it's Steve Ganski. Seeing him again after all this time immediately triggers old memories: Ganski was the officer who found J.D. and me, after we got beaten up by Perry White and his asshole buddies. He's come up in the world since then; Mom told me a while back that he's now Oakland's sheriff.

"Mr. Ganski?" I ask, too thrown by his presence here at this hour to even say hello. "What's wrong?"

"Morning, Noah, good to see you," he says. "Heard you were in town. Can I come in?"

The years have been spectacularly uncharitable to him. His skin is almost as gray as his hair—except for his nose, which is a mottled blob of red and pink veins. He was always a big man, but his jowls now have jowls of their own, and his belly is so distended he looks like he's carrying quintuplets. I open the door as Mom appears at my side.

"Good morning, Steve," she says, sounding as surprised as me. "What can we do for you?"

"Morning, Virginia, sorry to disturb you so early." He takes off his hat. He used to have a major crush on her, and from the sudden color in his cheeks it looks like he still does. "This is a little awkward, but I'm looking for a young Asian lady who was apparently uptown with Noah a couple days back, in Edgerton's parking lot. A little lady with long red hair?"

Mom and I exchange a glance, and I can tell she's thinking, "Oh, shit," same as me. Did Bill Edgerton decide to press charges after all, for Janelle's shoplifting fiasco?

"That's my niece," Moms says warily. "Is there a problem? She and my sister are visiting from California."

Ganski plays with the rim of his hat. "Nate Snethen was the one who saw her and Noah together, which is how he recognized her when she came into his gift shop yesterday, by herself. I guess she kind of sticks out."

"I don't even know who Nate Snethen *is*," I say, bewildered. "How the hell does he know *me*?"

Ganski grins wryly as Mom shushes me. "Guess you've always stuck out a little, too, Noah," he says. "Nate was just a couple years behind you in high school. He said he knew you right away, since you look just the same as you used to."

Oh, for Christ's sake. This is exactly why I can never live in this town again. It's too damn creepy.

"Anyhow," Ganski says, his grin fading, "Nate says this girl bought some things from him, using a credit card. The sale went through fine, but first thing this morning Nate got a call from Visa's fraud department, before he was even out of bed. They told him the charge was being disputed by the credit card owner, who just noticed last night her card was missing. Nate called me right after he got done talking with Visa."

Mom's face is pale. She doesn't say anything, and neither do I. I'm not sure exactly how much trouble Janelle is in, but I think it's safe to say that she's upped her game a whole hell of a lot from stealing corkscrews.

"Can I ask what your niece's name is?" Ganski asks Mom.

"It's Janelle. Janelle Thomas."

"The name on the card she used was Bethany Paulson, and that's how she signed the receipt, too." Ganski grimaces apologetically. "I'm afraid I'm going to have to take her down to the station to sort this mess out."

Damn you, Janelle. Since when does a kleptomaniac use a fucking *credit card*? Mom must be thinking along the same lines; she asks what Janelle bought. It doesn't matter, I guess, but you have to wonder what my moronic cousin wanted so badly that she was willing to commit fraud for it.

"Quite a bit," Ganski says. "A bracelet, earrings, a couple of scarves, and a damn fine watch. Nate says it all tallied up to almost twelve hundred bucks." He hesitates. "Anything over a thousand is a felony."

"Dear God." Mom is actually wringing her hands. "It's likely she still has everything she took, Steve," she says, floundering. "If she returns it all immediately, would that help? Or what if she pays Nate for everything, in cash?"

Ganski clears his throat. "I'm sorry, Virginia. Even if Nate was willing to let this go—which isn't likely—there's no way in hell Visa won't prosecute. I don't really have any choice but to arrest her."

Mom looks at me with tears in her eyes, and I look back helplessly. She takes a shaky breath, then turns back to Ganski. "Do you mind if I tell my sister first, before we get Janelle up?

It might make things a little easier on everybody, if Cindy is the one who wakes her."

Ganski looks like he wants to object, but Mom's tears are too much for him and he eventually gives a reluctant nod; at this point, she could probably ask him to shoot himself and he'd do it. "Sure, take your time," he says. "I'm not in any big rush."

"Do you want me to tell Cindy?" I ask Mom.

She sighs, pressing my hand for a second. "No. I'll do it."

Ganski and I stare at each other as she heads upstairs. I feel bad for him; I know he's just doing his job, but it's kind of hard to make small talk with a man who's here to arrest a family member. Then I remember how decent he was to J.D. and me after we got our asses kicked, and how he came to check on us in the hospital, and how he watched over us after we got out, too, making sure no one touched us again. The least I can do is be polite, I guess, so I ask him how he's doing.

"Hanging in there," he says. "You still in Rhode Island?"

"Yeah, Providence."

We're both keeping our ears cocked for what's going on upstairs, but so far it's quiet.

"Providence, huh? Nice town."

I agree, scratching a bug bite on my knee, and we both fall silent. I want to ask what happens next with Janelle, after he arrests her. I assume we'll have to get a lawyer and bail her out, but I don't know what kind of timeframe we're looking at before a judge sets her bail. A day? Two days?

"You in town for long?" Ganski asks.

"That's currently under negotiation," I say, sighing. "Mom wants me to stay until at least Labor Day, but I'm pretty sure the ceasefire's going to fall apart any second now."

He chuckles. "Glad to see you've still got a sense of humor. You always were a funny kid."

"Sadly, not everyone would agree with you." I pause, and in

the quiet I can hear Mom and Cindy talking upstairs, though not what they're saying. Their voices are enough alike that I have a hard time distinguishing them. The volume of their exchange grows quickly though, and a second later it's definitely Cindy who cries out in agitation, "She did *what?*"

Ganski and I look at each other as we're hearing running feet, and a door banging open with enough force to make us both cringe.

"Janelle!" Cindy screams. "What have you *done*, you stupid, *STUPID* girl!"

"In retrospect," I tell Ganski, "it may not have been a good idea to wake up Cindy first."

He sighs. "Yep."

CHAPTER 7

If I ever bitch about needing more excitement in my life, please feel free to make me swallow my own tongue. Sure, I get sick of my daily routine, when there's nothing more interesting going on than a spat with an annoying coworker or an inconsequential blowjob from a stranger, but even so, I much prefer boredom to the nonstop weirdness and emotional upheaval of the last few days. If I took a blood pressure reading right now, the cuff would explode off my bicep and punch a hole through the wall.

We managed to get Janelle bailed out of jail early this afternoon, and now she's back up in her room, licking her psychic wounds and snarling at anybody who comes near. She's completely screwed, and we all know it: She's being charged with not just one, but *two* felony counts—unlawful possession of a credit card, and forgery of the card owner's name. The forgery charge is a complete dick move on the part of the DA, since the unlawful possession charge is already more than enough to ruin her life, but given Janelle's shoplifting history, neither the DA nor the judge who set her bail were inclined to cut her any slack. Cindy had to cough up twelve thousand dollars just to get her mentally deficient daughter temporarily out of jail.

Needless to say, today hasn't been much fun.

Cindy hasn't sat still for more than fifteen minutes at a time since we got home four hours ago; she keeps trotting upstairs to try to talk to Janelle—who either yells at her to go away, or ignores her completely—then she comes back downstairs and bawls her eyes out in the living room while Mom tries to console her. I've been hiding in the kitchen all afternoon, perched on a barstool at the island and doodling in my sketch pad. Most of what I've done is crap, but I no longer care: Happy hour officially started half an hour ago, and I'm now on my second gin and tonic. At the moment, Cindy is upstairs again, and Mom is molesting a big ball of pizza dough on the counter for tonight's supper. I set down my charcoal pencil and rub my hand.

"Want some help?" I ask.

She looks over her shoulder and shakes her head. "I'm nearly done." She slaps the poor dough a few last times for good measure, then wanders over to check out the sketch I just finished. "Wow," she says, leaning over my shoulder. "That's really good. I assume it's from yesterday?"

"Yeah." I evaluate the drawing with a more critical eye than hers; it's a profile of J.D., sitting on the bleachers with his elbows resting on his knees. It's decent, I guess, especially for working from memory, but it could be a whole lot better. The knuckles in his left hand are too pronounced, for one thing, and I also bungled the muscles in the side of his neck. I haven't drawn or painted J.D. in years, but his body is still as familiar to me as my own.

"He looks more careworn than the last time I saw him," Mom says. "But he's still beautiful."

I don't want to tell her that he looked a whole lot better before I told him about her ALS, so I just nod. "Yeah, for an old guy I guess he's not too bad."

She smiles for the first time all day. "He's younger than you, Methuselah."

"Don't remind me. It's too depressing."

Mom starts to say something else but then there's another eruption upstairs from Janelle, howling at Cindy to leave her alone; Cindy wails back something incomprehensible. Mom and I wince.

"Can we please sedate those two?" I ask.

She sighs. "I keep telling Cindy to just let her be, but she seems bound and determined to add matricide to the list of Janelle's felonies."

The dryness of her tone tickles me. "Uh-oh," I say. "Looks like that inappropriate humor your doctor warned you about is starting to kick in."

We grin at each other, in spite of everything, but it doesn't last; the caterwauling in Janelle's bedroom is getting out of hand. "Do you think I should go up and try to referee?" Mom asks.

"Absolutely not," I say. "How about I make you a gin and tonic instead, and we go outside for some peace and quiet?"

Before she can answer, there's an operatic crescendo upstairs, followed by a door slamming. In the charged silence that follows, we listen for Cindy's feet on the stairs, but apparently she's decided it's more fun this time to just stay where she is, presumably rending her garments as she glares at Janelle's closed door. Mom takes me up on the offer of a drink, and we head to the front porch with our glasses. The second we sit down on the top step and start to relax, though, a gray and rusty Honda Accord pulls up and parks across the street from us. Its windows are rolled down and "Hotel California" is blaring from its speakers.

"Oh, for pity's sake," Mom says, glowering at the teenage driver, who's alone in the car. "That's obnoxious."

I put my glass down and climb to my feet. It's Leo.

The boy waves at us tentatively, turning off his engine and killing the music. In the sudden quiet, I hear Sadie barking behind the Overtons' house. I wave back and Leo gets out of the car.

Mom is frozen in place. "Dear God," she breathes. "Is that—"

"Yep, sure is." I pull her up beside me as Leo crosses the road, looking self-conscious. He's dressed in cargo shorts, sneakers, and a short-sleeve shirt. His shirt is open down the front, and he's fumbling to button it as he walks.

"Dear God," Mom says again. "I thought you were exaggerating about how much he looks like you."

"Nope. I think he's my clone."

Her hand is trembling in mine. "I'm not sure how to handle this, Noah." Her voice is uncharacteristically timid. "Do you think Carolyn knows he's here?"

I seriously doubt it, but there's no point in saying so. "Just come say hello," I tell her, tugging her down the steps with me. "I told him you don't bite, so don't make a liar out of me." We meet Leo at the midpoint of our sidewalk.

"Hey, Leo," I say. "Welcome to the Island of Misfit Toys."

"Hi, Noah." He gives me a nervous smile, but he really only has eyes for Mom. "Hi, Great-Grandma. I'm Leo."

Mom clears her throat. "Hello, Leo. Just call me Virginia." She suddenly steps forward and takes him in her arms. "I'm so happy to meet you."

He seems surprised by the warm reception, but also pleased. "Me, too," he says. "I'm sorry I didn't tell you guys I was coming."

"Don't be silly," Mom says. "You're always welcome here." She pulls back but still grips him gently by the shoulders. "Please tell me, though, that your grandmother knows where you are."

He flushes and starts to stammer. I'm irritated with him for not waiting a couple of days like I asked, but I'm also not surprised at all.

"Oh, Leo," Mom says. Her voice is way milder than it ever is when I fuck up. "I think you should call her right now. We mustn't go behind her back."

"I told my dad," Leo protests. "I sent him a text a few minutes ago."

"Well, that's a start, I guess." She finally lets him go. "What did he say?"

"He's pissed because now he's the one who has to tell Grandma."

I can't help but laugh, which makes Leo grin, but Mom is still fretting. "I really don't want to upset Carolyn. Are you sure you shouldn't be the one to call her?"

"She'll just yell if I do," Leo says. "Dad and Grandpa are the only ones who can talk to her when she's mad." He's doing his best to sound unconcerned, but I can tell he's worried that Mom is going to insist. "Dad says hi, by the way, and he can't wait to meet you."

Mom runs a hand through her hair. "That's very sweet, and I want to meet him, too." She sighs. "I want very badly to meet *all* of you, but I think it's wiser to wait until Carolyn is ready to join us."

"It's a little late for that now," I remind her. "Leo's already here."

"Yes, I'm aware of that, son, thank you," Mom says acerbically. "And I'm glad he came. I just hope Carolyn will understand." She looks at the boy again and her expression softens. "What do you like on your pizza, Leo?"

Before he can answer her, a bloodcurdling scream from the second-floor windows makes us all jump. His eyes get big as he looks at us for an explanation.

"Don't worry," I tell him. "There's a crazed felon on the loose in the house, but she's unarmed."

"That's not funny, Noah," Mom says, but her face is doing that twitchy thing it always does when she wants to laugh but doesn't think she should. "Come on inside, Leo. This has been a pretty terrible day for us, but now that you're here maybe things will go a little better."

* * *

Oddly enough, Leo's presence in the house does seem to help. Cindy pulls herself together enough to leave Janelle alone for a while, and although Janelle declines to join us for supper she accepts a couple of pizza slices that I take up to her room. She even talks to me for a minute, brokenly apologizing for all the turmoil. I tell her that Leo is downstairs and ask if she wants to meet him, but she just shakes her head and closes the door again, fresh tears welling in her eyes.

I can't say I blame her. I'm sure she's aware that Leo knows what's going on; Mom and I didn't have much choice but to tell him. His only reaction was to say "Wow," but I was still dreading introducing the two of them, since Janelle is so fragile at the moment and I was worried Leo might inadvertently set her off.

Anyway, I just rejoined everybody else at the kitchen island a few minutes ago. Cindy is subdued and teary while we eat, but I'm impressed at how she still tries to put Leo at ease, joining in the conversation now and then in spite of her own heartache. Leo doesn't quite know how to deal with the overall weirdness of the situation, but he clearly likes Mom, and doesn't balk when she starts giving him the third degree about his life. In short order, we find out that Carolyn hates her job as a dental hygienist, Ben is a retired state trooper, and Oliver (Leo's dad) is a carpenter. Mom's interrogation grinds to an abrupt halt, though, after she asks about Leo's absent mother. Leo tells us that she was killed in a car accident when he was in kindergarten, and Michael was just a baby.

Mom blanches. "I'm so sorry, Leo. That's awful."

"It's okay. I don't really remember her." Leo fiddles with his napkin. "Anyway, that's why we live with my grandparents, because Dad needed help with Mike and me when we were little. I wish we'd get a house of our own again, but it's never going to happen. Dad likes living there because Grandma takes care of everything."

He reaches for his third slice of pizza; the first two went down in a single gulp. Mom's pizza tonight is a work of art, with jalapeños, green olives, and a garlicky cream sauce that's more sensuous than a hot bath, and Leo's face is rapturous as he stuffs his mouth again. Mom is enjoying watching him eat; I think she misses the days of feeding ravenous teenage boys. I'm expecting her to ask him why he doesn't want to live with his grandparents anymore, but she restrains herself—she probably figures it's not a good idea to encourage bitching about her own daughter—and changes the subject by asking what Michael is like.

Leo shrugs. "He's okay, I guess. He's really good in school, but he's kind of a spaz, and the only thing he's interested in is Legos. We don't hang out much."

He's getting over his shyness; when dinner started he kept his gaze mostly on his plate, but now that he's got some food in his belly he's looking around the room with open curiosity. The old painting I did of Mom and J.D. is behind Mom on the wall—it's the same one that Janelle commented on the other day—and I watch him comparing Mom to her earlier likeness. She follows his eyes, turning on her stool to see what caught his attention.

"Noah did that when he was only a littler older than you," she says. "It's my favorite early painting of his."

"Wow, you did that?" Leo asks me. "It's really good."

I thank him, reaching for another slice of pizza before he inhales the whole damn thing. Mom's got a second one waiting in the oven, but the way this kid eats I'm not taking any chances.

"Who's the guy with your mom?" he asks.

"My first boyfriend, J.D.," I say. "He used to live with us."

Leo seems taken aback, but quickly recovers. "That's cool."

I doubt he's a homophobe—most kids his age don't give a crap these days about other people's sexual thing—but Fall River isn't exactly Key West, and maybe his family is more conservative than I imagined. I hope not, obviously, because if Carolyn and Company have a problem with homos, the wheels are coming off this family-reunification cart pretty damn fast.

"You didn't realize Noah was gay?" Mom asks, apparently also picking up on his surprise.

Leo reddens. "Maybe, I guess. I wasn't sure."

"No one ever thinks I'm gay because I'm such a macho stud," I say.

Mom snorts, and Leo relaxes enough to grin.

"Uh, son, how do I put this delicately?" Mom says drily.

"No, seriously, you wouldn't believe how often I get accused of overt masculinity," I tell her, flexing my muscles. "Take a gander at these guns."

She rolls her eyes, making Leo laugh. I tell them they're hurting my feelings and they both laugh harder. Even Cindy manages a wan smile for a moment, but then Janelle's plight hits her again and she sobers. She abruptly excuses herself and takes her plate to the sink. Mom's face tightens with concern as she watches Cindy's back, and she starts to apologize for fooling around at a time like this.

"Don't be silly, Ginny," Cindy says, cutting her off. "I'm the one who should apologize for spoiling Leo's visit. I'm just not fit for company tonight. Forgive me."

She goes back upstairs, and a minute later we hear her knocking on Janelle's door.

"Oh, good," I mutter. "Round thirty-seven, coming up."

Mom rallies enough to offer Leo more pizza, and while he's cramming down another five slices we try to resume our conversation, but Cindy and Janelle are indeed going at it again and communication is limited to grimaces and small talk. I suggest that the three of us take a walk just to get the hell out of the house, and they agree immediately. We put the dishes to soak and scoot out the door, leaving a note on the counter for Cindy and Janelle, telling them where we've gone.

* * *

It's a pleasant August evening once we get some distance from the battlefield. It's almost sunset and the sky to the west is a stunning collage of reds, oranges, and yellows. A cool breeze cuts the heat and sets loose an orgy of fragrances—lilacs, chrysanthemums, freshly turned garden soil, newly mown grass. People are out in their yards or on their front porches, watching the world go by and shooting the shit with their family and neighbors. The sidewalk is too narrow for all three of us to walk side by side, so we wander down the middle of sleepy side streets, hugging the curb for the rare passing car. We don't talk much at first, lost in our own heads.

"This is a sweet little town," Leo says after a while. He's walking between Mom and me. "It's really pretty."

"It's okay," I say, distracted by two psychotic black squirrels chasing each other around the trunk of an oak tree. "But it's a lot less attractive if you live here every day."

Mom sighs. "Noah has a contrary streak when it comes to Oakland, but he didn't always. He used to love it here, when he was your age."

I make a face. "I also used to love Ayn Rand's novels when I was his age."

She ignores me, taking Leo by the arm and changing the subject, asking him what's been going on at his house since his family found out about us.

"I hope you don't mind me asking," she says when he hesitates. "This is all so new, and I have no idea how to behave. Is there anything I can do to make things easier for everyone?"

He stays silent for a few steps, considering, then turns his head and grins at her. "You could shoot Grandma," he says. "The rest of us will pay you whatever you want."

I laugh, and Mom's mouth twitches. "That's not exactly what I had in mind," she says. "Is she being difficult?"

"Yep, but that's not just because of you guys," he says. "She's always like this."

A litany of complaints about Carolyn's foibles comes spilling out of his mouth when Mom asks him to tell us more. He says she's refusing to talk about Mom and me, and won't let the rest of the family talk about us, either. He also says that she's a neat freak, vacuuming and dusting the house daily and refusing to go to bed at night if there's a single dirty spoon in the sink; he tells us that she's always in a bad mood when she gets home from work, because the dentist she works for is messy and it pisses her off; he says she never laughs, unless she's had a lot of white wine, which is the only alcohol she likes; he says she's bossy as all hell, and yells a lot at him and Michael.

"And she's a hypocrite," he continues. "Like, she doesn't let me or Mike eat popcorn, because she's scared we'll break our teeth, but she eats a gigantic bowl of the crap every single night when she watches television. She also yells at us for chewing on pencils, but every single pencil in the house already has *her* stupid teeth marks all over it. She's like a freaking *beaver*."

Mom gently steps in to defuse his tirade. "I'm sure she's not perfect, Leo, but honestly she doesn't sound so bad. You should hear what Noah says about me when he doesn't know I'm listening. He told Janelle the other day that I'm the lovechild of Lady Macbeth and Hannibal Lecter."

I smile at her. "What makes you think I didn't know you were listening?"

Mom laughs, startling Leo. "You're way cooler than Grandma," he tells her. "If I said anything like that to her, she'd go ballistic."

"Noah pouts when I don't laugh at his jokes, so I've found it's easier just to humor him," Mom says. "Tell us something good about your grandmother."

I expect him to do the typical aggrieved teenager thing and deny that she has any redeeming qualities, but he surprises me.

"She can be really sweet sometimes," he says. "Like I really suck at math, and she always helps me with it. She also helps

Grandpa in the garden, even though she hates being outside because of all the bugs. She's a good cook, too, but not as good as you."

Mom thanks him, though I can tell she's uncomfortable with him favoring her over Carolyn. She changes the subject by pointing out the entrance to North Park. The public swimming pool is there, and also a baseball diamond, used by all the local clubs and kids' leagues. It's almost dark now but the pool is still open, and we wander up to the wire fence surrounding it and watch about a dozen kids messing around in the water. There are underwater lights as well as overhead ones, so everything inside the fence looks like it's in a different time zone. Most of the kids are high schoolers, but there are also a couple of middle schoolers off by themselves in the shallow end, playing catch with a Nerf football.

"Did you used to come here when you were a kid?" Leo asks me, eyeing a large, chubby boy bouncing up and down on the high diving board.

"Just a few times," I tell him. The boy on the board does a spectacular cannonball and sets off a tsunami, drenching a couple of his friends on the side of the pool. "I only lived here my senior year and the year after, and J.D. and I always preferred going to the beach, even though it's a couple of hours away. We weren't exactly welcome here. People were afraid they'd catch our gay cooties."

"I'm pretty sure chlorine kills those," Mom says.

I grin. "Yeah, but not much cootie research had been done back then, so nobody knew."

Leo is studying me. "Were people really afraid of you guys?"

I shrug. "The pool always cleared out pretty damn fast when we got in."

"Maybe they thought you were peeing in the water," Mom said.

"Okay, you're starting to weird me out," I tell her. "You just said two marginally funny things in a row, and that's never happened before."

"I'm just showing off for Leo." She reties her ponytail while watching a long-limbed girl swim laps in the lane closest to us. "I almost wish I'd brought my swimsuit. I haven't been swimming in years."

It suddenly occurs to me that I have no memory of ever seeing my mother swim; I didn't even know she owned a swimsuit. "Do you want me to run back to the house and get it?" I ask, intrigued by the novelty of watching the New Hampshire Poet Laureate at play in a public pool. "We could all go swimming. I've still got an old pair of trunks in my dresser that Leo can use, and I can just wear soccer shorts or something."

Leo says that sounds like fun, and Mom actually seems to be considering it for a minute, but then she shakes her head. "The pool's probably going to close soon." She leads us away from the fence, looking a little wistfully over her shoulder at an attractive young couple sitting with their feet in the water, the girl's head on the boy's shoulder. "Besides, I'd be half a century older than anybody here, and I'm pretty sure that an old lady in a swimsuit would clear the pool even faster than gay cooties."

"We could conduct an experiment," I say.

She snorts. "Maybe another time."

The fireflies are out now, flickering around us as we start making our way home. Cicadas and crickets are engaged in a battle of the bands, and I also hear a solitary owl, hooting mournfully in the distance. Mom says she's worried about Leo driving back to Fall River this late in the day, and invites him to stay overnight, but he says he never goes to bed until two or three in the morning anyway, and he'll be home before then. He says he also doesn't want to piss off Carolyn any more than he already has. We fall into a companionable silence, watching the night descend.

"Are you any good at science?" I ask Leo after a while.

"I'm okay, I guess," he says. "How come?"

"I was just wondering why a firefly's ass lights up."

There's a long pause, then Leo and Mom both get tickled; it's oddly pleasing to hear them giggling together in the darkness like naughty preschoolers savoring a bit of potty humor.

"I'm serious," I tell them. "I mean, if I could choose any part of my body to light up, it would definitely be my ass, but what do you suppose *their* reason is?"

"Is he always like this?" Leo asks Mom.

"Sadly, yes."

We turn the corner onto Main Street a couple of blocks from home, and can see lights on in our house, both upstairs and down. There's also enough moonlight to clearly see the road in front of the house, and I notice something at the same time as Leo.

"Uh, where's my car?" he asks.

CHAPTER 8

Far be it from me to question the child psychiatrist who initially diagnosed Janelle as a borderline kleptomaniac, but I'm beginning to suspect that my cousin's chronic case of sticky fingers is only the tip of her Titanic-destroying psychological iceberg.

She's gone, along with her suitcase, Leo's car, and ninety-some dollars in cash from my wallet, which I foolishly left on my dresser. She apparently crept out the front of the house while Cindy was sitting on the back porch steps, watching the night sky and trying to calm down after their latest brawl. Janelle didn't steal my credit card, thank God, and while I'd like to think this was an act of kindness on her part, I'm fairly certain the only reason she didn't take it is because she now knows how easy it is to track a stolen card.

Mom, Cindy, Leo, and I are all in the kitchen, and Leo just dialed his father on his phone.

"Hi, Dad," he says when Oliver answers. "Uh, we've got kind of a problem here."

Mom and I are drinking gin bucks, I just gave a can of Pepsi to Leo, and Cindy is ignoring a cup of chamomile tea at her elbow and staring vacantly at the island counter.

"My car got stolen," Leo tells Oliver. "No, I'm not kidding, Janelle took it. She's, uh, Virginia's niece, and we don't think she's coming back." He pauses. "I'm not being disrespectful, Dad. She wants me to call her Virginia, not Great-Grandma. Anyway, it's kind of a long story, but Janelle was already in deep sh—uh, I mean she was already in trouble with the cops before she took my car. She stole some other stuff a couple days ago and got arrested, and Aunt Cindy—that's her mom— just bailed her out this morning, and thinks she's decided to make a run for it." Another pause. "No, I've still got my car keys. She hot-wired it."

"I can't believe Janelle knows how to hot-wire a car," Cindy murmurs, raising her head. She looks deranged, with her hair askew and her eyes puffy and wild. "Where in God's name did she learn to do that?"

Mom and I both stay quiet, but it seems pretty obvious at this point that Janelle isn't exactly an ingenue when it comes to larceny.

"Yeah, Noah called the sheriff's office," Leo says. "I guess the state police are out looking for her, too." He winces, muting his phone. "Grandma is giving Dad holy hell," he tells us. "She wants to talk to me but he won't let her." He unmutes. "I'm fine, Dad. Virginia said I can stay here tonight, and Noah will drive me home in the morning."

He rolls his eyes and re-mutes. "Grandma's going ballistic. She wants Dad to come get me right now, even though it's a four-hour drive."

"Carolyn has every right to be concerned, Leo," Mom says. "You're with people she doesn't know, and your car has been stolen, and she's probably worried sick."

He makes a face. "Yeah, I know, but she's being dumb. Even if Dad left right now, we wouldn't get back to Fall River until dawn. Grandpa and Dad are both trying to tell her that, but she's not listening. Oh, crap, she got Dad's phone." He un-mutes again. "Hi, Grandma. Don't worry, I'm fine."

We can hear Carolyn haranguing him, and he apologizes for not asking permission to come here in the first place. His tone is more sullen than apologetic, however, and I can't really blame him; from the sound of it, she's reaming him out so badly it probably feels like an anoscopy. Mom looks appalled: This is definitely not how she wanted her daughter to get to know us.

"But it doesn't make any sense for Dad to come get me tonight," Leo says. "He'd be on the road all night long. Why can't Noah just bring me back tomorrow?" He cringes as she yells some more. "No, he can't drive me back tonight. He's had a few drinks." He looks at me apologetically and raises his voice in exasperation. "No, Noah's not a drunk, Grandma! I'm just saying it's safer for everybody if we wait until morning."

Truer words were never spoken, but I'm not thrilled that my sister is accusing me of being a lush at this stage of our relation-ship.

"Tell her we're going to play beer pong as soon as you get off the phone," I tell Leo, and he fights to keep from laughing.

"Hush, Noah," Mom says. "She's just worried about him, that's all."

Leo tries another tack. "They're really nice people, Grand-ma. You'd like them a lot if you'd just give them a chance." He mutes his phone again and sighs as Carolyn unleashes another lengthy tirade. "Now she says she wants me to go to a motel. She thinks I'll be safer there."

Mom chews on her lip for a second, then holds out her hand and asks Leo for the phone.

His eyes get big. "Are you sure?" he says. "She's nuts right now."

"Everything will be fine," she says, but she takes a deep breath before she unmutes the phone and clears her throat. "Hello, Carolyn. This is Virginia." There's dead silence on the other end, and Mom tries again. "I'm so sorry that we're speaking for the first time under these circumstances. My niece has thrown us all for a loop today, but I can assure you this is not the way things usually go around here."

She waits once more for a response, but none is forthcoming; she frowns a little.

"Leo is a fine young man, and I'm so happy to get to know him," she says. "I hope you'll consider letting him stay here tonight with us, instead of at a motel. Our little town only has one motel to offer, and it's neither sanitary nor safe. I wouldn't recommend it."

I raise an eyebrow at her. She's lying through her teeth, capitalizing on what Leo told us about Carolyn being both a neat freak and a worrywart. Though I've never been inside Oakland's solitary motel, at least from the outside it looks both clean and quiet, and I've never heard anything negative about it. I suppose it could be a dump inside, but I doubt it, since Mom is avoiding my eyes.

Carolyn finally answers, but I can't hear what she's saying. Mom listens intently, and I wonder how it feels to hear the adult voice of the baby girl she was forced to give up so many years ago. My guilt for not taking her with me to meet Carolyn is suddenly sharp again; their first conversation was bound to be awkward no matter what, but if I'd given them a choice in how and where it took place, at least they would've been spared this negotiation over where Leo's going to spend the night.

He'd also still have his goddamn car.

"I understand your concern," Mom replies after a moment. "But even if Janelle were to come back tonight—which is highly unlikely—she's not dangerous. She just . . . steals things. Leo will be completely safe, I promise."

Leo leans on the counter next to me and sips his Pepsi, waiting for his fate to be decided. "I can't believe Grandma isn't yelling at her, too," he whispers to me, sounding genuinely awestruck. "It's a freaking miracle."

"Mom's really good on the phone," I whisper back, amused by his reverent tone. "She used to moonlight as a phone-sex operator."

Pepsi spurts from his nose and I pat him on the back to ease his coughing. Mom snaps her fingers at us for distracting her, and Leo's ears turn red. Mom apologizes to Carolyn and asks her to repeat something she missed.

"Maybe this isn't the best time to be a comedian, Noah," Cindy murmurs, helping Leo mop up the counter. The gentleness of her reproof makes me feel like an ass.

"You're right," I tell her. "I'm sorry."

Leo wets a paper towel and dabs at a stain on the front of his shirt, and I lean close so we can talk without bothering Mom. "Sorry I got you in trouble," I say in his ear. "That was totally my fault."

He grins and whispers back, "You're kind of a dick, Uncle Noah."

I come dangerously close to spitting up my own drink, but the strained look on Mom's face as she listens to whatever Carolyn is saying keeps me in line, though barely. Leo is clearly pleased with himself as he watches me struggle for self-control.

"Welcome to the family, jackass," I finally manage to say. "You're going to fit right in."

Mom is talking again. "Of course, Carolyn, if that's what you want. I'll make sure that Noah and Leo leave here by no later than eight tomorrow morning. But may I make a counterproposal?" Her voice is steady, but the hand holding her drink has a slight tremor. "What if you and your family were to come up here for a late lunch tomorrow? We could all have a picnic in the backyard, and get to know each other, and Leo could go home with you afterwards. I completely understand if you don't feel comfortable visiting yet, but I just want you to know that you're welcome here, and I'd love to meet you. I'm sure you must have a lot of questions."

I can see how badly Mom wants to make a connection, and I find myself holding my breath with her, waiting for Carolyn's response. Leo, too, is now watching Mom with a sober expression, as is Cindy—who, in spite of having her entire world fall apart tonight, is still somehow managing to care about Mom's stuff. It makes me speculate again about Mom and Cindy's relationship, and why they've gone so long with so little contact, when they clearly still love each other. On impulse, I reach for Cindy's hand and squeeze it, glad she's here in spite of her daughter's aggravating crime spree. She looks at me and smiles sweetly, her fingers tightening on mine.

"I understand," Mom says, her face falling. "Another time, then. I'll make sure Leo calls you as soon as he and Noah get on the road tomorrow." She swallows, and her eyes meet mine briefly; her disappointment is palpable. "I'll give you back to Leo, now. Good night, Carolyn."

She returns the phone to Leo and drains the rest of her drink in one long pull. Leo listens impatiently to another long diatribe from Carolyn, then finally manages to say goodnight and hang up. We all look at each other for a minute, then Mom goes to the fridge for more ice.

"It was worth a try," I say. "At least now she knows you really want to see her."

"It's a lot to take in all at once," Cindy chimes in. "Give her time."

Mom nods but doesn't answer. Her back is to us, and there's a fragility in the set of her shoulders that hurts my heart. Leo clears his throat.

"I'll make sure she comes up here soon, I promise," he tells her. "I'm sorry she's being a pain in the butt."

Mom glances at him over her shoulder. Her eyes are red, but

she's not crying. "Please don't be upset with her, Leo," she says. "She has every right to be wary. I was the one who left her, after all, not the other way around."

"Yeah, when you were *twelve*," I blurt. The injustice of her shouldering the guilt for something her sicko father did makes me indignant. "That evil son of a bitch didn't give you any choice." She shoots me a warning glance but it's too late; Leo is frowning as he watches us.

"Who are you guys talking about?" he asks.

Oh, for Christ's sake. Me and my stupid mouth, yet again.

Mom sighs, no doubt internally cursing me as she tries to decide how much to reveal. "My father," she says reluctantly, then glances at Cindy. "Our father, I mean."

"Our father," Cindy repeats sourly. "Dear old Dad. What a charmer."

The bitterness in her voice is jarring.

"Amen," Mom says, clinking her glass against Cindy's teacup. She turns back to Leo. "Our dad wasn't a very good man, but let's leave it at that for now, okay? I'm not comfortable sharing too much family history until your grandmother and I have a chance to talk."

"Sure," he says, wise enough to see it's useless to press for more tonight. "That's fine."

Mom mixes herself another gin buck—two parts gin, three parts ginger ale—and looks at her sister. "I've heard that gin goes nicely with chamomile tea. Want to give it a try?"

Cindy pushes her cup across the island. "Fill 'er up."

A soft knock wakes me early in the morning.

"Rise and shine," Mom says, sticking her head in the room as I roll over in bed and blink at her with lizard-like somnolence. "If you and Leo are going to be on the road by eight o'clock, you better get a move on. I want you looking presentable before you leave the house."

"What time is it?" I grunt.

"Six forty-five, but you both need to shower and shave before breakfast. I promised Carolyn I'd have Leo in the car by eight, and I intend to keep that promise."

"God forbid we leave at 8:05," I mumble.

"Wake Leo after you shower, and don't come downstairs until you're sure he's up."

"Yes, Drill Sergeant," I say, putting my pillow over my face. "Does he need to do calisthenics, too?"

I hear her bare feet padding across the floor to my bed, then a second later she pokes me in the stomach, making me curl up like a pill bug. I pull off the pillow and scowl at her. "You're a very bossy person, did you know that?"

"Don't make me drag you down the hall by your ankles," she says. "Get up."

"Okay, fine, whatever, I'm awake," I say. "Go away."

She doesn't budge until I sit up in bed with a sigh, picking sleep from my eyes. "That's better," she says, pivoting on her heel and disappearing down the stairs. I stare around the room, still groggy, then pull on my boxers and wander down the hall to the shower, passing the closed doors of our two guest rooms. Cindy is staying directly across from Mom, and Leo's room—which just yesterday was Janelle's—is across from the bathroom. I shower, shave, and brush my teeth, then wrap a towel around my waist and knock softly on Leo's door, trying not to wake Cindy. There's no answer, so I stick my head in his room.

He's sound asleep and snoring lightly, one arm over his eyes and the other across his chest; his sheet is pushed down to his belly button and his feet are sticking off the end of the bed. There's a small pile of clothes at the base of his nightstand, and all his windows are open, with sunlight streaming across the floor. Despite the earliness of the day, it's already hot in here; his thin torso is shiny with sweat.

"Hey, Leo," I say quietly. "Time to get up."

He stirs slightly but then resumes snoring. It was a late evening for all of us last night—we stayed up talking past midnight—and I wouldn't be surprised if he, too, like me, messed around on his phone for a while before going to sleep. I raise my voice and say his name again, and this time he spazzes, flailing comically. He raises his head and gawps at me.

"Shit, Noah, you scared me! What's wrong?"

"Morning, sunshine," I say. "There's a gestapo poet downstairs, threatening to write a sestina about unpunctual teenagers. Better get your ass out of bed."

He drops his head back on the pillow and rubs his eyes. "Okay." He looks at me again, blinking balefully. "What are you talking about?"

I grin. "Mom wants us on the road at precisely eight o'clock, looking and smelling like angels. After you take a shower she's going to make breakfast for us."

"I don't need a shower," he says.

"Apparently you missed the part about smelling like an angel. Don't take this personally, kid, but right now the stench of unwashed armpits is wafting around the room."

He makes a face and sits up, yawning; he's wearing blue boxers. "I can't imagine why you're still single," he grumbles. "You're so considerate of other people's feelings."

I laugh. "Mom put out a clean towel and a toothbrush for you on the bathroom hamper, and if you need a shave you can use my razor. She's serious about you looking well tended when you get home."

"Yeah, okay." He swings his legs over the side of the bed and yawns again before standing up. "It won't make any difference to Grandma, though," he says. "I could show up in a tux and she'd still be pissed."

I've fulfilled my duty to get him on his feet, so I tell him I'll see him downstairs and I turn to go get dressed. He stops me before I get out of the room.

"Can I borrow a clean shirt?" he asks. "I've only got the one I had on yesterday."

It's funny that he's now worried about what he's going to wear, when he didn't even think he needed a shower until I gave him a hard time about it. He must be more sensitive than I thought.

"I was only teasing when I said you stink, Leo," I tell him. "I'm sure your armpits smell like roses."

He snorts. "No, you were right. I don't want to gross out your mom."

"That's wise," I say. "She's even meaner than I am about personal hygiene issues." I tell him to help himself to whatever clothes he needs from my dresser.

"Thanks," he says, studying me shyly. "Are we the same size? How much do you weigh?"

I tell him 137; he says he's 135. We compare height as well: I'm five seven; he's five eight. On a whim, I wander over to a large mirror on the closet door and gesture for him to stand next to me. We look back and forth between our reflections, hunting for differences, but our bodies are even more alike than our faces.

"Holy doppelgängers, Batman," I say.

"Your nose is a little bigger than mine," he says. "But our arms and shoulders are exactly the same."

I pat my stomach and sigh. "I think I've solved the mystery of those two extra pounds."

"At least you've still got all your hair," he says matter-of-factly. "Dad's going bald on top." His eyes meet mine in the mirror. "Why do I look so much more like you than him?"

I shrug. "Blame it on Darwin. Mom's genes must kick serious butt in utero."

"Guess so." He shakes his head and looks at me directly. "It kinda freaks me out, to tell the truth, and not just because we look the same." He runs a hand through his messy hair and gazes around the room. "I just got here yesterday, but it already feels like I've been coming here my whole life. I like you and your mom better than anybody I've met in a long time." He blushes a little, avoiding my eyes. "Sorry, I'm being weird. I'll shut up now."

His embarrassed sweetness touches me. "Mom and I like you, too, Leo," I say. "She told me last night that you're a great kid, and Carolyn should be proud to have you as a grandson." He gets even redder hearing this, but the corners of his mouth twitch with pleasure. I grin at him and nudge him towards the bathroom. "She'll change her mind fast, though, if you go downstairs smelling like a toilet bowl."

He laughs and gives me a shove. "Yeah, yeah, okay, I'll go shower."

"Hurry up," I tell him as he crosses the hall. "I'm hungry, and Mom makes the most amazing breakfast on the planet."

Mom is at the counter chopping stuff when I walk in the kitchen. Her back is to me and she's listening to music on the radio, but she still hears me. She turns her head and gives me the once-over.

"You should maybe wear a nicer shirt today," she says.

My shirt is a dark green button-down, and it's perfectly fine, so I ignore her. "What are you listening to?" I ask.

"Bach's Violin Partita in D Minor. Did you shave?"

I sigh, pouring myself a cup of coffee in the monkey mug. "Yeah, but I seriously doubt Carolyn will get close enough to notice. She's probably praying I'll just drop off Leo on the corner."

She waves her knife impatiently. "Make sure to say hello, even if she's less than welcoming. I'd like for her to know that I raised a son with some manners, and if she also happens to notice that you clean up nicely, so much the better. Maybe she'll be more open to meeting me if she realizes we're respectable people."

"Why don't you just come with us today, and force her hand a little bit? It's not as if she's going to sic a pack of Dobermans on us if you show up."

She returns to the chopping board. "She's not ready to see me. Leo coming here against her wishes already upset her, and I'm not going to make a nuisance of myself." She lowers her voice as I lean against the counter next to her. "Besides, there's no way I can leave Cindy alone today, and I'm certain she won't leave the house. She's still hoping Janelle will turn up."

"Fat chance," I murmur. "She's probably in Tijuana by now, if Leo's car didn't break down."

Mom doesn't bother to reply; she knows I'm right.

I have no idea how many times I've stood in this same spot over the years and watched her cook, but it's probably in the thousands. When she's feeling calm she takes her time, but if she's agitated, like this morning, she goes warp speed, and it's both impressive and terrifying to behold. Her knife flies as she dismembers a red bell pepper and a yellow onion in about a nanosecond, then she starts grinding up some garlic, olive oil, salt, and black peppercorns with a mortar and pestle, turning the mixture into a thick paste. I ask if she wants help and she hands me the mortar.

"Add a big handful of parsley to that, and a little more oil," she says.

"What are you making?"

She shrugs. "I'm still debating." She often starts preparing a meal like this, grabbing random stuff out of the fridge and cabinets with nothing more than a vague notion of the final product. She has a genius for culinary improvisation that I definitely didn't inherit. "Do you know if Leo likes spicy food?"

"He'd better, or he's dead to me." My phone buzzes in my pocket and I dig it out, wondering who the hell is calling so early. I don't recognize the number, but it's from Fall River, Massachusetts. I show Mom the screen and she freezes for a second, then nervously tells me to answer it.

"Hello?" I say cautiously.

"Hi, Noah, it's Ben Fortier."

His deep, slow voice is affable as we exchange good mornings; I tell him Leo is taking a shower, and we're still planning on being on the road by eight o'clock.

"Lucky I caught you before you left," he says. "Hey, is it too late for us to accept your mom's invitation to come up for a picnic today? Carolyn and I talked things over, and decided it was a great idea. Leo can just come home with us afterwards, so you don't have to shlep down here."

Mom's face is right next to mine as she listens intently to the conversation, her head cocked to one side like Sadie, our neighbor's spaniel.

"Tell him yes," she blurts, then grabs the phone from me before I can obey. "Hi, Ben, it's Virginia. Yes, please, do come for a picnic! We'd be absolutely delighted to have you."

I reclaim my coffee mug and listen as they chat about logistics. Leo wanders into the kitchen, wearing one of my old RISD T-shirts and a pair of chino shorts from that same woebegone era of my life.

"What's going on?" he whispers, eyeing Mom's animated face as she talks to Ben.

"Looks like we're going to have a family get-together today, after all," I tell him.

He looks thunderstruck. "No shit?"

"Yep. Carolyn must've had a change of heart."

I ask him if he wants some coffee and tell him to help himself when he says yes. I smash parsley and olive oil in the mortar as he fills his mug and stands next to me, both of us eavesdropping on Mom's side of the phone conversation. It sounds like Oliver and Michael are coming, too. Carolyn, apparently talking through Ben, is insisting on bringing some of the food for the feast, and Mom keeps saying things like, "Oh, that would be lovely, but there's no need to go to so much trouble, unless she really wants to." They go back and forth for a while like this and finally settle on a menu and a start time for the festivities—three o'clock—then Mom says goodbye and hangs up. She stands there with my phone in her hand, looking both pleased and stunned as she stares at Leo and me.

"What happened?" Leo asks. "I thought Grandma and Dad both had to work today."

Mom shakes her head. "I don't know. Ben just said everybody is looking forward to the trip." She tugs at her hair and nervously eyes the clock on the stove. "Dear God. We have so much to do before they get here."

I return to smashing parsley in the mortar. "Can we eat breakfast first? We've got almost the whole day to get ready, and Leo and I can help you with everything. Cindy will help, too, I'm sure."

Mom blinks. "Oh, no, poor Cindy. I didn't think how this might affect her. Having a party today is probably the last thing she'll want to do."

"Maybe it will help to take her mind off things." I step back to the cutting board on the counter and ask what else she needs for breakfast, but she just keeps standing there, looking addled. I doubt she ever really allowed herself to believe that she'd actually get to meet Carolyn; the reality of their impending reunion must be seriously frying her brain. I reclaim my phone gently. "Hey, don't go into a fugue state, okay?" I say. "Leo probably thinks you're going to start speaking in tongues."

Leo protests that he wasn't thinking that at all, prompting a smile from Mom; she regroups, ordering me to the fridge for eggs and chorizo. "Start browning the chorizo while I go wake up Cindy," she says. "After we've had breakfast I'll make a list of everything I need you boys to do today."

Naturally, it's not enough to mow, trim, and rake the grass to the satisfaction of the anal-retentive maniac who spawned me: She also wants all the flowerbeds weeded and mulched for the first time ever, which means ripping out fourteen billion hostas growing wild in every square inch of earth bordering the house, garage, fishpond, and driveway. It's another blisteringly hot day, and by late morning Leo and I are nowhere near finished with Mom's yard list from hell. We're also bug bitten, sunburned, and covered head to toe in sweat and dirt, both of us stripped to the waist and looking like characters from *Lord of the Flies*. Mom and Cindy are inside, cleaning the house and preparing food for the picnic, but Mom is periodically checking on us to make sure we're sticking to her Obergruppenführer timetable.

"Jesus, this is sadistic," I grunt at Leo, yanking out yet another plant by the roots and tossing it in an overflowing wheelbarrow. "If Zeus really wanted to punish Sisyphus, he should've introduced him to hostas." We've been on our hands and knees for the past two hours, save for brief trips with the wheelbarrow to the far side of the garage, adding to a compost heap that's starting to resemble Mount Kilimanjaro. I ask him if he hates us yet.

He grins at me and straightens for a minute, wincing as he stretches his lower back. "Nah," he says. "But whoever's been doing the gardening around here sucks."

I laugh, dropping my trowel and tugging off my work gloves. "I need a breather. If I don't drink some water I'll pass out."

The front and sides of the house are finally done and we're in the backyard, clearing an oval, brick-lined flowerbed that's midway between the fishpond and driveway. It's been a tangled patch of jungle for years, and I'm absolutely certain it would've remained like that forever if Carolyn weren't coming today. I climb to my feet, and as I stretch my own back a red two-door Nissan pulls in our driveway. The sun is shining directly on the windshield so I can't see who it is, but the Fortiers aren't due for several hours. The car engine turns off and the driver's door opens.

It's J.D.

He grins as he gets out of the car, and I gape at him as if he's a heat mirage. He's dressed casually, in a blue polo shirt, white shorts, and brown boat shoes, and he looks clean and cool, making me feel even grungier than I already did.

"So," he drawls, closing the door and leaning against it, "I guess we're even now, for you just showing up the other day without warning." His grin widens. "I sure hope I didn't have the same dumb look on my face that you do right now."

I grin back in spite of my shock. "As a matter of fact, you looked like the village idiot."

The passenger door pops open and my smile becomes forced as Bruce gets out. Well, shit. I should've realized he wouldn't let J.D. drive up here alone. I hate to admit it, but he's an attractive man. He's got royal-blue eyes, curly red hair, and a lean, long-limbed body that probably looks even better naked than clothed. Thank God his chin is weak and his ears stick out, otherwise he'd be revoltingly beautiful.

"Hi, Bruce," I say with as much civility as I can muster. "How are you?"

"Hey, Noah," he says warily. "Good to see you."

He and J.D. are staring at Leo, having no clue who he is. Leo is still on all fours, self-consciously pretending to struggle with a hosta, but he keeps darting looks at these strangers in the driveway, equally curious about them.

"Take a break, buddy," I tell him. "I want you to meet my old friend J.D., and his husband, Bruce." Leo sets aside his trowel and stands up slowly, brushing off his knees, and I turn back to J.D. and Bruce. "This is my great-nephew, Leo Fortier."

J.D. blinks, digesting this, then blinks again as he gets a closer look at the boy. "Hi, Leo," he says, shaking his hand. "My sympathies for being related to Noah. I'd tell you to deny it but you guys look too much alike for anybody to believe you."

Leo nods. "I've been considering plastic surgery ever since I met him."

"Oh, good," J.D. says, snorting. "You also sound like him." He steps over and gives me a hug, despite the fact that Bruce is watching us, and I'm filthy. He squeezes me hard before pulling back, smiling. "Blech, you're a mess. What are you guys doing?"

I scratch an insect bite under my ear. "Long story, but Carolyn and the rest of Leo's family are coming for a picnic this afternoon, and Mom's going nuts, since she hasn't met Carolyn yet. I think she's deluded herself into thinking we can make the place look like Versailles. Oh, and my cousin Janelle got arrested for credit card fraud, stole Leo's car, and skipped town last night. The cops are looking for her as we speak, and Aunt Cindy is probably out twelve thousand bucks in bail money."

His mouth falls open comically. "Holy crap. Are you kidding?"

I shake my head. "Boy scout's honor."

"Holy crap," he says again. "No wonder Virginia is flipping out." I start to answer but he's too wound up to let me. "And Carolyn's really coming here today? Jesus. I've been dying to know what happened when you went to Fall River. Was it weird? How come Leo's here by himself, if Carolyn hasn't even met your mom? Is Cindy still here?" He pokes me in the chest and scowls. "Why didn't you call me, you asshole? Was your mom as pissed as I said she was going to be for not telling her about Carolyn? I almost texted you a thousand times that night but I didn't want to interrupt if she was eating your entrails. I hope it hurt, and I hope she took pictures."

"Wow." I shake my head, enjoying him. "Sorry, can you repeat all that? I've never seen a human mouth flap so fast and I got distracted."

"Shut up," he says. "I'll just ask Virginia to fill me in on everything. Is she inside? I want to catch her by surprise, too."

I glance at the house and sigh when I see Mom already at the back door, peering through the screen. "Too late," I say.

She must've just realized it's J.D. I'm talking to, because she's frozen solid, staring out at him. Her hand drifts slowly up to her mouth, then she bursts out the door with a wordless cry. J.D.'s fingers find my shoulder and tighten for a second before he runs to meet her halfway. My throat closes as I watch them collide and spin in a circle. They haven't seen each other since J.D. and I split up, sixteen years ago. That's my fault, of course: Though I've told each of them many times it's fine if they want to hang out without me, they both think that I don't really mean it, and worry I'll feel excluded.

They know me too well.

Mom kisses him on the cheek and looks him up and down, and her face is practically on fire with joy. "It's about damn time," she says, crying as she pulls him close again. "Oh, how I've missed you."

"Me, too," J.D. says, and suddenly there are tears on his cheeks as well. "Me, too."

I've made peace with most of the could-have-beens in my life, but seeing the two people I love the most in the world clinging to each other like this, here in this place, where we were once a family, tears me up inside. If I hadn't been such a dumbass, it's likely J.D. and I would still be together—or at least there's a damn good chance of it. It should've been me today in the passenger seat of his car, coming here to visit Mom; it should've been me sharing his life, and his home, and his bed, all these years. Did I really believe, back then, that I'd be happier on my own?

I swallow thickly, trying not to feel like the world's biggest loser, and I turn to Leo for a diversion. He's watching Mom and J.D. with a bemused smile on his face.

"I guess they know each other," he says drily.

I clear my throat. "Nah, they're just super friendly people." Miraculously, my voice comes out somewhat normal.

"I was sorry to hear your mom is sick, Noah," Bruce says

quietly from behind us, surprising me. "She means the world to Jason."

If he's pissed that I snuck around Wellesley to see J.D. in private at the high school, he's hiding it well; I tell him thanks. I'm not exactly ecstatic that he's here, but as long as he continues to play nice, so will I.

"I think it's safe to say she feels the same about him," I say, then raise my voice so Mom and J.D. can hear me. "I'll introduce you to my mother as soon as she and your husband stop making out." They half turn toward us, grinning through their tears.

"Don't be a dick," J.D. says.

Mom snorts, wiping her eyes. "He can't help it. It's congenital." She moves toward Bruce, still clinging tightly to J.D.'s wrist; I doubt she'll let him go for a century or two. She offers Bruce her free hand and he takes it; the smile he gives her is a lot more genuine than the one he dredged up for me.

Mom is barefoot, as usual, and she's got her hair tied back with a blue bandana, and she's wearing a white T-shirt and a pair of dirty cutoffs. When she came outside about an hour ago to check on Leo and me, she was looking tired, sweaty, and harried, but her extreme pleasure at seeing J.D. has transformed her: She's so radiant it's a wonder we're not all blinded. J.D. is clearly thinking the same thing; he keeps searching her face as if he can't believe someone so damn pretty can also have a fatal disease.

"I'm sorry about our timing," he says. "Noah just told us about everything that's going on, and I should've called ahead. Should we come back another—"

"Absolutely not," she interrupts, with a finality that J.D. knows as well as I do. "Your timing is perfect. I'm scared to death that Noah and I might frighten Carolyn away, but she'll adore you, no matter what she thinks of us." He mounts a feeble protest and she shushes him with a finger on his lips. "I swear to God I'll shoot you if you try to leave."

He grins, wisely surrendering to her bullying. "Well, okay then. I guess that's decided."

Bruce looks more than a little annoyed, and I guess I can't really blame him, since J.D. didn't bother to ask for his input. He'd probably prefer a bowel resection to staying here and dealing with (A) me, and (B) this byzantine little family drama that makes about as much sense to an outsider as a Puccini opera. He mumbles something about not wanting to intrude on our privacy, and really needing to get back to Wellesley by mid-afternoon.

J.D. frowns, belatedly clueing in on his husband's irritation. "Oh, I'm sorry, honey," he says. "I should've asked if it was okay, but I thought you had the day off."

He never called me "honey" when we were together, and it sounds odd coming from him. Our endearments were more along the lines of "butthead" and "shit-for-brains."

"Yeah," Bruce answers, "I forgot I had a meeting at four o'clock today. I'm sorry." For a lawyer, he's a horrible liar; he's actually blushing. "Besides, Mrs. York and Noah have a lot going on, and I really don't think we should get in their way."

"Call me Virginia, please," Mom says. "I appreciate your thoughtfulness, Bruce, but please don't worry about us. As far as I'm concerned, J.D. has walk-in privileges here for life, which means you do, too." She reclaims Bruce's hand and beams up into his face, slathering on the charm like mayo on a hoagie. "I'm so pleased to finally meet you. I hope you brought an appetite; my sister and I are cooking enough food to feed the entire town, and Carolyn is bringing even more. It would be criminal to let it go to waste."

J.D. is applying his own brand of blunt pressure as well, gazing at Bruce with a hopeful, waif-on-the-doorstep expression that even Stalin couldn't resist.

"Well, I suppose I can reschedule the meeting," Bruce says, apparently too dense to realize that nobody believed he had one in the first place. "It's not really that important."

Mom says wonderful, then tells us all to come inside for a quick bite to tide us over until the picnic. She leads the way to the back door but stops Leo and me at the base of the porch steps. "You two go hose off," she orders. "You're much too disgusting to come in my clean house."

I grin at Leo. "Isn't she sweet?"

"Yep," he says. "I'm really touched."

Everybody laughs and Mom shoos us away, leading J.D. and Bruce inside, but J.D. hangs back for a minute at the screen to taunt us. "Let this be a lesson to you poor unwashed heathens," he says. "Cleanliness is next to godliness."

I cheerfully flip him the bird. "I bet you don't even know the name of the tight-ass who originally came up with that asinine aphorism."

"Teddy Roosevelt? No, wait. It was Alice Cooper."

"Nice try, bonehead. It was John Wesley."

"Wasn't he the guy who used to sit out in front of the drugstore, picking his nose?"

"No, that was you. John Wesley never picked his nose. He was a Methodist, and Methodists frown on anything to do with boogers."

We used to go on with juvenile idiocy just like this for hours, and the sparkle in his eyes is exactly as I remember it. Without warning, my sense of loss kicks in again, but I manage to keep my tone light, telling him to make himself useful and pour me a cold beer from the fridge while I'm getting cleaned up.

He gives me a playful salute, but then lowers his voice. "You sure it's okay with you if we stick around?"

Of course he noticed my mood change; I could never hide anything from him. I glance at Leo, feeling self-conscious discussing this with him here, and I'm grateful to find that he's already wandering off to give us some space, pretending to be fascinated by the sight of Sadie straining to get off her chain in the Overtons' backyard. I turn back to J.D.

"Are you kidding?" I ask him. "You've made my day. I haven't seen Mom this happy in years."

He fiddles with the hook latch on the screen door. "It's so good to see her again. I should've come to visit a long time ago." He stares out at the yard. "Everything looks pretty much the same as the last time I saw it. I was just telling Bruce on the way here about when we dug out that big-ass fishpond over there. Remember?"

"Of course." I wipe sweat from my forehead, leery of taking a trip down memory lane right now. "It's not every day that you find a bridal gown and a tuxedo buried in your backyard."

Bruce's voice calls from behind him in the house, and J.D. yells back that he's coming. He hesitates, however, and when he speaks again I can barely hear him. "I know it's hard having us here," he says. "It's hard on me, too, believe me. But I had to come see your mom. I've been really worried about her since we talked."

I nod, glad I'm not the only one struggling with our past. "It's fine, truly. And for what it's worth, I agree with Mom about you always being welcome here." I pause. "But I also feel it's my duty to mention that Bruce's ears make him look like a cross between Yoda and a llama."

He narrows his eyes but he's trying not to laugh. "Asshole. Go get cleaned up. You stink."

He disappears abruptly, and I sigh. Today was going to be complicated enough with just the Fortiers on hand, but the chances of it turning into an absolute clusterfuck have just increased exponentially. I shake my head and join Leo; he looks at me sympathetically, like he can hear the warning siren going off in my head.

"You all right?" he asks.

"So far," I say, shrugging as I lead him toward the hose. "But the day is young."

CHAPTER 9

Leo and I go back to scrabbling in the dirt after lunch, and Mom puts J.D. and Bruce to work as well, running errands for her and setting up tables and chairs in the backyard, in the shade of two maple trees. Cindy is trying her damnedest to help out and stay cheerful, but she looks lost and broken; her eyes are red and puffy from crying and she spends a lot of time standing around, staring at nothing. Mom is watching her anxiously, and I know she's conflicted about going ahead with the picnic while Cindy is so clearly hurting.

"Please don't feel there's any need to be social today, dear one, if you're not up to it," she tells her as they carry dishes and silverware to a table near where Leo and I are working. "You get a free pass to do whatever you want, even if that means tossing rocks through every window in the house and screaming your lungs out."

If there's such a thing as karma, my felonious young cousin Janelle has a gigantic asteroid of shit headed her way in the not too distant future. I guess it's possible that Cindy did something in the past to deserve getting stiffed for twelve grand by her own daughter, but it's hard to imagine.

"I'm okay, Ginny," Cindy says, smiling feebly. "I'd rather be with other people instead of moping in my room." She takes some plates from Mom and starts setting the table. "I just hope Carolyn understands if I'm not exactly the life of the party."

"Of course she will," Mom says. "Everyone will."

J.D. and Bruce are at Edgerton's, buying ice, and Leo and I are spreading cedar mulch in the cleared flower beds. We're finally almost done with this gardening crap. It's about time, too, because the Fortiers are due in half an hour and we still have to shower and make ourselves presentable before they get here. I wearily rip open the last bag of mulch and dump it at our feet, but just as we're starting to kick it around I glance up and see the familiar, shaggy-haired, lanky figure of Walter Danvers, Mom's quasi-boyfriend, strolling around the side of the house.

I see Mom when she spots him, too, just in time to catch a flash of consternation on her face. She quickly replaces it with a fond, welcoming smile. "Walter! I thought you weren't due back till Monday."

Walter's face relays no such mixed signals; he trots toward her with all the dignity of a besotted beagle, barely sparing a glance for the rest of us. I've always had a soft spot for Walter. He's been nuts about Mom from the instant he met her, and his ardor never shows any signs of lessening. He's a little older than she is, in his early seventies, but he's still neat and trim, and his boyish devotion to her is endearing.

"My last workshop got canceled late yesterday," he tells her, bestowing a rare public kiss on her cheek; they're seldom affectionate even when I'm the only one around. "I caught an early flight home." He greets me with a big, friendly wave. "Hey, Noah, great to see you, son. I'd hug you but you're too gross. Is that dung all over your body, or just dirt?"

"Hi, Walter." I grin back at him; our relationship is largely based on making fun of each other. "I see you're still in your Goth phase."

He almost always wears a black shirt, and today is no exception, in spite of the heat. At least this one's short-sleeved, and he's got the top button undone.

"Mouthy brat." He looks at Cindy and Leo with interest. "Did you bring these nice people with you?"

"Walter, this is my little sister, Cindy, and that's Leo over there next to Noah," Mom says. "I've got a lot to catch you up on."

Walter blinks. "Your sister? Really?" He steps over to Cindy with a look of wonder and warmly takes her hand. "I never thought I'd get the chance to meet you." He eyes Leo over her shoulder. "Virginia told me you had a daughter, but I didn't realize you had a son, too."

Cindy clouds up at the reference to Janelle, and Mom intervenes. "Leo's not with Cindy, Walter. He's my great-grandson."

Walter blinks. "Uh, come again?" He stares hard at Leo once more, then back at Mom. "I don't understand. *Your* great-grandson?"

"We've had a strange week while you were away," Mom says. "Noah found Carolyn."

His jaw goes slack. "Carolyn? You mean the baby girl who . . ."

Mom nods as he trails off. "Yes. The baby girl I gave up for adoption when I was a child. Leo is her grandson."

"My God." Walter recovers his manners, walking over to offer his hand to Leo. "Pleased to meet you. You're the spitting image of Noah when he was your age."

"That's just because of the dung," Leo says, making both Walter and me laugh.

"Yes, well, it looks much better on you," Walter tells him.

"Come with me, Walter," Mom says, taking him by the arm. "I'll bring you up to speed."

Her tone is light, but as she leads him toward the house she glances back at me with a strained expression, and I suddenly remember that Walter doesn't yet know about her ALS. Since everybody else showing up today does, however, she obviously has to tell him—either that, or send him home before somebody accidentally lets the cat out of the bag. I watch them walk up the porch steps hand in hand, chatting, and though I feel bad for both of them, it's Walter I'm more worried about in the short term. Mom can survive anything, emotionally, but I'm fairly certain Walter Danvers will never again be so lighthearted.

The snack Mom made for us earlier (when J.D. and Bruce first arrived) started off awesome, but ended up sucking balls. J.D., Mom, and I did all the talking, as Cindy was grieving the loss of Janelle, Leo was shoveling food in his face with unsightly abandon, and Bruce was sulking. Leo and I sat dripping on one side of the counter, naked to the waist and seated on towels, our shorts soaking wet from the hose; J.D. and Mom sat directly opposite us, with Bruce beside J.D. and Cindy next to Mom. Our three-way conversation was in no way impeded by the silence of the others; we yapped nonstop about whatever happened to pop into our heads, just like in the old days. It was so familiar and comfortable that I couldn't blame Bruce for feeling left out, though I admit it tickled me when I caught him staring with a quickly repressed scowl at my painting of Mom and J.D.

Yeah, I know: My pettiness isn't pretty, but it has its pleasures.

I couldn't shake the feeling that this was the way things were supposed to be in my life, every day. I watched Mom reach up and ruffle J.D.'s hair and tell him he needed a haircut; I fork-wrestled J.D. for a fat, juicy slice of tomato on a tray in the middle of the counter, and he gloated when he won; I listened to the sound of our voices filling the kitchen, talking over each other and finishing each other's sentences with eerie frequency. We were speaking English, of course, but in a dialect based on facial expressions, body language, and subtle tonal variations as much as words: an intimate, complex way of communicating we'd invented together, years ago. J.D. was finally back where he belonged, and a long dormant part of myself—the part that still had access to joy—started waking again, like a scraggly, disoriented groundhog stirring in its burrow on the first day of spring. The return to consciousness was amazing; I was hyper-aware of everything—the vibrant blue and white pattern on the rim of the plate in front of me, the fresh tang of red onion, avo-cado, and garlic hummus in a flour tortilla, the scent of earth and lilies wafting through the open windows on a breeze that tickled the hair on the back of my neck. I'd been asleep forever, it felt like, and I couldn't stop smiling from the sheer pleasure of being alive.

But of course it didn't last, because midway through lunch J.D. casually reached for Bruce's hand while saying something about their house in Wellesley, and the sweetness of the gesture spoke volumes about their relationship. It made me feel like puking, but it was exactly what I deserved for forgetting real-ity, even for a moment. The ceiling fan whirring above the counter caught my attention right about then with a faint click-ing noise, saying over and over *he is not yours, he is not yours, he is not yours.*

Go fuck yourself, fan: I already got the memo.

Mom looks remarkably composed as she watches the For-tiers pull in the driveway in a purple minivan, but given the cir-cumstances I'd wager a case of my favorite lube that she's a complete wreck on the inside. If so, she's not the only one struggling here. Cindy keeps wandering out to the road every few minutes and looking both ways, in the vain hope that Ja-nelle will return, and poor Walter has aged ten years since Mom gave him the bad news about her health. To tell the truth, I'm not doing so great myself. Ever since J.D. and Bruce came back from their run to the grocery store, holding hands and making goo-goo eyes at each other, my insides have been roiling with nausea, depression, jealousy, and barely containable malice. So far I've managed to keep from making an ass of myself, but if Bruce doesn't stop fondling J.D.'s goddamn knee soon I'm going to completely lose my shit.

Oh, this is going to be such a fun picnic.

We're sitting in lawn chairs in the shade of the trees, snacking on chips and salsa to stave off hunger before the main event. Leo and I are clean and dressed again, and I have to admit that all the work Mom made us do was worth it, at least from an aesthetic standpoint: The yard is now so manicured and coiffed that the other lawns in the neighborhood probably feel bad about themselves. Mom and the rest of us get to our feet as the Fortiers pile out of their van. Ben, Oliver, and Michael are all smiles, but Carolyn's face is expressionless. As she and Mom approach each other, I can't imagine what they're thinking. What in God's name are they supposed to say under these circumstances? "Oh, hello there, stranger, remember when we were connected by an umbilical cord fifty-six years ago? Good times."

They stop a couple of feet apart, and the rest of us are silent as we watch them study each other. J.D.'s eyes meet mine and I can tell he's worried about how this will go, too. Carolyn's wearing a light green blouse, a yellow skirt, and sandals; Mom's in a sky-blue summer dress, and of course she's barefoot. Carolyn is a pretty woman, but her face isn't as fine-boned as Mom's, and her stockier build makes her appear less graceful even though she's a couple inches taller. I'm sure Mom can see herself in Carolyn's features, and I'm guessing she also sees traces of her/their father, which is ample reason for both the wonder and the sadness in her eyes. Carolyn's control slips a bit; her face is still unreadable, but I can see her hands start to tremble.

"Hi, Carolyn." Mom's voice is so soft I can barely hear her. "I'm so happy you came."

"Hello," Carolyn says, polite but reserved. She glances at me for a second, almost as if seeking reassurance, and my heart goes out to her. She looks back at Mom. "Thank you for inviting us."

Mom steps forward tentatively. "Can I give you a hug?"

"Sure."

They come together awkwardly—like they've heard about hugs, but have never actually seen one performed—and Mom whispers something in Carolyn's ear. Carolyn doesn't answer, but her shoulders loosen a little, and when they step apart she manages something close to a smile, which gives the rest of us permission to relax. As Mom goes over to embrace Ben and the other Fortiers, one after another, everybody starts talking at once.

"Hey, Leo!" Michael says. "I can't believe your car got stolen!"

"Yeah," Leo says. "It kinda surprised me, too."

"Hi, Noah," Ben says, taking my hand gently in his giant paw. "Good to see you again." Oliver and Michael greet me, too, then Mom introduces everybody else. She starts with Cindy and Walter, who dutifully make the rounds without incident, but when Mom gets to J.D. and Bruce—calling J.D. her "second son"—Carolyn raises an eyebrow. Before Mom can explain, though, Cindy goes on an apology tour about Janelle's grand larceny, which makes everybody really uncomfortable, since she's sobbing as she talks. Ben saves the day by putting his arm around her shoulders and telling her it's not her fault; he says Leo's car was pretty beat-up, anyway, so it's not a huge loss, especially since it was insured. Carolyn surprises me by coming over and giving me a quick hug, but before I have a chance to say a word she goes into alpha mode with her family, sending Oliver and Leo to go get the food from their van and ordering Ben and Michael to help Mom with whatever else needs doing.

It's not a bad start, all things considered.

Mom lets everyone know where to find the bathroom if they need it, then recruits Walter and me to help Ben and Michael cart out all the stuff she and Cindy made—platters of fried chicken, a vat of German potato salad, a charcuterie plate, tapas, ham and bean salad, guacamole with pita chips, chocolate-walnut brownies, peach pie, apple pie, etc. It's already an absurd spread for only eleven people, so by the time Carolyn unloads her gigantic cooler, too—tuna salad, pasta salad, a cheese plate, and a fruit pizza with cream cheese, strawberries, and kiwi— there's barely room at the tables for anybody to sit. As if that weren't enough, Ben brought a separate, big-ass cooler full of beer, white wine, and soda, to go with Mom's big-ass cooler full of beer, hard cider, and sparkling water.

"Jesus Christ," I mutter at Walter, after we finish hauling the food from the kitchen. We're standing to one side, a little apart from everyone else as they mill around the coolers, chatting and getting drinks before sitting. "This is a bulimic's wet dream."

I was hoping he'd smile, but I don't think he even heard me. He's still shellshocked from his earlier conversation with Mom, and I can't bear to see the pain in his eyes. I nudge him and try again. "Looks like we're going to need a vomitorium."

He finally comes out of his daze enough to reward me with a ghost of the usual smirk he employs when I say something stupid. "Ignoramus," he says. "A vomitorium isn't for vomiting. It's an exit ramp in Roman amphitheaters, designed to disgorge large crowds quickly."

"Really? How fascinating." I grin. "Has anyone ever told you how much you suck at small talk?"

He tries to hold on to his smirk, but his heart is clearly too heavy for our usual back-and-forth. "I'm sorry, Noah," he says, looking away. "I appreciate what you're trying to do, but I'm going to be pretty lousy company today, I'm afraid."

"No worries." I touch his arm. "You should've seen me when I got the news."

He nods but doesn't say anything else. I ask if he wants to be left alone, but he shakes his head, so I stay beside him, using the silence to study everyone else.

We've got two picnic tables pushed together lengthwise, and an extra card table for the overflow of dishes. Oliver and Cindy seem to have hit it off and are the first to sit, side by side. Carolyn is fussing with the arrangement of the desserts, and Mom is back inside with Ben, getting bug spray and citronella candles. Leo and Michael are talking to J.D. over by the coolers, and Bruce is hovering in the background, looking ill at ease but smiling a little bit and doing his best to fit in. J.D. has always been good with kids (apart from his pain-in-the-ass little sister when I first knew him), and he just asked the boys what music they listen to. Leo readily lists several seventies bands—Boston, the Doobie Brothers, Kansas, Fleetwood Mac—and Michael says he likes all of those, too, which annoys Leo.

"Since when?" he asks. "You only listen to crap like Jacob Sartorius."

Michael blushes and stammers, and J.D. steps in effortlessly, saying he's not familiar with Sartorius but will check him out. J.D. knows everything about music—including just how shitty Jacob Sartorius is—so I'm sure he's only trying to spare Michael's feelings. It works, too; Michael gives Leo a vindicated look and regains his normal color. Leo asks J.D. what music he likes, and J.D. starts reeling off an itemized list of about ten thousand bands neither boy has ever heard of. He's not showing off; he's just a walking music library, and gets excited talking about the stuff he loves—very much like Mom gets with poetry. The difference between them, though, is that J.D. quickly realizes he's being a bore and stops, laughing at himself. One of the main reasons everybody likes J.D. is because he's fully aware that he's a geek, and has no shame about it. From the way both boys are talking to him without constraint, I can tell he's already won them over.

Carolyn is chatting with Oliver and Cindy, but she's watching her grandsons as well, and eavesdropping, just like me, on their conversation with J.D. Her face is curious, and I remember that she still doesn't know who J.D. is, or why he's here. I tell Walter I'll be back soon and wander over to her side. We say hi bashfully, then stand there like a couple of wallflowers at our first prom. I guess it's going to take a while to adapt to this brother/sister thing. I see her looking at J.D. again and it frees up my tongue.

"He's my ex," I explain. "He used to live with us, so he and Mom got really close."

She looks a little surprised, but if it bothers her to find out I'm gay she doesn't show it. "I see." She hesitates. "I didn't realize there were going to be other people here besides you and your mom, and Cindy. Is anyone else coming?"

I shake my head. "This is it. Sorry we didn't warn you about the extended guest list. Walter was out of town and got back earlier than we expected, and J.D. and Bruce just showed up a couple hours ago, completely out of the blue. Mom insisted that everybody stay."

She glances at me, maybe sensing my own aggravation with Bruce. "Do J.D. and his husband visit a lot?"

I sigh, lowering my voice. "No, thank God. This is the first time J.D.'s been back since we split up, and Mom's never met Bruce until today."

"I see," she says again, and we both fall silent once more. Her eyes drift to the house as Mom reappears with Ben. The two of them are getting along famously, smiling and jabbering, and Carolyn's sigh echoes mine.

"You all right?" I ask. "I'm still really weirded out by all this family stuff, myself."

"Good," she says. "I'd hate to be the only one." She watches

Mom intently. "The worst part is that I still have no idea if I'm actually who everybody else seems to think I am."

I grin at her, suddenly finding her skepticism funny. "You mean like maybe the adoption agency accidentally switched bassinets with you and the real Carolyn Thatcher?" I touch her hand. "I hate to break it to you, but given how much you and Mom look alike—not to mention Leo and me—I think you may be stuck with us."

She gives me a very Mom-like snort that obviously means she's not convinced, but she doesn't pull away from my touch. "Stranger things have happened. I'm just saying we should get a DNA test done, sooner rather than later."

"That's an excellent plan," I say, nodding. "Though once we know for sure we're related, we need to talk about all the birthday gifts you owe me from my childhood."

Her eyes go wide for a second, then a laugh escapes her, husky and contagious, making her sound far more likable than I'd given her credit for being. It seems to catch her family off guard, too; Leo, Michael, and Oliver all stare at her like they can't believe their ears, and Ben actually winks at me. Mom is pleased, too, though I'm not sure why: For all she knows I might be telling Carolyn all sorts of outrageous lies about her. J.D. smiles and rolls his eyes a little, holding up four fingers, and I grin when I figure out he means *four minutes*. I'd forgotten that he used to accuse me of having an almost pathological need to make new people laugh within five minutes of meeting them.

Bite me, I mouth at him, and he laughs.

Bruce sees our exchange and frowns, not knowing what's going on, and it irritates me when J.D. leans over to explain. I know they're married, for Christ's sake, but does Bruce need an interpreter for every damn thing that passes between J.D. and me?

Carolyn is still chuckling, and Michael asks her what's so

funny. She waves a hand, looking embarrassed. "Nothing, honey. Noah just caught me by surprise."

"He's good at that," Leo says. "He made Pepsi come out my nose yesterday."

The affection in his voice touches me. Regardless of what else has happened in the last few days, it appears I've made a friend. That he also happens to be my great-nephew is oddly satisfying. It saddens me that Janelle didn't choose to stick around longer; I think we might've been friends, too, given a little more time.

Maybe we can still be pen pals, after the cops catch her and toss her butt in prison.

Everyone is on their best behavior when we all get seated, so the talk is limited to insipid crap like work and the weather, and oh, this salad is amazing, and can I have another slice of that fabulous peach pie, please, and this fried chicken just melts in your mouth, doesn't it? Ben is at the head of the table, and to his left are Carolyn, me, J.D., Bruce, and Michael; to Ben's right are Walter, Mom, Cindy, Oliver, and Leo. This puts me directly across from Mom, with J.D. on my left and Carolyn on my right. We're pressed together for space, which I'm finding hugely distracting, since I haven't felt J.D.'s bare leg against mine since before he got married.

Ben is the first to climb out of our stultifying conversational hellhole, telling Mom that since he found out about us he's been reading a lot of her poems. He lists a couple he really likes—"Autumn 1914" and "Grace After Midnight"—and I tense up, sure he's also going to mention "The Lost Soul." He doesn't, praise God, but probably only because he no doubt remembers me bitching about it at their house the other day, and he's nice enough not to rub my nose in it.

"Thank you, Ben," Mom says. "It's sweet of you to read my poems."

"I really like 'Autumn 1914,' too," J.D. says, then gives me a sly grin. "But of course, 'The Lost Soul' is my all-time favorite."

I choke on a bite of chicken, and his grin just gets bigger as he pats me on the back. I lean over to whisper in his ear. "You bastard."

"Beg pardon?" he says. "I didn't catch that."

Mom, looking highly entertained, jumps on the Noah dog pile, too. "For some reason, Noah doesn't care for that poem, J.D. I can't imagine why."

I scowl at both of them, but they're so pleased with themselves for yanking my chain in tandem that it's hard to glower properly. It also doesn't help that Ben is hiding a smile behind his hand, and Leo is laughing aloud at his end of the table.

"Can we talk about something else?" I ask plaintively. "Anything at all?"

Oliver steps in, blessedly, asking Cindy if any of Mom's poems are about her.

"None that I'm aware of," Cindy says, "but until this week we haven't seen each other in a long time, and Ginny seldom writes about her personal life, anyway." She gives me a sympathetic look. "With one major exception, of course."

"Lucky me," I grunt.

"Have you read all her books?" Ben asks Cindy.

"Yes, I love them. I've always been so proud of her."

Mom rests her head against Cindy's and tells her thanks. Mom's long, mostly black hair makes a vivid contrast to Cindy's short white hair, but their faces aren't all that different, in spite of the roundness of Cindy's cheeks and chin. Carolyn is watching them closely, and asks how long it's been since they've seen each other.

"Twenty-eight years," Mom says, looking uncomfortable at the surprised reactions from everybody except J.D., Walter, and me.

"Seriously?" Ben asks. "Why so long?" He catches himself. "Sorry, that's none of our business."

"It's fine, Ben," Mom says. "I know how strange it sounds, but the years somehow just got away from us." She hesitates. "We were very close as girls, and have always stayed in touch, but we could never seem to find the time to get together. I don't know why we let that happen, but we did."

She's being cagey, but I don't blame her: Any real explanation of their long separation has to include memories of their father, Carolyn's birth, and God knows what else.

Cindy follows Mom's lead. "Living on opposite sides of the country certainly didn't help," she says, "nor the fact that we were both workaholics. But those are poor excuses, I know." She looks around the table with a disarming smile. "Family should always come first."

It's a nice pivot—if smarmy—but I can see by the speculative look in Carolyn's eyes that she's not buying it. She's not stupid, and likely recognizes a smokescreen when she sees one. Fortunately, she doesn't choose to pursue it; she just asks Walter how long he and Mom have been together.

Walter makes an effort to pull out of his funk. "You better ask Virginia," he says, grinning sideways at Mom. "At least half the time she wasn't talking to me, so I don't know if that gets included in the total."

He's joking, but it's also true; Mom runs hot and cold so often with him it's a wonder he doesn't have both frostbite *and* first-degree burns all over his body. She'd ordinarily scowl at him for making a comment like this, but today she just takes his arm indulgently.

"We started dating when Noah was a senior in high school," she tells Carolyn. "That was also when J.D. came into our lives, so it was an important year for all of us."

"Oh!" Carolyn says, turning to me. "I didn't realize when you said J.D. was your ex that it was that long ago."

"Yep, prehistoric," I say. "There was even a bloodthirsty cavewoman involved."

J.D. snorts as everyone stares at me. "He's talking about the girl I was dating when we met. She wasn't nearly as bad as he makes her sound."

"She had a necklace of human teeth, and decorated her cave with the vital organs of children," I say.

Everybody laughs, including Bruce, which surprises me; until this very second, I wasn't sure he had a sense of humor. To be fair, I don't know him well at all—and given my history with his husband I probably never will—but J.D. wouldn't love him if he wasn't a good person. I also have to admit that it's hardly Bruce's fault that I bring out the worst in him; I seem to have that effect on a lot of people.

Mom asks Carolyn and Ben about how they met, but I entirely miss what they're saying because even though I'm pretending to listen I can't seem to focus on anything but J.D. I'm watching him from the corner of my eye, and he's watching me exactly the same way, like when we were kids and couldn't get enough of each other. I reach for my beer and drain half the can in one go, trying to distract myself from the feel of his warm thigh sticking to mine under the table.

Ben and Carolyn finish whatever they were saying, and a short, awkward silence follows, but alcohol quickly comes to the rescue, loosening tongues. Oliver asks Cindy about Sonoma County, where she lives, and Bruce starts talking about a trip he and J.D. took there a few years back. Walter and Carolyn get chatting about Walter's two cats, Parsnip and Onions, and Mom leans behind Walter to grill Ben about his years as a state trooper before he retired. Leo and Michael aren't drinking booze, of course, but are now comfortable enough to start sniping at each other in the insular language of brothers, half rancor and half affection, so I have no idea what they're talking about. Bruce keeps trying to draw J.D. into his Sonoma story, but J.D. just smiles and nods, which is what I'm doing, too, whenever anybody looks my way.

And meanwhile, the two of us are attached knee to hip like

Siamese twins, eyeing each other covertly and knowing nothing has changed between us, nothing at all.

I remember something I meant to tell him earlier and lower my voice so only he can hear me. "I ran into Perry White when I first got to town this week. He actually apologized for beating the crap out of us."

That surprises him enough that he turns to face me full on. "Really?"

I nod. "Yeah. I think the asshole even meant it."

His beautiful blue eyes study me. "What did you say?"

"Nothing. I just glared at him until he drove away."

"Good. I was worried you might've forgiven the son of a bitch. I still have nightmares about that day."

The bitterness in his quiet voice makes me wish I could reach for his hand. "Really? I hadn't thought about it in years, until I saw him."

"You're tougher than me," he says, shrugging. "You always were. Hell, you tore off half his damn face. All I did was get my ass kicked."

He's wrong about me being tougher, but now he's got me wondering why that day didn't affect me much, in the long run. We'd been outnumbered two to one, and they were all the size of goddamn gorillas, but in spite of almost losing an eye I'd never felt like a victim. Is that only because I had the great good fortune to get hold of one of the bastards and do some damage of my own? If so, I'm not sure I like what that says about either my character or human nature in general. Shouldn't inflicting suffering on another person—no matter how richly the prick deserves it—come with a cost? Sure, my attack on White was self-defense, but I'd be lying if I said it hadn't also given me enormous pleasure to bring him to his knees, screaming. Did that act of savagery somehow vaccinate me against long-term trauma?

Sigh. Noah the Barbarian.

"You had three of them on you," I remind J.D., "and I had

one. The only reason I got loose was because nobody was expecting me to fight dirty."

His mouth twitches. "I could've warned them, but they didn't ask."

"What are you guys whispering about?" Bruce says, leaning in and putting a possessive arm around J.D.'s waist.

J.D.'s eyes linger on mine for a couple of seconds before he turns away, smiling. "Just reminiscing, sweetie. Noah ran into an old acquaintance of ours the other day."

"Who was it?"

"Nobody important." He looks across the table at Cindy and Oliver. "I'm sorry, I missed part of what Bruce was saying about our trip to Sonoma. Did he tell you about the Gloria Ferrer Winery? That was my favorite."

Bruce must know about Perry White, so it's interesting that J.D. didn't tell him who we were talking about. His nonanswer isn't setting well with Bruce, though, because he's now looking at me behind J.D.'s back with a distinctly unfriendly expression. My more charitable thoughts about him when he laughed at my joke earlier now slide out of my head, and I contemplate asking if the reason he doesn't have a chin is because he's part manatee. I bite my tongue and turn away, grateful that I haven't had much to drink; I need to stay sober if I don't want to cause a scene.

Ben excuses himself to use the bathroom and Walter rises to get himself another beer, leaving Mom and Carolyn momentarily silent as they appraise each other across the table. I admire Mom's self-discipline, because I know she's dying to get to know Carolyn better, and her normal way of dealing with strangers is to interrogate them like murder suspects. She's playing it cool, though, probably afraid of pushing too hard, too fast. Carolyn shifts a little on the bench beside me and clears her throat.

"I have a lot of things I want to ask you, Virginia," she says quietly, with a furtive glance down the table to make sure Leo and Michael aren't listening. "But I don't feel I really have the right to ask until I know for sure you're my birth mother."

"Of course you have the right," Mom says carefully. "And I'll tell you everything I can, whenever you feel like talking." She hesitates. "But it would probably be best if we spoke alone, or with only Ben present."

The fact that she phrased it that way—*I'll tell you everything I can*—says to me that she still hasn't figured out how much to share about Carolyn's origins. I don't envy her having to dance around that particular nest of snakes, and I'm grateful she's not asking me to be there, given that I don't have a very good poker face and might reveal more than she wants Carolyn to know. I can sense J.D. listening in on my other side, even as he pretends to be riveted by whatever inanity Bruce is spewing at Oliver and Cindy, and from the abstracted gaze on Cindy's face, I wouldn't be at all surprised if she's eavesdropping, too.

"Either way is fine with me," Carolyn says. "But if there's any way we can talk today, I'd appreciate it." She drops her voice to a whisper. "I have the feeling it's not going to be easy, and I'd prefer to know the worst upfront, rather than letting my imagination run wild."

Mom studies her closely then nods, reaching across the table to touch her hand. "In that case, we can go talk as soon as you're done eating. Everybody will understand if we disappear for a time." She looks at me, and though she's putting on a good show of imperturbability I can see she's nervous by the brightness in her voice. "Do you mind holding down the fort, Noah?"

I shake my head. "Not at all. This particular fort is well-stocked with booze, so there's no place else I'd rather be."

Bruce is still talking to Oliver and Cindy, but now he's recounting a story—for no discernible reason—about when he and J.D. went car shopping, and how J.D. wanted the red Nissan they drove here today, but Bruce wanted a blue Volvo instead, so they ended up buying both because they couldn't make up their minds. The story doesn't really have an ending, nor a point—except maybe to boast about having two really nice cars—and when J.D. gently teases him for telling it, Bruce gets embarrassed and emits an apologetic donkey bray of laughter. I wince reflexively, and Mom's mouth twitches.

"Better not drink too much," she warns me, with a raised eyebrow for emphasis.

Everyone helps clear the tables and clean up the kitchen after we finish eating, then Mom and Carolyn, looking solemn, shuffle into the living room while the rest of us return to the backyard. As we drink and talk in the shade the general vibe is relaxed, but we're all keeping a watchful eye on the house, wondering how the heart-to-heart is going.

Oliver and Walter are chatting as comfortably as a pair of old army buddies, seated side by side with an impressive pile of empty beer cans quickly accumulating between their lawn chairs. Apparently they've discovered a shared passion for antique coins, and I'm happy to see Walter showing a spark of life again, even though their talk about doubloons and drachmas makes my eyes roll up in my skull. I haven't figured out Oliver yet, but he seems like a good guy, both unassuming and sincere, if a tad unexciting.

Ben is sitting on the ground, looking perfectly comfortable with his back against an old oak tree; he's so solid himself that I'm not sure if he's leaning on the tree or vice versa. Michael is lying on his back in the grass next to him, playing a game on his phone, and Ben is talking to Cindy, who's perched on a chair nearby, getting quietly shitfaced on Chardonnay. They're reminiscing about movies they loved as kids—*Paint Your Wagon*, *The Graduate*, *The Dirty Dozen*—and though Cindy is holding up her end of the conversation, she can't stop digging her phone out of her pocket every few minutes, willing it to ring.

Leo and I are both on the ground, a few feet from J.D. and Bruce, in chairs. I'm stretched on my side, propped on an elbow, and Leo is nearby, sitting with his ankles crossed and his arms wrapped around his thin legs. J.D. and I are doing most of the talking, in spite of our occasional attempts to include Bruce and Leo in the conversation; we've never been good at shutting up when we're together. J.D. just noticed that Leo is wearing one of my old T-shirts—black, with a gold Guinness Extra Stout label on the chest—and he asks if I remember where I got it in the first place.

"Sure," I say, laughing. "You bought it at that Saint Paddy's Day parade over in Portsmouth, and I stole it from you as soon as we got back home. Sorry about that."

"You're not forgiven. You always took my favorite shirts." He looks at Leo. "It's uncanny how much you remind me of Noah at your age, but I can tell you're a way nicer kid, who would never dream of resorting to common thievery."

Leo grins. "I was actually thinking about stealing this shirt from Noah. I like it."

"Fair enough," I tell him. "Finders, keepers."

Bruce is smiling, but it looks strained. "You guys are funny," he says, running a hand through J.D.'s hair and glancing briefly at me. "I'd never take Jason's clothes without asking—it would feel disrespectful—but I guess the rules are a lot different in a marriage than in a high school romance."

I eye him, wondering if he's baiting me. He's looking all innocent, so maybe I'm just being paranoid.

"I stole just as much stuff from Noah as he stole from me," J.D. tells him. "I even still have a couple of his old CDs."

"Really?" I ask. "Which ones?"

"Probably more than a couple, actually, now that I think of it," he says. "But the only ones I know for sure are yours are Springsteen's *Nebraska*, and the first Jayhawks album."

I snort, flinging a clump of mulch at him. "You dick. I thought I'd lost those when I dropped out of RISD."

"You did. You left them in my car when I helped you move out of the dorm. You should be more careful with your things."

We grin at each other like fools, and it suddenly occurs to me
that we're pretty close to the secluded spot where we first had
sex—just about thirty feet from here, on the ground, beneath a
couple of Scotch pines and an old maple tree, right next to a
stone bench and a Victorian birdbath: all still there, along with
my vivid memories of that cool autumn night, with a half-moon
and a billion stars overhead, and a breeze rustling through dead
leaves, smelling of earth and pine, drying the sweat on our bodies. Our sex was clumsy, a little painful, and almost unbearably
sweet, and it changed my life forever. Having him here again is
making me feel both slaphappy and horny; if Bruce weren't sitting right next to him I'd probably charge across the lawn and
jump his bones in front of God and everybody. J.D. sees where
I'm looking and his grin gets bigger. Our eyes lock for a moment but then he abruptly turns back to Bruce and starts telling
him about the croquet course we used to have out here. Bruce
makes all the right noises as J.D. talks, but he's watching me
suspiciously all the while.

Shit, this is torture. I drain my beer—number four thus far,
but who's counting—as Leo stirs beside me.

"How do you think it's going inside?" he asks.

"No clue," I say, relieved at the diversion. "But the house is
still standing, so that's a good sign."

He shrugs. "Maybe." He lowers his voice. "I wish you'd tell
me what they're talking about."

I hesitate. "I would if I could, Leo. But it's not mine to tell."

He looks around the yard, making sure no one is listening.
"But all of you guys know, right? I mean, Cindy does, obviously, and Walter, and J.D."

I may have underestimated this kid.

"You don't miss much, do you?" I ask. He smiles a little, but
stays quiet, waiting for an answer as I play with the tab on my
empty can. "Yeah, we know at least part of the story. But Mom
and Carolyn are the only ones who have a right to share it with
anybody else."

He scowls. "I knew you were going to say that."

I nudge him in the ribs. "Sorry to be so predictable." He still looks dissatisfied, so I nudge him harder, making him topple over on his side. "Oops," I say.

"You butthole," he complains, laughing in spite of himself.

"Language, Leo," Oliver chides.

There's a jingle of tags over by Michael and Ben, and I belatedly spot Sadie, off her chain yet again and now drooling on Michael's knee. Michael squeals in surprise, then sits up to pat her. "I didn't know you guys had a dog," he says to me. "What's its name?"

"She's not ours, she belongs to—"

"SADIE! GET BACK OVER HERE!"

Everyone else jumps a little at Freddie Overton's yell, but I was half expecting it, so I barely even react. He's at the edge of his property, clapping his hands like a madman and looking thoroughly disagreeable. Jesus Christ. I'm starting to think the poor bastard is turning Sadie loose himself, just so he has an opportunity to pick a fight.

Sadie ignores him, trotting over to say hi to Ben and Cindy, then J.D. and Bruce.

"SADIE, COME NOW!" Freddie bellows, now running toward us.

His shirt-and-shorts combination today is red and blue, and his bald head and face are even redder than his shirt. Sadie glances at him nervously, tongue lolling, but makes one more quick detour to greet Leo and me before hanging her head and ambling back toward her berserk master. Freddie has almost reached us by then, and bends down to snatch her up near the fishpond, rough enough to make her yelp as we all gawk at him.

"Oh, don't hurt her, please!" Cindy says.

"I've asked you time and again not to encourage her to come over here!" Freddie snaps at me, ignoring Cindy.

I sit up. "It's not exactly our fault, Freddie. She just shows up."

"And you fuss over her every time! How many times do I have to ask you to stop doing that?"

This clown is getting on my last nerve. I climb to my feet with a grimace and go over to him, wanting to steer him away from the party as fast as possible. "How about we take a look at her chain together, and I'll see if I can help you fix it?"

"There's nothing wrong with her chain!"

I glance at J.D., who stares back at me with raised eyebrows and a *what-the-fuck* expression that makes keeping a straight face impossible.

"You think this is funny?" Freddie demands.

"Not at all," I say. "I just can't help smiling whenever I see you, because you're always so pleasant."

"Don't you dare be sarcastic with me, mister!" he snarls. "I won't put up with it!"

"Is everything okay, Noah?" Ben asks from behind me. He's still sitting with his back against the tree, but eyeing Freddie unfavorably.

"It's fine," I say. "It's just a misunderstanding."

I look back at Freddie, not sure how to proceed. My natural inclination is to push every button in his pot-bellied body, but I guess that's not the best plan, since Mom wants to make a good impression on the Fortiers today.

"Look, Freddie," I say. "I apologize. We really aren't trying to encourage Sadie to come over here. We just like dogs, and it feels mean to chase her away when all she's doing is saying hello."

"Are you saying I'm being mean to her?" he snaps.

"Of course not." My self-restraint begins to fray, and I stare down at the goldfish swimming in the pond a few feet away, picturing how Freddie would look if I tossed his obnoxious ass in there. "I'm saying that if you buy her a better chain, we'll never need to have this conversation again."

"Are you deaf, or just stupid?" he asks. "I keep telling you there's nothing WRONG with her chain."

I shrug. "Maybe not, but her owner is definitely missing a few links."

"That's not helpful, Noah," Cindy cautions in her best counselor's voice, but she's slurring her words a little at this point, so it doesn't have quite the effect she's probably going for.

"This is your last warning," Freddie hisses. "Not one more word." He looks so pathetic, clutching his squirming spaniel in one arm and shaking his other fist in impotent fury, that I almost feel sorry for him.

Almost.

"Has anyone ever told you that you're a belligerent wingnut, Freddie?" I ask.

His punch comes a lot faster than I'm expecting, but I still manage to duck it. He loses his balance and falls on his knees, dropping Sadie, who has the good sense to run off. Freddie, bellowing, dives for my legs and dumps me on my butt on the ground, but before he can try to swing again, J.D. drags him off and steps between us as we both scramble to our feet.

"Are you crazy?" J.D. yells in his face. "What the hell do you think you're doing?"

Freddie sputters incoherently and tries to shove him aside, but Ben has reached us by now, too, and with ridiculous ease he immobilizes Freddie in an armlock. Freddie squeals in alarm.

"I don't know the whole story here, buddy," Ben tells him amiably, "but what you just did is called assault, so you'd better calm down." He turns to me. "You okay, Noah?"

I nod, embarrassed that things have gotten so out of hand. "Yeah, I'm fine, thanks. Sorry about this."

"Let go of my husband!"

Oh, good. Faith Overton just burst out of their house and is scurrying across the lawn, as fast as she can move in sandals and a confining pink dress.

"Not just yet, ma'am," Ben calls out, "but I promise I won't hurt him." He eyes me again. "Do you want to call the police, Noah? I'll back you up if you want to press charges."

I look at Freddie, safely incapacitated in Ben's strong grip. He's still spitting mad—the veins on his bald head are writhing like worms on a plate—but he's not likely to try anything else, with Ben and J.D. guarding me. Faith is now there, too, at Freddie's side, and her hand on his arm seems to have a calming effect.

I sigh. "No, it's okay. Let's just forget it."

Ben gazes at Freddie sternly. "If I turn you loose, can you keep from trying to murder my brother-in-law?"

"Only if he can keep a civil tongue in his head," Freddie grinds out.

I narrow my eyes, but before I can say anything J.D. clamps a hand on my mouth with startling speed. "Just nod your head, Noah," he suggests.

The feel of his warm palm on my lips is more than enough to make me completely forget whatever wiseass remark I was going to make. I nod obediently, docile as a lamb, but he doesn't let go until Ben turns Freddie over to Faith and she starts dragging him back toward their house.

"For Pete's sake, Freddie," she huffs. "Can't I even leave you alone for five gosh darn seconds?"

"This isn't over!" Freddie barks over a shoulder, but not until he's well out of Ben's reach.

Ben shakes his head, sighing as he turns back to me. "Some folks never learn." He taps me gently on the chest with a knuckle, grinning. "Looks like my wife isn't the only one in the family with a sharp tongue," he says.

I blush, feeling like an idiot, but he's so good-natured I can't help but grin back at him. "Sorry, Ben. I didn't handle that well at all."

J.D. snorts. "Ya think?"

"Good reflexes, Jason," Ben tells him. "Looks like you've had some practice shutting Noah up."

"I was worried I'd lost my touch, but it was just like riding a bike," J.D. teases, draping an arm over my shoulders. "Virginia usually puts a muzzle on him when he goes out in public, but she must've forgotten today."

I wrap my arm around his waist, marveling at how natural it still feels to be held by him. "I'm overdue for my distemper shot, too, so you better watch yourself."

"Uh, Jason?" Bruce pops up on J.D.'s other side, looking seriously miffed. "I know you're having a good time, but we should probably think about taking off." He eyes me coldly. "Can I have my husband back, please?"

Ben murmurs something about getting another beer and makes a discreet exit—I'm really starting to like that man—as J.D. and I separate a little guiltily, realizing too late how our affection for each other must've appeared to Bruce. J.D. is flushed, but he keeps his smile. "It's still early, sweetie," he says softly to Bruce. "And I don't want to leave before Virginia and Carolyn have finished talking. Would you mind if we stick around for just a little bit longer?"

Everybody else is trying to give the three of us a little privacy, pointedly not looking in our direction, except for Michael, who's probably wondering at the sudden tension in the air.

"I'd rather not," Bruce says. "Noah's neighbor might come back for a rematch, and I don't want you in the middle of it again, just because Noah can't control his mouth."

He's not wrong, of course, but the holier-than-thou tone in his voice pisses me off.

"As a matter of fact, I'm controlling my mouth right now," I say.

He throws up his hands. "You always have to get the last word in, don't you? You're such a juvenile."

"Nuh-uh," I say. "Poo poo pee pee."

J.D. abruptly turns his head away, shoulders shaking, as Bruce glowers at both of us.

"My God, Jason, you act like a child, too, whenever Noah is around," he says. "It's really gross, and I'm embarrassed for both of you."

J.D. sobers at once. "I'm sorry you feel that way," he says stiffly. "But please stop attacking Noah, just because you're mad at me. He hasn't done anything wrong."

"I can't believe you're defending him," Bruce snaps, loud enough to make it hard for everybody else to pretend nothing is going on. "I knew it was a huge mistake to come here today."

This guy has a stick up his ass the size of the Florida Panhandle, and I'd like nothing better than to point this out to him, but I don't want to make things worse for J.D. I start edging away, deciding to make myself scarce, like Ben did.

"Can we please go talk about this somewhere more private, Bruce?" J.D. asks, before I get far. "This isn't appropriate at all."

"Oh, *now* you're worried about what other people think?" Bruce demands shrilly. "Just five seconds ago you and Noah had your hands all over each other, even though I was just two feet away! I'm sure that made a *wonderful* impression, as did the fact that you almost got in a fistfight with a perfect stranger, just to protect Noah's stupid ass!"

J.D. is getting angry, too, turning red and breathing hard. "I'm sorry I upset you, but that doesn't give you the right to act like a jerk in front of these nice people! What is *wrong* with you? Can we please go for a walk now, and talk about this?"

Bruce fumes like a truculent toddler for a couple seconds, then shrugs. "Fine, but it won't change anything."

J.D. mutters an apology to me and marches down the driveway, not even waiting to see if Bruce follows. Bruce does, but slowly, and as he passes by he gives me a look so full of venom that I can't resist goading him, just a little.

"My ass isn't stupid," I tell him. "I can fart in three languages."

For the second time in less than ten minutes I get tackled

around the knees. This time, though, I'm too close to the fish-pond; I tumble in with a spectacular splash, unable to control my fall because Bruce is still clutching my legs. The water is only about a foot deep, so my butt, elbows, and head all hit the concrete bottom of the pond, hard enough to stun me. I come up gasping and spitting. Bruce is half in, half out of the water, and he finally lets go of me and flops over on the grass, his shirt drenched and algae in his hair.

"Dammit, Bruce!" J.D. bellows, sprinting back. "Have you completely lost your freaking mind?"

Like magic, Ben is already by the pond, bending down to help me out. "You sure know how to throw a party," he says, taking my hand and pulling me to my feet with a grunt.

I rub the back of my head, wincing, as I step out of the water. One of my sandals is floating in the pond and the other is missing; I'm soaked to the skin, and everybody is gaping at me like I'm the creature from the black lagoon.

"We aim to please," I say, torn between hilarity and humiliation, as Leo, Walter, and Cindy wander over to make sure I'm okay, shaking their heads. Leo and Walter are repressing smiles.

"Please tell me you didn't just do that," J.D. says heatedly to Bruce. "Tell me you didn't just knock Noah into the fishpond because he made a fart joke."

"I didn't mean for him to fall in the water!" Bruce cries. "But that's not why I did it, and you know it!"

"Are you hurt, Noah?" J.D. asks, ignoring him. He comes over and touches my arm. "You look a little rough."

I shrug. "I'm probably less traumatized than the goldfish."

Bruce isn't enjoying the attention I'm getting; he's back on his feet at once. "Give me the car keys," he orders J.D. "I'm leaving right now, with or without you."

"Seriously?" J.D. stares at him, gobsmacked. "You're giving me an ultimatum, after pulling a stunt like that?"

"Maybe you can't see what's going on here," Bruce says, "but I can, and I'm sick of it. You need to remember who you're married to, Jason." He holds out his hand. "Give me the keys."

J.D. looks at him for a long moment, then his face whitens; he digs out the keys from his pocket and slams them in Bruce's hand. "Fine, leave," he says. "When you're ready to stop acting like an idiot, let me know."

Bruce bursts into tears, stomps to their little red Nissan, hops in, slams the door, and cranks the ignition. He peels out, spraying gravel all over the yard and tearing down the driveway. Once the car disappears around the corner at the end of the street, no one says anything for at least half a minute. J.D.'s eyes are brimming over as he finally turns to all of us.

"I am so sorry about this, everyone," he says. "I don't even know what just happened." He looks at me as if for reassurance, but as I limp over to him he gets an almost panicked expression on his face and shies away when I reach out to him. "Don't, Noah. I can't be around you. You're a human wrecking ball, and you never change."

He hurries off, vanishing around the side of the house.

Cindy removes a clump of green slime from my bicep and pats me on the back. "He just needs a little time by himself," she says. "You should go get cleaned up. You're a mess."

I nod, wondering idly why everyone is staring at me like I'm going to fall apart, too. "I'll be fine," I tell them. "Believe it or not, this is pretty much par for the course around here."

Walter snorts, clapping me gently on the shoulder. "Except for the bit with the fishpond," he says. "That was new, and kind of entertaining."

He returns to his seat beside Oliver; Cindy wanders off to check her phone again, leaving me with Ben and Leo. I bend down to fish my sandal from the pond, and Leo trots over to retrieve its missing partner—it somehow flew halfway across the yard. I thank him when he gets back and hands it to me.

"I don't much like Bruce," he says. "He's kind of a twat."

"Language, Leo," Ben says. "People do dumb things when they're jealous." He grins at me. "Especially when the person they're jealous of keeps poking the bear with a stick."

I wince, sighing. "I swore I was going to be nice today, but he just rubs me the wrong way. I'm sorry you guys had to see that."

"Not to worry. Want a cold beer to take with you to the shower?"

"Yes, please."

He sends Leo for the beer and I'm gratified at how soon he returns with a cold can in his hands. I decide to enter the house through the front door, because it's closer to the stairs and should allow me to sneak up to the bathroom without disturbing Mom and Carolyn. I'm assuming they're still deep in conversation in the living room, because nothing else could've kept Mom from intervening in the two loud, impromptu wrestling matches I just instigated in the last fifteen minutes. I leave my sandals on the porch and step inside as quietly as I can, dripping scummy fishpond water all over Mom's clean floor.

As I tiptoe through the entry toward the stairs, I can hear voices from outside through the open windows—Cindy and Oliver, I think—along with birdsong and the faint buzz of a distant lawnmower, but the house is completely silent, save for the steady whirr of the ceiling fans. From where I'm standing I can't see in the living room, but if I took a couple of steps to my left I could. I wait at the base of the stairs, listening for signs of life as water puddles at my feet. As soon as Mom or Carolyn starts talking, I'll try to scoot upstairs unnoticed.

A full minute goes by, but there's still no noise whatsoever, aside from the ceiling fans and my own breathing: I may as well be in a tomb.

Why the hell aren't they saying anything?

Another minute creeps by, and impatience gets the best of me:

I inch my way over to the doorframe and peer around the corner, prepared for a tongue-lashing if Mom catches me skulking.

Carolyn is sitting on the couch, with Mom directly across from her in the armchair. They both look dreadful. Carolyn's face is a silent shout of shock and pain, and her hair is a wild tangle, like she's been attempting to tear it from her head, strand by strand; Mom's eyes are dark and haunted, and her cheeks are wet with tears. Mom is watching Carolyn intently, but Carolyn can't seem to meet her gaze, as if she fears getting turned into a pillar of salt.

If I were smart, I'd back away right now, but God only knows how long they've been sitting like this. I bite my lip, not liking my options, then step in the room.

"What's going on?" I ask quietly, and they both jump.

"Not now, Noah, please," Mom says. She doesn't sound pissed, but her voice is thick with grief and anxiety. "Can you give us a little more time by ourselves?"

She clearly could use some support—the fact she doesn't even notice I'm sopping wet speaks volumes about her current state of mind—but the look she gives me is a silent plea to let her handle things herself, so I turn to go, ashamed at how relieved I feel.

"Sure," I say. "I'm sorry I interrupted."

"Why do we need more time alone?" Carolyn asks, before I can withdraw. "Is there more to tell me than what you already have?"

Mom shakes her head. "No, there's nothing else. I just thought you might find it easier to talk with just the two of us here."

Carolyn grimaces, and when she answers I'm surprised to hear anger creeping into her tone. "I don't think anything will make this any easier. Do you?"

"I suppose not."

"Then you might as well stay, Noah."

Mom shrugs helplessly when I look at her and I hesitate, no

longer knowing what to do. I'm not exactly sure what's causing Carolyn's anger, but I take a stab at it.

"None of what happened was Mom's fault," I tell her. "You know that, right?"

"Of course I do," she says, glowering at me like I'm an idiot. "She was just a little girl." She drops her face in her hands for a moment, her shoulders shaking, and when she raises her head again the desolation in her eyes is appalling. "But she's not twelve anymore, Noah, and what's happening *now* is another matter. For the love of Christ, why did the two of you come looking for me? Why couldn't you have just stayed away from me, and my family?"

I cringe at the growing fury in her voice, and Mom turns pale.

"Please don't be upset with Noah," she says faintly. "I asked him to find you. You're my daughter, and I wanted you in my life."

"Yes, well, thank you very much for that." Carolyn barks a corrosive laugh with a tinge of hysteria in it. "Do you have any idea how much I wish we'd never met?"

Mom flinches like she's been slapped, and though part of me understands Carolyn's desire to lash out, there's no way in hell I'm going to let her continue making Mom feel like garbage.

"Back off, Carolyn," I say. "Do *you* have any idea how hard it was for Mom to tell you this stuff? Do you really think she's causing you pain on purpose?"

"Don't, Noah," Mom begs. "Just let her be."

Carolyn leaps to her feet, eager for a fight with anyone willing to give her one; her temper looks to be the equal of Mom's. Mom is in no shape to take her on, though, so it's me who ends up nose to nose with my enraged sister.

"It was selfish and cruel to come looking for me!" she snaps. "I've been perfectly fine my entire life without knowing anything about my birth family, and now I'm just supposed to be

okay with hearing that my father was a pedophile and a rapist?"
She rounds on Mom. "Why for the love of God did you tell me
about this?"

"Because you asked her to!" I snap back in exasperation.
"You already knew you weren't going to like what you heard,
but now you want a do-over, because it's worse than you
thought it would be?" The obstinacy in her expression makes
me want to shake her. "Jesus, Carolyn, what do you think it
was like for Mom? She's the one who *lived* it, for fuck's sake!"

"I *know*, goddammit!" Carolyn cries. "But does that mean I
have to suffer, too?" She turns to Mom and lowers her voice
with an effort. "Oh, why couldn't you have just left me alone?"

The pain in Mom's eyes makes Carolyn's face crumble, and
she begins to sob. Both Mom and I instinctively reach out to
comfort her, but she jerks away from us and starts to wail.

"I'm sorry, Virginia, Noah, honest to God I am! But I can't
do this! Can't you see I can't do *any* of this?" She lurches toward the door without warning. "Please, *please*, don't ever contact me again!"

And then just like that, she's gone. Mom and I stare at each
other in horror, and she starts to cry. I put my arms around her
and try to tell her it will be okay, but she shakes her head
against my shoulder.

"No," she says. "No, I don't think it will."

CHAPTER 10

It's mid evening now, and Mom, Cindy, and I are the only ones still here. The Fortiers took off hours ago (in an anxious blur of hurried hugs and/or handshakes from Ben, Oliver, Leo, and Michael, as Carolyn sat stone-faced in their van), and Walter went home at dark, as soon as Mom told him she'd prefer to sleep alone tonight. He took the dismissal pretty well, considering he clearly wanted to stay over, but I could see he was hurt. I don't blame Mom, though. If he'd stayed, I'm sure he would've made every effort to comfort her—not only for her ALS, which they've had little time to process together, but also for the dismal failure of her talk with Carolyn—yet given Walter's own emotional state about Mom's lack of a future, it's more likely she would've ended up doing most of the comforting, and she's not up to that tonight.

The yard and kitchen are back to normal, but it's creepily silent inside, like a home with a corpse in the parlor on the eve of a wake. Cindy's already in bed—she pretty much blacked out an hour ago, and I had to help her upstairs; she gave me a drunken kiss on the tip of the nose and told me everything would be fine in the morning, she was sure of it, then she started sobbing about Janelle again and passed out. I just got back from my third walk of the evening, searching for J.D., who apparently has his phone turned off. Mom is sitting on the porch swing when I walk up the front steps.

"Still no luck?" she asks. Her voice sounds tired and bruised, but at least she's talking again.

"Nope." I join her on the swing. "I don't know where else to look."

"I'm sure he'll show up soon. He had a bad day, too." She rubs my neck. "It's been a rough week, hasn't it?"

"Nah," I say. "I mean, aside from your whole terminal disease thing, and Janelle stealing everything but the silverware, and us finding Carolyn and losing her again, and J.D.'s husband trying to drown me."

Unbelievably, she laughs in the darkness. "You forgot Freddie."

"Oh, God, that lunatic. Let's pray he doesn't own any firearms."

She barely even chastised me earlier for turning our family picnic into a reality TV show about lowlife bare-knuckle brawlers. She did ask why there'd been so much yelling going on while she and Carolyn were inside, but when I explained she just sighed and said, "I guess I should be grateful nobody died."

I know her decision to come clean about everything with Carolyn is still eating her up inside, but what else could she have done, aside from lying her ass off? I tried to tell her that earlier but she wouldn't listen: After the Fortiers left she barely spoke for hours. The worst of her despair now seems to have passed, thankfully, but I doubt very much she'll get any sleep tonight.

We sit in silence, staring out at the night and hoping to hear J.D.'s returning footsteps on the sidewalk. The usual choral battle between the crickets and cicadas is going on, and I kick off my sandals and draw my knees to my chest. The movement causes the swing to rock gently beneath us, the rusty chains squeaking a countermelody to the insects.

"I know it's hard to sort things out right now," Mom says after a while, "but before things went completely to hell, what did you think of Carolyn? For the life of me, I can't figure out if it's even worth trying to patch things up, at this point. Do you think she may ever get past this, and learn to love us?"

The uncertainty in her voice is so uncharacteristic that I wish I could tell her yes without feeling like a liar. "I'm not sure," I say carefully. "She's not exactly warm and fuzzy, but Ben loves her, and Leo's a great kid, so I figure she must be a decent person. Maybe she'll come around, eventually."

She nods, but I know she hears my doubt. "I get the feeling she's always pretty guarded, even when the circumstances aren't so . . . unusual. The only time she really relaxed today was when the two of you were talking by yourselves. You even got her to laugh before we ate." She pauses. "All I did was make her cry and yell."

"She shouldn't have taken it out on you. She wanted to know the truth, and you told her. You didn't do anything wrong."

There's enough starlight to see her shrug. "I suppose. But I certainly understand why she was so upset. Who in their right mind wouldn't be?"

"Yeah, but she still shouldn't have yelled at you," I say. "I should've just jammed a sock in her mouth when she started in on you."

"Yes, well, perhaps it's for the best you didn't," she says drily. "You may have ended up in the fishpond again."

Sometimes I adore this smartass old woman so much I can't even stand it.

"Yeah, okay, have your fun," I tell her, grinning. "But in my defense, that only happened because Bruce was being a complete douche-wad."

"I don't doubt it. But I also suspect you were too busy being clever to care about the consequences of shooting off your mouth."

My grin fades. "You mean like J.D. calling me a human wrecking ball, and disappearing for six hours? Yeah, I probably could've toned things down a little."

She takes my arm and squeezes it. "He'll be back."

I sigh, giving in to self-pity. "And then what? If he hasn't already made up with Bruce, he will tomorrow, then he'll go back to his life in Wellesley. They love each other, and that's that."

It's the first time I've ever admitted to her how much I wish things were different.

I mean, I'm sure she didn't need to be told that I'd give anything to go back in time and fix things with J.D., but we've never talked about it before because it was just too damn hard. Between the day J.D. and I split up until the day he finally gave up on me, there were a million times I could've changed everything—like the time we saw each other in Boston the year after we separated, or when he came to see me in Providence and first told me about Bruce. Or any other goddamn day in the calendar from 2005 to 2007. All he ever needed to hear me say was "Please come back to me," and we could've started over. But something was wrong with my brain back then; I can't even begin to explain what I was thinking. I'd love to blame my dysfunction on someone else—like maybe I was abducted by aliens, and the little green bastards unplugged my cerebellum, just for shits and giggles—but it's all my fault. And though I'm well aware it's an epic waste of time, and spirit, to wallow in regret, I can't seem to help it.

Just five simple words: *Please come back to me.* How fucking hard would they have been to say?

"I know it hurts to see J.D. and Bruce together," Mom says.

"I don't much like it, either, to tell the truth." She rests her head on my shoulder. "Remember when you told me you'd broken up with J.D.?"

Like I could ever forget. We were in the kitchen when I gave her the news, and she started off with an earsplitting *"You did WHAT?"* then proceeded to inform me I was "a masochistic, emotionally-stunted imbecile," and "a shortsighted, self-destructive little dunce"—among many other equally inventive epithets. At one point she decided it would be a good idea to empty the dishwasher while she was still verbally eviscerating me, and she got so pissed that she broke three plates by slamming them down on the counter. I yelled back for a while, but could match neither her outrage nor her volume, so I eventually put my tail between my legs and scampered from the house.

"Sort of," I tell her now. "I still have PTSD from that fight."

She sniffs. "Yes, well, I was rather upset with you. But do you remember what I said was going to happen one day?"

I sigh. "You said I'd come to hate myself for letting him get away." I pause, grimacing. "Feel free to gloat about how right you were."

"That's only the first part of what I told you." She squeezes my arm again. "I also said that the two of you would never be happy without each other, and someday you'd both realize it at the same time."

I blink back tears; it's been a long day. "It will never happen, Mom. There's no way in hell he'll give up Bruce. As much as I hate to admit it, I think they have a good life together, and J.D. is already plenty happy."

"Maybe, but there's a reason Bruce got so jealous today. It's obvious how much J.D. still loves you."

"Yeah, but I can't offer him anything that compares to what he already has. They've got a great home, lots of friends, a long-term marriage, plans for growing old together, etc.—the whole freaking kitchen sink." I rub my temples, fighting a headache.

"It also doesn't help that Bruce is gorgeous, and makes fifty times as much money as I do."

"I'm absolutely certain J.D. would rather talk to you than Bruce any day of the week, and you know full well he doesn't care how much money you make. He's not wired that way." She pauses. "I also doubt he finds Bruce more attractive than you. Your looks are much more interesting."

I laugh. "Thanks, I think."

"I'm not being snide. I understand that whatever I say about your looks is highly suspect, since I'm your mother, but you really have no idea what those long eyelashes of yours and that damn impish smile can do to people. Anyway, J.D. couldn't stop watching you today, even though he did his best to pay attention to Bruce instead. Call me crazy, but I think he's still in love with you."

I don't say anything for a while, content to just sit with her leaning on my shoulder. She may be feeding me a load of crap, but it makes me feel better. I know it's childish to want so badly to believe her, but I can't help it. I'm also uneasily aware that I'm forcing her into the role of comforter—just as Walter probably would if he were here—but she doesn't seem to mind, at least not with me.

I yawn loudly, surprising myself. As much as I want to be awake when J.D. finally shows up—*if* he shows up—I may not be able to keep my eyes open much longer.

"I object to the characterization of my smile as 'impish,'" I say, through yet another yawn. "'Sexy' is a more appropriate adjective, don't you think?"

She pats my knee. "Dream on, son."

"Hey."

I wake with a start, flat on my back on the porch, my feet on the steps. J.D. is sitting beside me, barely visible in the darkness.

"What time is it?" I croak.

"I'm not really sure. Late." He shifts, looking over his shoulder at the house. "Virginia must've just gone to bed, though. I saw her bedroom light go off when I came around the corner."

At some point in the evening, Mom and I moved from the porch swing to the steps, but I fell asleep soon after and have no idea how long she stayed with me.

"The heartless strumpet left me out here alone?" I say, rubbing my eyes. "I could've been eaten by dingoes."

J.D. snorts. "Unlike me, she was smart enough to sneak off without waking you."

He and I used to come out here all the time when we were kids—often in the wee hours of the night, just like this, to talk and stare up at the sky—and I almost wonder if I'm still asleep, dreaming. He sounds sad and tired, and I'm sorry for that, but being here together again, however briefly, feels like a miracle.

"I wasn't sure if you were coming back tonight," I tell him, sitting up. "Mom said you would, but I was beginning to think you'd called Bruce and had him come get you."

"I'm still too pissed to talk to him." He sighs, running a hand through his hair. "He hasn't called me, either, so I guess he feels the same way."

"How do you know?" I ask. "Your damn phone was off all day."

"Good point." He bumps his knee against mine. "I just listened to all the messages you left on my voice mail. You were getting pretty annoyed by that last one. I've never been called a *turd worshipping fart fucker* before."

I grin. "Mom came up with that."

"Huh. That doesn't really sound like her."

"The ALS is affecting her mind." I flick his thigh. "Where were you? I looked all over the place."

He shrugs. "Everywhere. I bet I walked twenty miles. The blisters on my feet have blisters."

For the first time I notice his feet are bare. "Where are your shoes?"

"Out there on the grass somewhere. I kicked the damn things off the second I got back on our lawn." He pauses. "Your lawn, I mean."

"You were right the first time," I tell him. "Home is where you lose your shoes."

He takes my right hand in both of his and gently kneads the muscles in my palm. "So how did Virginia's talk go with Carolyn? Are they both okay?"

"Not really." My voice comes out hoarse; his touch is doing what it always does to me. I tell him about the blowout in the living room and what happened afterwards: how the Fortiers collected their things in a chaotic rush, while Mom watched them, devastated. Leo argued with Carolyn about leaving and I thought she was going to smack him, and when he hugged Mom goodbye he had tears in his eyes because he felt so bad for her. He hugged me, too, and told me he'd be back soon, regardless of what happened with the rest of the family. Oliver and Michael shook hands with all of us, but Carolyn just got in their minivan without saying goodbye to anyone. She was crying as she shut the door, though, and Ben engulfed Mom and me in a bear hug and told us they'd get things sorted out eventually.

J.D. sighs when I finish talking. "I know it must've been hard for Carolyn to hear the stuff about her dad, but leaving like that was a shitty thing to do to your mom."

"Yeah. After they took off, Mom just stood there like a statue for about fifteen minutes. It was awful. It reminded me how quiet she used to get before her breakdown."

"Really? It was that bad?"

He sounds disturbed, and for good reason. He's the only person besides me who knows just how bleak things got back then—the loaded silences, disconnected conversations, unpredictable eruptions of temper, despair, and finally a total collapse, topped off by a bloody self-mutilation and screams that still give me nightmares.

"She's not in danger of having a relapse or anything," I say, reassuring him. "It was just hard to see her hurting again."

He raises my hand to his mouth and kisses the base of my thumb. My breath catches in my throat and I cradle his chin with my fingers.

"We better stop," he whispers, leaning into my touch. "I'm not thinking straight, and I don't want to make a huge mistake."

"You started it," I say.

"I know." He kisses the inside of my wrist. "Are you sleeping with anyone these days?"

"Not sleeping, no."

"Let me rephrase. When was the last time you had sex, and were you careful?"

"A couple of days ago, and yes. I'm on PrEP, and we used condoms."

His lips had traveled from my wrist to the crook of my elbow, but now he stops. "A couple of days? Seriously? Since you got back here, you mean?"

"Yeah. Some guy I met on Grindr. I needed a distraction."

"You are such a slut. So are you doing a lot of hookups these days?"

I shrug. "Not a huge amount, no, but some. And I'm always careful."

"Have you met anybody special?"

I feel myself flush, which I'm glad he can't see in the dark. "You sound like Mom."

"I'm not trying to piss you off. I just have ulterior motives for asking." He runs a hand over my bicep and slips a finger inside the sleeve of my T-shirt, tickling my armpit hair. "I know

I don't have the right to complain, but to tell the truth, I don't much like the idea of you fooling around with other guys."

His voice is as hoarse as mine. I lean closer, so our faces are only about an inch apart. "Yeah, well," I say, " just so we're clear, I'm not too crazy about the whole Bruce thing."

He rests his forehead against mine. "Right at this moment, neither am I," he says. "I want to kiss you so much, but I think that's a terrible idea."

"Not to play devil's advocate, but how come?"

"For one thing, I'm married, and I don't want to be a jerk."

"Those are two things."

"Shut up." He untangles his hand from my shirt and rests his palm against my cheek. "Your breath smells like stale beer."

"Yours isn't exactly a floral bouquet, either."

"Good. I'd hate to be the only one suffering."

Our lips meet and we stop breathing. He pulls back after a second, though, with a weak bleat of protest. "Goddammit," he says shakily. "We shouldn't do this, Noah."

"Because you love Bruce?"

"Yes."

"More than you love me?"

"It's not that simple." He touches my face again and I'm startled to see tears spilling down his cheeks. "It's not a contest."

I put my arms around him and hold him tightly. "Crybaby. You didn't answer the question."

He's sobbing, now, hard enough that he can't talk, but he shakes his head against my shoulder, telling me what I need to know. I start crying, too.

"You're messing up my shirt," I tell him.

He makes a noise more blubber than laugh, but he gradually quiets as I rub his back. He nuzzles my neck, and after a while his hands begin traveling my body.

"Damn you, Noah York," he murmurs. "Why can't I stop touching you?"

His fingers drift inside the leg of my shorts and tickle the tip of my penis.

"I don't know," I gasp. "But do you hear me complaining?"

His voice in the darkness of my bedroom, the salt of his sweat on my lips, his head on my stomach as we rest. His hands on my hips, his tongue circling the rim of my belly button, his knees between my thighs. His fingertips tracing my ribs, his big toe brushing my ankle, the strength of his arms as he shifts my weight to make me more comfortable, the creak of the bed frame as he straddles my chest for a time, pinning my wrists to the mattress. A catch in his breathing, a moan, the heat of his groin on my face, his habitual gentleness. The change of positions, the exploration of every centimeter of each other's skin, the brief discomfort as he enters me, the intense pleasure and growing frenzy of our coupling, the slow, languorous kiss afterwards. Muffled laughter, spooning, dozing. Waking half an hour later to his lips at the base of my spine—

I've done all of this with other people, but what a difference love makes.

It's fair to say I'm a big fan, in general, of copulation, but the only true magic I've ever experienced has been with this man now sleeping beside me. The magic was there when we were boys, too, but it's even stronger now, aided by the grace of long experience and an intimate knowledge of each other's needs and wants. I don't know what tomorrow is going to bring, and neither does he, but right at the moment, I don't care.

J.D. Curtis is in my arms again: Abracadabra.

It's almost ten in the morning when I wake up. J.D. is sleeping on his stomach and I'm on my back; his arm is draped across my belly. His face is turned away from me and he's lightly snoring. I stare at the ceiling for a few minutes, deliriously happy to discover that last night wasn't just a feverish, crazy-erotic dream. I run my hand over his arm and listen to him snore, wondering how he's going to feel about waking up in our old bed today. I hope he doesn't regret it, but I fear it's likely, given his struggle with the idea of cheating on Bruce. To be honest, I'm not exactly sure how I feel about my role in this three-way drama, either. I've never slept with a married man before—at least not that I'm aware of—and in theory it's not something I aspire to: too many complications, too much potential for causing harm. Yet whatever twinges of conscience I may have, I'd be lying if I said I wouldn't do the same thing again, in a heartbeat.

But unlike J.D., I'm not in love with two people at the same time, nor am I half as decent a human being as he is. From my perspective, what we did was perfectly justifiable, because (A) we love each other, and (B) Bruce is even more of an asshat than I am. But J.D. won't let himself off the hook so easily. We didn't speak last night about what, if anything, sleeping together might change; it's all too possible it will change nothing at all, and we'll never do this again. If I thought groveling at his feet would convince him to leave Bruce, I'd already have rug burn on my elbows and knees, but pressuring him at this point might do more harm than good. I guess if he and Bruce had a different kind of marriage we could talk about an open relationship, but I'm damn sure that's not in the cards—particularly since I doubt I could handle it any better than Bruce.

His snoring breaks off as he stirs a little. I keep stroking his arm and after another couple minutes he turns his head to face me.

"Morning," I say.

"Morning." His smile is a little strained, but there's a tenderness in his gaze that moves me; at least he's not jumping out of bed in a frenzy of puritanical remorse.

"How'd you sleep?" I ask.

"Really well, actually." He clears the gunk from the corners of his eyes and yawns. "Man, I need a shower."

"Me, too."

He props himself on an elbow, looking around the room. "It's surreal to be back here. It's almost like I never left."

"Yeah, I'm experiencing a little temporal displacement myself."

He rests a hand on my ribcage. "Do you think Virginia and Cindy know I'm in here with you?"

"Most likely," I say. "Mom would never let me sleep this late otherwise."

He sighs. "Great. So much for this staying our little secret."

I keep my voice as neutral as I can. "Is that what you want it to be?"

"I don't know." He frowns, playing with one of my nipples. "I'm a complete mess right now, just in case you're wondering."

"I'm sorry." I founder for words; not sure what he needs to hear, if anything. "Do you want to talk about it, or will that just make it worse?"

He draws a line with his index finger down the center of my torso to my navel. "I don't know." He looks up at me. "What do *you* want?"

"Do you really need to ask?" I touch his face. "I want you back, dumbass."

"I was afraid you were going to say that." His eyes fill. "I was almost hoping you'd kick me to the curb again, so I wouldn't have to make a choice."

I get a lump in my throat. "I'm not about to do something that stupid again. It was the worst mistake of my life." I brush a tear from his cheek. "It's up to you this time. I'm here as long as you want me. I wish you didn't have to choose, but whatever happens, I'll love you forever."

"God damn you," he says. His hand drifts below my waist as he kisses me. "Damn you, damn you, damn you."

I struggle to control my breathing. "Swearing at someone is generally more effective if you're not fondling their genitals."

"Shut up."

We eventually shower and get dressed, then head downstairs, our bare feet drumming the wooden steps. Mom is sitting alone at the island in the kitchen, cupping a mug of coffee in her hands, and she's staring sightlessly at the steam rising from it. She looks over at us as we enter the room—her eyes going first to me, then J.D.—and a huge smile breaks out on her tired face.

"It's about damn time, you two idiots," she says. She opens her arms wide to J.D. and he steps into them, looking a little sheepish.

"Morning," he says, stroking her hair. "Sorry I vanished yesterday."

"You had good reason, from what I hear." She gives him another hard squeeze, then releases him. "Are you boys hungry?"

"Starving," I say, pouring coffee for J.D. and me. "Sorry we missed breakfast."

"Fortunately for you, I'm feeling peckish. All I had earlier was a piece of toast." She goes to the fridge and starts rooting around in it. "Any requests, J.D.?"

I'm expecting him to tell her not to go to any trouble, but I underestimate his greed; he always loved Mom's breakfasts.

"I'd kill for one of your Greek omelettes," he says. "I've been trying for years to make mine taste like yours, but they're never even close."

She calls me over and loads me up with eggs, kalamata olives, feta cheese, bread, butter, and a bag of spinach. I unburden myself at the counter and she goes to work immediately, mincing a red onion and garlic. J.D. asks if he can help and she sends him outside for fresh tomatoes and herbs from a planter on the south side of the house.

"You look like a different person this morning," she tells me as soon as he's out the door. I blush a little in spite of myself and she laughs, leaning over to kiss my cheek. "Dare I ask where things stand now?"

I sigh. "Still to be determined." I tell her that J.D. hasn't talked to Bruce since yesterday, and I'm scared to death that once he does they'll patch things up. "He's really conflicted, and he feels guilty. I thought he was going to paint a scarlet A on his chest this morning."

She nods. "I don't envy him. Someone he loves will get hurt, no matter what."

"Yeah, I know." I start breaking eggs in a bowl. "Am I a bad person for hoping it's Bruce?"

She snorts. "Yes. But I don't blame you."

I ask where Cindy is and she says the front porch, pretending to read a book but actually keeping an eye out for Janelle. Her return flight to California is only a couple of days away, but Mom says she doesn't want to leave without knowing if Janelle is going to reappear or not.

"I told her she can stay as long as she wants, of course," Mom tells me. "But between us, I think the only way Janelle will come back here is in handcuffs."

J.D. reenters with an armful of tomatoes, dill, and parsley. "Sadie is off her chain again," he says. "She came to say hi, but I was too scared to pet her even though Freddie was nowhere in sight."

"Good call," I say. "I bet he was watching you from behind a bush, waiting to pounce."

"Sadly, that may not be far from the truth," Mom says. "I forbid both of you from ever speaking to that man again, by the way. Let me handle him, if there's another incident."

J.D. grins at her stern tone. "Why am I forbidden? All I did was pull him off your smartass son when the two of them were rolling around on the ground."

She grins back. "Yes, I know. But I haven't given you an order in ages and I've missed it terribly, so humor me."

He laughs. "Yes, Mom."

The omelettes only take her about ten minutes to make, and the smell as she's cooking is enough to make me drool. We're just finishing eating when J.D.'s phone rings in his pocket. He gets a strange expression on his face, half-relieved, half-despairing, as he digs it out and looks at it.

"It's Bruce," he says, meeting my eyes. "I guess I better take this."

He touches my shoulder and excuses himself, then hurries outside again for privacy. My stomach turns to lead as I hear him open their conversation with, "Hi, honey."

Mom and I look at each other, and she takes my hand.

"Don't freak out," she says. "Wait and see what happens."

CHAPTER 11

It's early afternoon, on a Monday. Mom and I are at Jenness Beach, a couple hours from home. She made me bring her here because she said she was sick of watching me mope around the house, throwing a pity-party for myself and drinking all her booze.

No, I don't want to fucking talk about it.

The only reason I didn't put up more of a fight about leaving the house is that I was shocked she actually asked me to drive her to the coast. As far as I know, she hasn't been near the ocean since a couple of years before Dad died, when they took a weeklong vacation to St. Bart's. I wasn't invited—I was likely the main reason they needed a vacation—and they came back with dark skin and dopey smiles for each other. They took no pictures of the trip and never talked much about it, except to say it was "wonderful." I didn't resent being left out of the fun, though, because even though I was only fifteen they trusted me to stay by myself all week, free to come and go as I pleased for the first time in my life. Anyway, I'm pretty sure they humped like ferrets and fell in love all over again on that trip, and I'm also pretty sure that's why Mom hasn't wanted to go to the beach since, because she doesn't want to be reminded how much she's lost since Dad died.

Hence my surprise when she insisted we come here today.

I haven't been to Jenness Beach in years. It's a breezy, sunny afternoon, with an achingly clear blue sky, but even though it's ideal weather for a day at the beach, it's not as crowded as it would be on a weekend. It still takes about twenty minutes of walking, however, to find a semi-isolated spot to put down our blanket. Mom packed a big canvas bag full of drinks, sandwiches, towels, and sunscreen, which I've been toting. We spread all our stuff out and eat in silence, staring at the blue and green waves rolling in.

Mom's dressed in a blue halter top, white shorts, and a straw sunhat, and she looks damn good for an old lady. She rarely goes out in the sun but doesn't burn very easily. Neither do I—thanks to our Portuguese ancestors we've got olive oil in our veins instead of blood, so mostly we just brown, like beef in a skillet—but we put on sunscreen anyway. She tucks her hair behind her ears and sits with her arms wrapped around her knees, humming quietly to herself. She notices me watching her and raises an eyebrow in question.

"Do you remember the last time we were on a beach together?" I ask her.

She thinks for a minute. "Lake Michigan. You were just a little boy."

"Yeah, first grade. How come we never went back? I always wanted to, but you and Dad weren't into it."

She reaches for an apple and polishes it on her shirt. "We were afraid the temptation to drown you would be too great."

In spite of the heaviness in my heart I laugh. "Nice. Kick a guy when he's down, why don't you?"

She rests her hand on my back; her palm is warm on my skin. "It's good to see you smile. I thought you'd forgotten how."

I sigh, bleakness returning. "It's only a reflex. Like the Lazarus sign."

"I don't know what that is."

I can't remember the last time I knew something she didn't; I actually pause in surprise before answering. "It's when a person on life support dies," I say, "and their corpse crosses its arms over its chest, all by itself, even though the brain is completely dead."

She makes a face. "How appalling," she says. "Is that truly a thing?"

"Cross my arms and hope to die."

She gives me a shove. "I prefer you when you're catatonic. Go take your morbid self for a walk and let me sit here in peace."

The beach may be the best place in the world for a broken heart. The sunlight and salty air on my skin, and the sound of the waves rolling in, and the feel of the cool wet sand beneath my feet at the ocean's edge, and the smell of seaweed, and the cries of seagulls and piping plovers—none of it takes the pain away, but it's such a sensual feast that it lures me at least partway into the world again, rather than being utterly lost inside my head like I've been for the past two days.

I know I said I didn't want to talk about what happened, but it's all I can think about anyhow, so what the hell.

J.D. took the bus back to Wellesley, a few hours after talking to Bruce on the phone. He said he had to get away from me since he can't think straight when we're together. He said he loves me but he's not sure at all that I'm good for him, and he needed to go home and clear his head. He also said he was going to do everything he could to fix things with Bruce, because he doesn't want to lose him, and I shouldn't hope for them to split up because it probably isn't going to happen.

I know how hard it was for him to say all this, because he

was bawling his eyes out at the time—he wasn't the only one, by the way—and though I guess it's possible he could still change his mind, he sure as hell seemed like he'd made his decision, and when I hugged him goodbye as he got on the bus it felt like the last time I'd ever see him.

Mom keeps telling me to not give up hope, but she was really low, too, after he left. He came unglued in her arms when they said goodbye to each other, and I know the only reason she didn't fall apart herself is because she had to take care of me. She's getting a little tired of my emotional fragility, though, and is now alternating between gentleness and impatience. The combination is oddly comforting; if she were nice all the time I'd probably start worrying that I'm in even worse shape than I think I am.

I feel bad for leaning on her so much, because I know she's still hurting about Carolyn, who may be gone forever, too. I got a text from Leo yesterday, asking how we were doing; I didn't want to dump all my angst on him so I just said we were surviving, but we missed him. I asked how things were going at their house and he said Carolyn was walking around like a zombie and crying a lot, but still not talking about whatever happened between Mom and her. He said he missed us, too. I told him I'll be heading back to Providence in a week or so, and he's always welcome to visit me there, especially since my apartment is only half an hour from his house. It's out of character for me to extend an open invitation like that, but he's better company than most and I'm weirdly comfortable with the idea of him drifting in and out of my life as he chooses. I'll have to warn him that I have no idea how to host a teenager, but maybe he'll inspire me to venture out of my comfort zone of museums, bookstores, and dinner parties with friends.

I haven't told Mom that I've made up my mind to return to Providence. I feel like a shit-heel, but it's not like I'm sticking her on an ice floe in Alaska and shoving her out to sea; I'll come back at least once a month to check on her. She'll still have Walter for company any time she wants, and Cindy—who left just this morning to catch her flight to California—is also planning to visit again soon. I have a feeling she'll be back a lot when Mom starts to gets worse, and I wouldn't be too surprised if she even moved in with her eventually, especially if Janelle is still MIA.

Oh, yeah. There's been some news on that front. The cops found Leo's car at a rest area in upstate New York; apparently Janelle figured out that driving around in a stolen vehicle might not be the best idea. She was also savvy enough to either ditch or disable her cell phone, so at this point she's pretty well untraceable—at least until her sticky little fingers get her in trouble again.

Anyway, it's been an eventful couple of days.

I stop walking and wander in the ocean up to my knees. Two skinny Asian boys in their teens are bodysurfing nearby; I watch them for a minute as they frolic in the water like a couple of sleek young seals. A huge wave catches them by surprise when their backs are turned and they disappear under the deluge, knocked clean off their feet; they resurface spluttering and laughing, punch-drunk and delighted by the force of the wave. They race to catch the next one, arms flailing for balance and calling out to each other. It makes me smile to see how much fun they're having, even though it's also bittersweet: J.D. taught me to bodysurf when we were about the same age as these kids, on a beach not far from here, and that was the day I fell for him. We weren't lovers yet, but I sure as hell knew I wanted to be.

Damn him.

And damn me, too, for believing I could have him back.

I'm desperately trying to be a grownup and do the whole "if you love something set it free" horseshit, but I'm about two seconds away from jumping in Mom's car, driving down to his house in Wellesley, beating on his door and making him choose between Bruce and me, right on the spot. The only thing stopping me is that he already knows everything I could tell him, and me causing another ugly scene won't exactly work in my favor if he's still on the fence about what he wants.

I turn to face the dunes and gaze back down the beach to where I left Mom. She's not on our blanket and I'm far enough away that it takes me a minute to find her. She's at the edge of the water, stooping over and apparently looking for shells. Even from here, her self-possession and grace are moving; she looks perfectly relaxed and content, like a Buddhist monk in a Zen garden. I know her peace of mind comes and goes as often as the tide, but I still envy her.

"Hey, mister, heads-up!"

I spin around at the warning yell from one of the kids, just in time to get hammered in the chest by a rogue monster of a wave, knocking me on my butt and pounding me to a pulp in the surf. I swallow half the damn ocean and come up coughing and spitting, but also laughing: What else is there to do when a primal force of nature turns you into a chew toy? The kids are laughing at me, too, but it's good-natured; I get back to my feet and wave as they run off again.

I look back toward Mom, wondering if she saw the show. She's sitting on the blanket again, looking the other direction, so she must not have. I'm relieved, because she no doubt would've started composing another damn poem about me—-the ocean as a metaphor for love, maybe, kicking the crap out of anybody dumb enough to turn his back on it.

Goddammit. My phone is in the front pocket of my soaked cutoffs.

When J.D. and I were still doing the long-distance relationship thing in college, we often spent the weekend together, in Boston or Providence. One time though, on a whim, we rented a car and hit the road, no destination in mind, and ended up poking around comatose little towns in southern Massachusetts. Just outside Freetown State Forest, near Assonet, we stumbled across Profile Rock—a gigantic mound of granite that was supposed to resemble, on one side, the head of Chief Massasoit. It was a great place to go bouldering, which J.D. was into. (I liked climbing stuff back then, too, but not half as much as J.D.; he must have a mountain goat in his ancestry.)

Anyway, we clambered around the rocks for a while before resting at the highest point possible, a bald spot presumably on the crown of Chief Massasoit's head. It was a sunny afternoon in early October, and the surrounding forest was awash in yellow, orange, gold, and red, the branches of a few thousand trees all stirring in a brisk breeze.

"Wow," J.D. said, breathing hard from the climb. "It's so beautiful up here. I'm really happy we found this place."

"Yeah," I said, "It's like being in the middle of a Monet painting."

We were sitting side by side, and he bumped his shoulder into mine. "You artists are all the same. Everything in the real world reminds you of a painting."

"Not everything," I protested. "For example, you remind me of a goiter."

He laughed, kissing me. We were always careful about being affectionate in public, because we'd learned the hard way it wasn't safe, but there were only a couple of other climbers nearby that day, and they were currently out of sight—somewhere in the vicinity of Massasoit's right nostril. We didn't break apart until we heard the climbers below getting close.

"Mmm, that was nice," I said, reluctantly sitting back. "What did I do to deserve it?"

"Not a damn thing," he said. "I just did it to shut you up."

We took the most challenging route back down to the forest floor, a nearly vertical face with few handholds. I got careless and almost fell when we were still twenty feet from the ground; my feet went out from under me and I was left dangling by the fingertips of one hand. I cried out in panic, and J.D., who was below me, calmly guided my feet back to a ledge.

"Thanks," I breathed, my heart pounding. "That was close."

"Nah," he said. "There's a reason I'm down here and you're up there."

"So you can look up my shorts?" I asked.

He laughed. "Yeah, mostly."

"Pervert."

"Yup."

And that was all either of us ever said about his saving me from a broken leg or a whole lot worse. We both knew that if he hadn't planted my feet in time, I would've fallen directly on him, plummeting from the heavens like a cartoon piano and tearing him off the face of the rock, too. It also went without saying that he would've attempted to catch me anyway, even though it would've been suicidally stupid. I don't know how we both knew this stuff without talking about it. All I know is what we did say to each other never mattered half as much as the things we didn't.

"Your hair is wet," Mom says as I rejoin her on the beach blanket. "Did you go swimming?"

"Not intentionally," I tell her. "A big bully snuck up on me and gave me a swirly."

She smiles, but she looks tired; I ask her if she's feeling okay. She shrugs, tucking her hair behind her ears. "I wear out faster than I used to. Mind if we head home?"

I keep my eye on her as we're packing up; she's moving slower than usual and seems a little unsteady on her feet. I get a bottle of water from the cooler and make her drink some, scolding her for getting dehydrated.

"Don't be a mother hen," she says. "I'm fine, son."

I pull on my shirt and we amble toward the beach entrance, not talking much, our bare feet kicking through the hot sand. We pause a couple of times for her to rest, and she breathes a sigh of relief when we reach the car. I open the passenger door for her and she gets in.

"You sure you're okay?" I ask, climbing behind the wheel and wincing at the hot upholstery on the back of my legs.

"I'm fine," she says again, crossly, then softens. "I overdid it a little. I'm still getting used to this whole body-falling-apart thing."

There's no self-pity in her voice, just a rueful acknowledgment of reality. "You're not falling apart," I tell her as we pull out of the beach parking lot and merge onto the highway. "You could still take Wonder Woman in a fair fight."

She snorts. "Not unless she's got ALS, too, and loses that damn lasso." She touches my shoulder. "Have you thought any more about moving back home?"

I only glance at her for a second, but it's enough for her to read the answer in my face.

"I see," she says quietly, her hand dropping back in her lap.

I swallow. "I'm sorry, Mom. I've thought about it a lot, but I can't do it." I keep my eyes on the road, afraid to look at her again. "I'll come visit once a month, though, and we can Skype every weekend. I'll pester you so much that you'll get sick of me, I promise."

She doesn't respond, and her silence makes me nervous. I risk another glance at her and feel awful when I see she has tears in her eyes.

"Please don't cry," I beg. "That's cheating."

"I'm sorry," she says. "I'm not trying to make you feel guilty, I swear. It's your decision, and you have a perfect right to say no. I'm just sad, that's all. I hoped we'd have more time together, and thought it might be a good thing for both of us."

Her lack of anger causes me to choke up, too. "I'm really

sorry," I tell her, reaching for her hand. "I know I'm being self-ish, but I'd lose my mind if I moved back to Oakland. I'd end up resenting you for it, and we'd both be miserable."

She doesn't answer, but she gently laces her fingers with mine as she looks out the window, getting herself under control again. I don't know what to say to make her feel better, so I don't say anything, either, grateful that our linked hands are more fluent than we are in the language of love and loss.

When we get back to Mom's house, we don't even have the cooler unpacked in the kitchen before there's a knock on the front screen door. We both peer down the hall and see Freddie on the porch, looking grim as he stares back at us through the screen. His wardrobe choices today are a light blue shirt and yellow shorts—Christ have mercy, he looks like he's made of Play-Doh.

"What the hell does that loony want?" I murmur.

"Let me handle this," Mom orders. "You stay put." She squares her shoulders and walks to the door. I know she's right to keep Freddie and me apart, but there's no way I'm letting him out of my sight, so I stand at the end of the hall like an edgy bodyguard.

"Hello, Freddie," Mom says. "What can I do for you?"

"My dog has been missing for several hours," he says curtly. I can no longer see his face because Mom is in the way, but I can hear how upset he is; he sounds close to tears. "Have you seen her?"

"No, I'm sorry, I haven't. Noah and I went to the beach today, and we just got back a few minutes ago."

"Yes, I saw you pull in the driveway," he says. "I was hoping you might have seen Sadie somewhere while you were out and about."

"I'm afraid not," Mom says. "Would you like some help looking for her?"

He hesitates. "That's not necessary, but thank you. I'm sure she'll turn up soon." He coughs. "Please let me know at once, though, if you see her. I know she likes coming over here."

The worry in his voice is actually making me feel bad for him. To this point, I haven't seen him show any affection to Sadie, but maybe he loves her in his own strange, Gollum/Precious sort of way. That being said, I don't blame Sadie one bit for wanting to get away from him; I just hope she's staying off the roads so no one runs over her.

Mom tells him that of course we'll let him know if we spot her, and he thanks her again, then leans around her to look at me.

"Hello, Noah," he says stiffly. "It seems Sadie's chain was broken after all. I apologize."

No shit, I almost say, but restrain myself. I have some idea how hard it was for him to admit he was wrong, so I guess there's no point in rubbing his nose in it.

"It's okay," I tell him. "Sorry I was such a wiseass."

He looks at me a little suspiciously—as if he can sense everything I'm not saying—but then nods and takes his leave, thanking Mom again for her time. After he's out of earshot, Mom turns around and comes back to the kitchen.

"I'm impressed," she says. "It must've taken every ounce of self-control you possess to let him off the hook like that."

"I think I actually sprained my tongue, saying sorry," I tell her. "I'm not a big fan of acting like an adult. It's unhealthy."

She snorts. "I wouldn't worry about it. In your case, a recurrence is highly unlikely."

It's late afternoon. Mom is upstairs, taking a nap, and I'm in the living room, dicking around on her laptop. I tried to stalk J.D. on Facebook a little bit ago but he hasn't posted anything since before he came up here, and neither has Bruce. My phone is drying out in a bowl of rice on the kitchen counter; I can't believe I was stupid enough to get it wet, because now if J.D.

changes his mind and tries to call me, he'll think I'm just blowing him off when I don't answer.

Who am I kidding? He's not going to call.

There's a light knock on the back door and my heart goes nuts for a second, thinking it might be him, but then I hear Walter's voice saying hello and the screen door banging shut behind him as he lets himself in. I call out a greeting when I hear his footsteps in the hall and he sticks his head in the living room.

"Hey," he says, smiling a little uncertainly. He hasn't been back since the picnic but I know he's talked to Mom on the phone, so I'm sure he knows the whole situation with J.D. "How are you doing, bud?"

"Not great," I tell him, but I smile back, glad to see that he's looking better now that he's had a chance to absorb the shock of the ALS news. "How about yourself?"

"Not great, but okay. How was the beach?"

"It was good, but Mom wore herself out. She's taking a nap."

He nods. "I know. She called me about an hour ago and invited me to dinner. She wanted me to wake her when I got here."

I look at the time on the computer screen; it's just past five. "Since when do we eat dinner this early?" His face reddens a little and I laugh, catching on. "Ah, I see. The hussy made a preprandial booty call, didn't she?"

He laughs sheepishly. "Something like that." He comes over and sits beside me on the arm of the couch, even though I know he's anxious to get upstairs. "I'm glad I caught you alone for a minute," he says. "Your mom told me about your decision to stay in Providence instead of moving home. Believe it or not, I think it's the right choice."

I blink, surprised. If anything, I would've expected him to try to change my mind.

"Really?" I study his gray eyes and his fragile, familiar face, and some of the guilt I've been carrying in my chest lessens. His opinion matters, because I know how much he loves Mom, and he'd have no qualms telling me if he thought I was wrong. "I still feel like a complete shit for telling her no," I admit. "She really had her heart set on me living here again."

He nods. "I know, but as I told her, neither of you is mature enough to handle cohabitation with the other. I have no desire to come over here someday and find you both dead on the floor, with your thumbs in each other's eye sockets."

I grin. "At least that would be more original than a gunfight."

"Good point," he says, grinning back. "Seriously, though, I think Virginia forgets that she's the textbook definition of a temperamental artist, and whether or not you know it, so are you. I was just looking at your website again the other day, and I can see how good you're getting—which is wonderful, of course, but this house is nowhere near big enough for two highly talented, overbearing, prickly artists. Especially given that Virginia is likely to become very unstable emotionally as her body fails her, and you're about the worst possible caregiver I can imagine."

I raise my eyebrows. "Thanks for the vote of confidence."

He pats my knee affectionately. "Sorry. Anyway, I just want you to know that I'll look after her as much as she'll let me, and when I see that it's time for you to be here, I'll let you know."

Just like Mom, I've undervalued this man far too much through the years. I feel a burning in my throat. "Mom doesn't deserve you," I tell him. "And neither do I, incidentally."

He nods. "Tell me something I don't know." He climbs to his feet. "Anyway, guess I'll see you in a while."

He disappears up the steps with a wave, his stork-like legs taking them two at a time; it's actually kind of adorable to see a man his age in such a hurry to get laid. I sigh, closing the laptop, and let myself out the front door, stopping to slip on my sandals. I'm glad Mom feels good enough to have sex with Walter, but I'll be damned if I'm going to stick around and run the risk of accidentally overhearing any of the proceedings.

I walk aimlessly, lost in thought. It's still stifling outside but I don't mind; the moist heat feels purifying, like sitting in a sweat lodge. It appears most people in town don't agree with me, however, since few are outside, evidently preferring air-conditioning. A couple of little girls ride by on bikes, and I pass an old shirtless guy mowing his lawn, but that's about it. On a whim I wander toward North Park, to see if there's a baseball game going on or anything, but before I get there a little gray car passes me from the opposite direction, then stops and backs up, the driver's window rolling down.

Shit. It's Jessie, aka Ajax.

"Hey, stranger!" he calls out.

"Hey, yourself." I cross the road reluctantly and lean down to talk. I know it's only been a few days since we hooked up, but it seems like centuries. He's sent me about a dozen messages on Grindr, but I only read the first two. He's still cute, blond, and dimpled, but the idea of sex with anyone but J.D. at the moment is oddly off-putting.

"I thought you'd left town," he says.

I forgot I lied to him about when I was going back to Providence. "Plans changed. An old boyfriend came for a surprise visit."

"Oh, that's cool," he says, but his dimples become markedly less pronounced. "Is he still around?"

"Nope."

He brightens a little, and his eyes bore into mine. "So what are you up to right now?"

"Just out walking, but I'm heading home soon for dinner."

"Want a ride?"

I shake my head, knowing if I get in his car he'll expect more than friendly conversation. "Thanks, Jessie, no. I'm in the mood to walk tonight."

"You sure?" His gaze wanders over me and he lowers his voice. "I could just give you a quick blowjob, no strings attached."

Something is definitely wrong with me. Ordinarily my answer to an offer like this from a sexy, decent man on a hot summer afternoon would be to leap feet first through his car window—like the guys on *The Dukes Of Hazzard*—and pull my shorts down, but I'm not even vaguely tempted. I shake my head, trying to act regretful. I know I don't owe him anything, but he's a nice person and I don't want to hurt his feelings: Rejection isn't any fun at all, as I've just been forcefully reminded.

"Sorry, man," I tell him. "I'm still kind of a wreck about seeing my ex, and I just need to be alone right now."

His face falls. "That's okay, I get it." He reaches out and runs a finger lightly over my jawline. "But let me know if you change your mind. I had a lot of fun the other day."

"Me, too. Take care."

He waves halfheartedly and drives off. I watch him go, still puzzling over my response. It's not that I've never turned down sex before with someone I find attractive, but this feels different. I'm ninety-nine percent sure my slutty libido will come roaring back soon, but what if it doesn't? What if my night with J.D. was so special—so full of love, sweetness, humor, lust, and trust—that shagging strangers is no longer something I'll want to do?

It's unlikely, but a little worrisome nonetheless.

Who would I become without sex in my life? I mean, I know I'd still be an artist, a son, a teacher, etc., and that these things are far more important, but I'm still not ready to hang up my dick spurs, so to speak; I thought I'd have at least another twenty or thirty years of accumulating Frequent Fucker miles before time and age turn me into a eunuch.

Oh, for Christ's sake. I'm being ridiculous. I'll get over J.D. eventually; I may even fall in love with someone else. It happens to other people all the time—why not me, too? All I have to do is get through today, then tomorrow, and trust that someday I won't feel like the best part of my life is already over.

Someday better come soon, though, because right now it's all I can do to keep one foot moving in front of the other.

I forgot to tell you about Mom and I saying goodbye to Cindy this morning. Mom had to drag me out of bed because it was only six fifteen, and I wondered why the hell I told her last night to wake me up so early when I could've just said my farewells then. I pulled on shorts and a shirt, yawning, and stumbled out to the backyard a minute later, where Cindy and Mom were already locked in a death-grip, both of them crying. Cindy looked sad, pale, and old, like the past week had aged her a decade.

The grass was wet with dew under my bare feet as I joined them, and in spite of being bleary-eyed and grumpy, my throat closed when I saw the fierceness of their embrace.

"Oh, why did we waste so many years?" Cindy sobbed, her chin resting on Mom's shoulder. "I've missed you so much."

Mom shook her head. "I've missed you, too, dear heart. Somehow we let ourselves forget how much we need each other, but we won't let that happen again." She kissed Cindy on both cheeks and pulled back. "This isn't goodbye. I'll come see you soon, I promise."

"And I'll come to you. Just give me a little time to pull my life back together, now that Janelle's gone. I don't have a clue who I am anymore."

"You're my little sister, that's who." Mom looked over at me and smiled through her tears. "And Noah's aunt, too, though I realize that's hardly comforting."

I made a face at her. "You're a very mean person. I'm not going to play with you anymore."

Cindy sobbed a laugh and came to me. I held her close and surprised myself by starting to cry, too. "Bye, Aunt Cindy. I'm really glad I finally got to know you. It's good to know there's one nice person in the family."

"I'm sick of being nice," she said, kissing me on the chin. "You and your mother have much more fun." She got in and started the car, then lowered her window and snapped a picture of us on her phone. "You have no idea how beautiful you are together," she told us. "Don't ever take what you have for granted."

I raised my eyebrow at Mom. "What the fuck is she talking about?"

Mom sniffed. "Damned if I know."

Cindy laughed again and we all said goodbye, then Mom and I watched her pull out of the driveway, all of us waving until Cindy was out of sight. I put my arm around Mom's waist and she leaned against me.

"And then there were two," she murmured, wiping her eyes.

It took me a second to get what she was saying, and she was right: The house was going to feel pretty empty with just us. I tried not to think about how it would feel for Mom after Labor Day, when I'd be leaving as well.

She's a big girl, I told myself. *She'll be just fine, dammit.*

About two blocks from home I spot Sadie, chatting up an elderly woman sitting on her porch. They both look like they're enjoying each other's company immensely—the woman is patting Sadie's head and cooing at her, and Sadie's tail is wagging fast enough to propel a pontoon boat. I'm tempted to just walk on by and leave them to the bliss of their mutual admiration, but my conscience stirs before I get past the house and I stop with a sigh at the end of the sidewalk.

"Hi there," I call out. "How are you this evening?"

"Fine, thank you. Aren't you Virginia York's boy?"

I nod, wondering yet again how everyone in this town knows me when I've never laid eyes on most of them. "Yes, I'm just here visiting for a few days. Looks like you've got a new friend."

"Yes, indeed. I can't read his tags to see who he belongs to, but he's a real sweetie."

"He's actually a she, and her name is Sadie." At the sound of her name, Sadie trots down the steps and comes to say hello. I bend to pet her. "She lives in the house next to my mom's, and her owner is looking for her."

"Oh, dear," the woman says. "Would you mind taking her back where she belongs?"

I don't know if Sadie will follow me or not, but I straighten and start to walk, calling to her. She looks conflicted, staring first at me, then at the woman, but when I pat my leg insistently and whistle she makes up her mind, prancing around me as we head towards home. The woman waves goodbye at me like I'm the nicest young man she's ever met, making me think she probably needs to get out more. Sadie almost runs in front of a passing car but I manage to catch her by the collar at the last second.

"Whoa there, spazmoid," I say. "If you turn yourself into roadkill before I get you back to Freddie, he'll think I pushed you." I'm pleasantly surprised when she lets me pick her up; she must be used to getting toted around. She even licks my chin and squirms with excitement when I kiss her head.

And then I feel a warm stream of urine soaking the front of my shirt and dribbling on my flip-flops.

"Son of a bitch!" I snap, setting her down as fast as I can without dropping her. I hold her collar while she finishes spraying the sidewalk, looking at me with mingled remorse and adoration. I sigh. We're less than a block from home, but I can't see Mom's house yet because it's still around the corner.

"I guess the damage is already done," I tell Sadie, picking her up again with a wince. "But just so you know, dropkicking you from here to your front yard is still a viable option."

She licks my chin again, unfazed by either my threat or the strong smell of her own piss. I scowl at the squishy sound of my flip-flops as we turn the corner; I better get a Nobel Peace Prize for this particular act of charity.

My feet stop moving. J.D. is sitting on the front porch with Mom and Walter.

My eyes fill as he sees me. I can't seem to remember how to walk but it's okay; he's already running this way, and it only takes him a few seconds to cover the distance. He nearly plows into me before he can stop himself, and there are tears on his face, too.

"Dumbass," he says, panting. "Your mom told me you went swimming with your phone. I've been trying to call you all afternoon."

I try to answer but the only thing that comes out is something between a frog's ribbit and a glottal stop. He's crying as hard as I am as he leans in to kiss me.

"Why the hell are you carrying Sadie?" he sobs, pulling back with a shaky laugh as the dog breaks us up by slobbering on our faces. "She's pissed all over you."

I finally regain the use of words. "Does you being here mean what I think it does?"

He kisses me again. "Yes. But there's a lot we need to talk about."

The sound of running feet makes us both turn. Freddie is barreling toward us, crying Sadie's name with joy and relief. "Where did you find her?" he asks, taking her out of my arms with surprising gentleness, even though he also cringes when he feels her wet fur and sees what a mess I am.

"She was visiting an old lady a couple of blocks from here. I wasn't sure she'd follow me so I decided to carry her."

"Why did she wet on you?" he asks. "You must've frightened her, or held her too tightly."

I sigh. Under ordinary circumstances I'd say something to rattle his cage, but right at the moment all I can think about is J.D. so I don't bother to respond. My silence has an unexpected effect on Freddie, who for once seems to realize he's being an asshole.

"I'm sorry. I didn't mean to criticize," he says awkwardly. "Thank you for bringing her back to me." He turns away abruptly as his chin starts to quiver. "Come on, girl, let's get you home and cleaned up."

J.D. and I watch him walk away, then look at each other again.

"Come on, boy, let's get you home and cleaned up," he says.

We head back to the house, holding hands. I keep looking over at him, and he keeps looking back at me, but neither of us seems able to speak; this sudden transformation in our relationship has made us shy with each other. Even from a distance, I can see my astonished happiness mirrored on Mom's face as she sits next to Walter on the porch; her cheeks are in danger of actually splitting apart from smiling. To see her so relieved and delighted touches me deeply. All she's ever really wanted was the best for me—even when we disagreed, vehemently, about what "the best" might look like: How is it possible for her to still love me so much, when she knows what a dick I can be?

"What the hell?" J.D. blurts out, which seems like a weird thing to say, then I see that he's looking down the street at a blue Volvo that's about a block away, but headed our way fast—much, *much* too fast for a residential neighborhood. J.D.'s fingers clamp painfully on mine. "Oh, Jesus. It's Bruce."

I don't even have time to answer; the Volvo has picked up speed and is tearing along like it's on the fucking Autobahn. It hits the curb on the side of the road about twenty feet away from where we're standing—hard enough to send its front hubcaps flying—and then it's on the sidewalk, barreling straight for us.

"Run, dammit!" J.D. screams, yanking me towards a towering old oak tree on the north corner of Mom's yard. I kick off my flip-flops and sprint barefoot. Mom and Walter are now standing at the bottom of the porch steps, looking terrified; I panic at the thought of Bruce maybe going after them, too.

"Get Mom inside, Walter!" I yell. "Call the cops!"

The Volvo is almost on top of us when we reach the tree trunk and dive behind it; Bruce veers at the last second and narrowly avoids smashing into the tree, shooting by with his brakes squealing. He's not so fortunate with the granite birdbath a few feet later, however, and he plows into it with so much force that the top of the birdbath takes off like a flying saucer, its pedestal toppling under the Volvo. There's a horrendous shriek of metal as the rounded base of the pedestal crunches into the car's undercarriage, bringing it to a complete stop, and through the open driver's window I watch Bruce get thrown forward in his seat, smacking his head on the windshield.

The Volvo splutters and dies, high-centered, its two front tires lifted almost a foot off the ground and still spinning slowly in the air. In the shocked silence that follows, I glance quickly at J.D., making sure he's okay. His eyes are about the size of the car's tires but otherwise he seems fine; he inspects me, too, then we both climb to our feet warily, watching Bruce and wondering how much fight he still has left in him.

"Shit," Bruce groans, holding his forehead. He sees us looking at him and swears again, leaning into the passenger seat and disappearing from sight. I'm too much in shock to have any idea what's going on, but it sounds to me as if Bruce is rooting around in his glovebox. A terrifying thought occurs to me.

"Please tell me he doesn't have a gun," I whisper to J.D.

"What? No. He's scared to death of guns."

The driver's door pops open and Bruce tumbles out, still cradling his head, which is bleeding. He apparently isn't aware that his front tires are no longer on terra firma, so he loses his balance and falls to his knees, crying out when the ground isn't where he expects it to be. He lurches to his feet immediately, but only takes a couple of steps before he falls again, ending up on his back this time, like an overturned turtle. One of his fists is clenched tightly around something, but I can't tell what it is.

"Fuck!" he cries, rolling to his side with a groan.

I don't know if his head injury is contributing to his coordination issues, but it's certainly not his only problem: Even from ten feet away he smells like he's been bathing in alcohol. I heave a sigh of relief; he's in no condition to be much of a threat now that he's no longer driving.

J.D.'s shock is wearing off, and rage takes over. He runs toward Bruce, red-faced and screaming. "You stupid ASSHOLE! You almost KILLED us!"

He's in such a fury that he's literally hopping up and down by Bruce's head; I start to worry that he might decide to kick the drunken fool into a coma. I rush to intervene, wrapping my arms around his chest and dragging him away.

"Let go of me, Noah!" he bellows.

"No way!" I say in his ear as he struggles to break free. "You'll hate yourself later if you hurt him. He's so wasted he probably doesn't even know where he is."

"I'm sorry, Jason!" Bruce wails. "I just wanted to talk to you, but when I saw you walking with that little piece of shit "—he glares at me with blistering hatred—"I couldn't take it anymore! I'm sorry! I just lost control!" He holds up his hand and unclenches his fist, revealing a gold ring on his palm. "Look, here's your wedding ring! I know I made you give it back to me, but it belongs to you and I want you to have it!"

His face is a mess of blood, tears, and snot, and he looks so pathetic that J.D.'s anger dissipates almost at once; I can feel it draining out of him like water from a sponge as he stops fighting me and goes limp in my arms.

"Jesus Christ, Bruce," he says, his voice raw. "Look at yourself."

"I'm sorry! I'm so sorry," Bruce blubbers. "I just want you back. Please don't leave me!"

J.D. rests his hand on my arm to tell me it's safe to let him go. He stands over Bruce again for a minute, conflicted, then kneels beside him, sighing.

"I'm sorry," he says, his eyes filling as he gently re-closes Bruce's fingers around the ring. "I never meant to hurt you, and I'm so sorry that I did. But I'm not coming back. You have to let me go."

Bruce starts to sob helplessly as a siren starts wailing in the distance. "But Noah is such an asshole!" he cries. He turns his attention back to me. "Why couldn't you have just left us alone, you son of a bitch?"

For once, I have no desire to make things worse. The pain in his voice is brutal to hear, and I know he believes I've ruined his life. The truth isn't that simple, of course, but no matter how I try to sugarcoat it, I'm still responsible for a large share of his suffering. I glance down Main Street as the siren grows louder; there's a cop car and an ambulance both headed our way.

Bruce's bad day is just getting started.

"I'm sorry," I tell him, and I mean it, even though I know it won't do any good.

"Fuck you, Noah," he moans.

EPILOGUE

After Sheriff Ganski and the paramedics leave with Bruce—he blew .15 on a blood alcohol test, plus he likely has a moderate-to-serious concussion—J.D., Mom, Walter, and I stand there on the lawn in a daze, staring after the ambulance. Bruce's Volvo is still on the lawn, but Ganski told Mom he'd send a tow truck first thing tomorrow morning to deal with it. J.D. and I didn't want to press charges but Bruce is in deep shit either way; Ganski said he had no choice but to arrest him for reckless endangerment and driving drunk. The look on Ganski's face as he made his second felony arrest on our property in the past week caused Mom and me to cringe, but he took it pretty much in stride, just saying, "Interesting week for you folks, huh?"

I shake my head now and sigh as the ambulance disappears up the road. "Can anybody tell me what the hell just happened?"

No one has an answer for me, but the spell of stupefaction we're all under is at least partly broken; we all turn together and wander back to the porch. J.D. takes my hand again as we walk, and in spite of the insanity of the past half hour, Mom smiles as she looks at us, and we smile back at her, and a second later Walter is grinning, too. Everybody seems to become aware at the same moment that I look absolutely ridiculous, with grass and leaves in my hair, grass stains on my knees and elbows, and a T-shirt that's still wet and stinking from Sadie's urine.

"You may want to reconsider the cologne you've chosen," Mom says, her nose wrinkling.

"I actually think it's an improvement," Walter chimes in.

"Ha ha, you're both very droll," I say, making a beeline for the hose on the side of the house. I peel off my shirt and rinse it on the sidewalk, then head upstairs to shower. J.D. comes with me, neither of us saying anything as I step out of my shorts, turn on the water and wait for it to warm up, but about two seconds after I get in the tub he strips off, too, and joins me. We stay silent as he washes my hair and lathers my torso with soap, and when I step under the faucet to rinse he gets behind me and wraps his arms around my waist. I lean back against him and he kisses my neck.

"So what's new with you?" I ask.

He laughs, but I can hear how somber and tired he is. I ask him if he wants to talk about what happened when he went home to Bruce, and he tells me that he tried really hard to convince himself, and Bruce, that he really wanted to make their marriage work.

"But I just kept thinking of you," he says, "and I couldn't stop crying. Bruce got really upset—and I don't blame him a bit—but then he got mean, too, and we both started acting like five-year-olds, with a lot of yelling and name-calling. It was incredibly ugly, and all my clothes ended up on the front lawn. It was such a cliché, and really sad, but I truly thought that would be the end of it. I never dreamed he'd do what he just did."

I tilt my head back so I can see his face. "I'm sorry."

He shrugs. "I hate that I hurt him so much. To be honest, though, I don't know what else I could've done, once I figured out I was lying to myself. It's pretty simple, really. I love you, not him." I turn in his arms and he leans down to nibble on my nose. "You are such a baby," he says. "You're crying again."

"I am not. It's just shower water." I kiss him. "Yeah, okay, I'm crying. It just occurred to me that I'm going to be seeing a lot more of you, and it's very stressful."

"Shut up," he says.

After we finish showering—it takes a while, because neither of us wants to get out—we go back downstairs for dinner with Mom and Walter. Mom made Moroccan chicken and we're drinking white wine, and for a while nobody talks about anything of substance; we just eat and enjoy each other's company, chatting and clowning. Bruce's vehicular assault was just too weird and unsettling for words, and I think we're all purposely avoiding the subject, even though there's still a blue Volvo out on the lawn with a birdbath jammed into its undercarriage like a stake through a vampire's heart.

Jesus, what a world.

J.D. is weighted down by worry and guilt over Bruce, but underneath that burden is also a lightness that keeps breaking out in his smile, or his laugh. I think he knows it's right for him to be here with us, but I'm pretty sure, too, that he'll be beating himself up with a lot of what-ifs for quite a while. The rest of us are trying to tamp down our own lightheartedness in deference to his internal struggle, but we're all just so damn glad to have him here that the only thing that really keeps us from dancing around the room is how physically and emotionally drained we are, now that the adrenaline from Bruce's appearance has left our bodies.

"Oh, Noah," Mom says after a while. "I completely forgot

until just now, but a letter came for you this afternoon while you were out walking. It's on the hall table."

I raise my eyebrows and ask who it's from; I can't think of anybody who might write to me at Mom's house.

"I don't know. There's no return address."

The angular, messy handwriting on the envelope isn't familiar, but the two-day-old postmark is from Ann Arbor, Michigan, and I do have a couple of friends who live there. Curious, I open the letter as I walk back in the kitchen, scanning the first few lines.

"Holy shit," I say, surprised. "It's from Janelle."

> *Hey, Cuz.*
>
> *I messed up pretty bad, huh? I don't know what else to say, so I'll just say sorry, and skip the bullshit excuses. I'll pay you back the cash I took from your wallet when I can. I'll try to pay Mom back for the bail money, too, but to tell the truth I don't know if I'll ever be able to come up with that kind of dough. Tell Leo I'm sorry I took his car, but I left it someplace public with a note in it saying who it belongs to, so I hope he gets it back eventually. If he doesn't, though, it's a piece of junk, anyway, so maybe he's better off without it.*
>
> *I'm in Michigan right now with a friend, but by the time you get this we'll be someplace else. I can't tell you where, just on the off-chance you're pissed enough to tell the cops. I'm 99.99% sure you'd never do that, but I know how much I deserve it so I have to be careful. The only thing I can tell you is I've got a plan, and it doesn't involve jail.*
>
> *I don't really know why I stole that credit card, or bought all that stupid shit. I didn't even want*

*any of it. But once I got caught I figured I was
screwed no matter what, so I decided to see how
far away I can get. So far so good, I guess. I'm
scared all the time, which kind of sucks, but at
least it's better than waiting for a trial for a few
months, while Mom stares at me like I'm the
biggest fuckup on the planet. Maybe once I get
somewhere safe I'll actually stop doing stupid shit
and start over.*

   *Or maybe I'll just keep being a fuckup, world
without end, amen.*

   *Anyway, I gotta go. I just wanted to say I
know I hosed you, and I feel bad about that. I
really liked you, and Virginia, and I hope you can
both forgive me for causing you trouble. It was
nice being a family with you, even if it was just
for a few days. I'll write my mom, soon, but for
now if you can just tell her I'm okay, I'd appreciate it.*

   Okay, time to go. Love from me.
—Janelle
*P.S. I liked seeing you naked, lol. Too bad you're
gay.*

I offer the letter to Mom after I finish reading it aloud, and
she accepts it gingerly, like it might be coated with anthrax.

"I guess I should call Cindy tonight," she says, sighing. "It
will make her miserable, but at least she'll know a little more
than she did." She raises an eyebrow at me. "Why did Janelle
see you naked?"

"I was going to ask the same thing," J.D. says, smirking.

I blush. "It was an accident. She came in my room one night
when I was in bed."

"Kinky," Walter says.

"Shut up, all of you," I say.

We speculate for a while about Janelle's destination. My own guess is she's going to try to slip into Canada somehow, since she's already in Michigan, but I suppose she was just as close to the border when she was here, so who the hell knows? Mom and I are both relieved to know that she's at least still alive, and appears to be traveling with a friend. Things are more likely than not to end up badly for her, but as screwed up as she is, she appears to be a survivor, so maybe she'll manage to beat the odds and eventually get her act together somewhere else.

Or like she said, not.

Mom changes the subject when we're halfway through the second bottle of wine, and finally gets around to asking what J.D. and I are planning to do now.

J.D. sighs. "We haven't gotten that far. I took a few personal days so we can sort things out."

Mom nods, feeding bits of dried wax into the burning candle flame in the middle of the table. "My guess is you'll need more than a few days."

She's not wrong, of course. We've got a lot to figure out, and some of it will be hard. For instance, J.D. says he's already signed his contract in Wellesley at the school and has to stay there until next May, even though Wellesley is too expensive for anybody who isn't rich like Bruce. J.D. could live with me in Providence and commute—it's only about forty-five minutes by car—but because of all his early morning rehearsals and evening concerts it would still mean a lot of time on the road. I could move to Wellesley, instead, and do the commuting, but we'd basically have to live in a hovel to stay on top of our rent. Life decisions like this usually make me nuts, but for once I'm not too worried about what will happen. As long as I have J.D. in my life, and time to paint, it kind of feels greedy to ask for more.

We bat around ideas with Mom and Walter as we clean up the dinner dishes and wander out to the front porch; Mom and Walter take the swing and J.D. and I sit on the top step. Walter stays until sunset, then says he needs to go home and work on some course syllabuses. He kisses Mom goodnight, then on his way past J.D. and me he bends down and kisses me, too, on my forehead. He's never done that before, and it moves me.

"What's gotten into you?" I ask, smiling up at him. "You must be getting soft in your old age."

"I'm just rewarding good behavior," he says. "You brought Sadie home even though you didn't have to, and you were civil with Freddie, and decent to Bruce, and you didn't piss off your mother all evening long. I can hardly believe it's Noah York sitting in front of me." He squeezes J.D.'s shoulder. "Welcome home, J.D. You have no idea how much our idiot boy missed you."

He heads for the corner of the house to go retrieve his car in the driveway. Mom watches until he's out of sight, then comes to sit between J.D. and me on the step.

"You should marry that man," I tell her. "He's way sweeter than you."

"I know," she says. "I'm considering it."

"Really?"

She shrugs. "We'll see." She rests her head on my shoulder and holds J.D.'s hand in her lap, sighing with contentment. "Not a bad way to end a day, is it?"

"Nope, it isn't." J.D.'s voice is full of love for her. "I hope you know that Noah and I are going to be around here a lot, whatever else happens."

"Noah's already promised to visit once a month. I know you had no say in that promise, but I'm holding you both to it, anyway."

He looks at me over the top of her head. "We can do a whole lot better than once a month. Most of my weekends are free, plus I have a ton of vacation days when the kids are on break."

Mom snorts. "I can feel Noah's blood pressure spiking, even as we speak."

I growl as they laugh. "Better call an ambulance," I mutter. "I'm stroking out."

The sun is well below the horizon, but there's still enough light to see a car headed our way, down Main Street, even though its headlights aren't on. It's coming at a sedate pace, though, so I don't really pay much attention to it at first—unlike the Volvo on our lawn, this car doesn't seem intent on chasing me down and flattening my skull on the pavement. When it gets about a block away, though, it starts to look weirdly familiar; I sit up straight when I'm sure.

It's Leo's gray rust-bucket of a Honda. Mom recognizes it at the same moment, and she puts a hand to her mouth.

"It's Leo," I tell J.D., who's watching both of us, puzzled by our reaction. "But how the hell did he get his car back so fast? I know the cops found it in New York, but I was sure they'd hold on to it for a while."

Mom's not listening to me; she's already on her feet. "There's someone with him," she breathes.

Leo parks the car where he did the other night, before Janelle used it as her getaway vehicle. He turns off the engine and waves at us, but it's not until he opens his door and climbs out that we're able to see Carolyn in the passenger seat, looking back at us. My eyes fill, for about the hundredth time this day. Jesus Christ, at this rate I may need to buy a wet vac to keep up with the overflow.

I never knew a sixty-eight-year-old poet laureate with ALS could move so fast, but Mom is across the road before J.D. and I can even stand up.

THE LANGUAGE OF LOVE AND LOSS

ABOUT THIS GUIDE

The suggested questions are included to enhance your group's reading of Bart Yates' *The Language of Love and Loss*!

1. Noah York has many attractive qualities, but also many flaws. What do you consider to be his strengths and his weaknesses?

2. Virginia and Noah's parent/child relationship is complicated, to say the least. How would you describe it? Does it seem unusual to you?

3. Most of Noah's narrative revolves around the three main characters (Noah, Virginia, and J.D.), but there are many minor characters who are also integral to the story. Of all these characters, who do you like the most, and why? Which character do you dislike the most?

4. When Virginia reveals to Carolyn the identity of her biological father, Carolyn reacts with horror and anger, and resents both Virginia and Noah for seeking her out in the first place. Is this an appropriate reaction, given the nature of what she's just learned?

5. Virginia's old Victorian house and the small town of Oakland, NH, are both arguably "characters" in the story as well. What does this quiet, intimate setting add to the novel?

6. Are there alternate themes to this book, beyond the "love and loss" indicated in the title? If so, what are they? How the past affects the future, maybe? Or perhaps just the general messiness of life? How would you characterize the book to someone who hasn't read it?

7. Noah is a witty person with a sharp tongue, who often gets himself in trouble by shooting off his mouth. Do you find his sense of humor off-putting? Endearing? When does he use humor to cope with anger or grief?

8. Aside from Noah and Virginia's relationship, there are many other interesting "pairings" to think about. Noah and J.D., of course, but also J.D. and Bruce, Cindy and Janelle, Noah and Leo, Carolyn and Virginia, etc. Which of these relationships appeals to you the most?

9. Did the story end the way you expected, or did you think it was headed in a different direction? If you could change anything about the ending, what would it be?

10. THE LANGUAGE OF LOVE AND LOSS is a stand-alone sequel to LEAVE MYSELF BEHIND, featuring many of the same characters and the same narrator, though now Noah York is a middle-aged man instead of a seventeen-year-old boy. If you read the earlier novel, how has Noah changed over the intervening twenty years? Do you think the younger Noah would like the man he has become?

Please turn the page for an exciting sneak peek of
Bart Yates's newest novel
**THE VERY LONG, VERY STRANGE LIFE
OF ISAAC DAHL,**
now on sale wherever print and ebooks are sold!

DAY ONE

February 17, 1926. Bingham, Utah

Each day is a story, whether or not that story makes any damn
sense or is worth telling to anyone else. If you live a long time,
and your memory doesn't completely crap out, you end up
with enough stories to fill a library; it's nearly impossible to
pick and choose a mere handful to write about—a stupid, arbi-
trary stricture I've been cowed into accepting by a dead bully.
Why I lack the testicular fortitude to just say no is a vexing
question, but what aggravates me even more is the fact that I
have no idea where to start.

Okay, I'm lying.

I actually do know, but it irks me beyond belief to give
Aggie the satisfaction of following her advice. That she now
only exists in my head is beside the point: I'd like to maintain at
least a smidgeon of autonomy in my own skull, for God's sake.
Is that so much to ask?

Sadly, in this case, it is.

You're very unattractive when you whine, Isaac.

That's what she'd say, of course, if she were still here. I find it both irritating and oddly comforting that I can hear her voice so clearly, without even trying. She may as well never have died, given that she's every bit as exasperating in my imagination as she ever was in person.

Just get on with it, and tell them about the giant.

Agnes and I were getting ready for bed—and fighting, of course, about whose turn it was to stoke the wood stove—when our mother lifted her head and told us to shush. Agnes was my twin sister, and Mama always claimed we came out of her womb mad as weasels, screaming hell and death at each other, same as every day afterwards. (The midwife hauled me out only a few minutes ahead of Aggie, who no doubt thought the whole sordid business was my fault, and something I should have warned her about.)

"Shush, both of you," Mama repeated. She was nursing Hilda, our baby sister, by the wood stove. "Did you hear that noise?"

"What noise?" Agnes asked.

"The giant," I said.

"Don't be ridiculous," Agnes said. "Giants aren't real."

"Shush!" Mama insisted.

I was eight, and had just read *Jack and the Beanstalk*. I was a timid kid with a perverse imagination, and long before the story of Jack and his magic beans came into my life I was jumping at phantom faces in every shadow. I believed the large rock beside our house was a troll turned to stone, waiting for the next dark of the moon to become flesh; I swore I could hear nymphs and demons battling for dominion in the restless water of Bingham Creek; I dreamt almost every night of warty, jaundiced witches, lumbering ogres, and pallid ghosts with milky eyes. Yet the old fairy tale about Jack the giant killer—a murderous, thieving boy who not only got away with his sins, but was actually rewarded for them—unsettled me in a way few things did. Whatever my mother may have heard that night, *I* heard a vengeful relative of Jack's slain giant, rousing to wrath somewhere up the canyon.

Agnes and I had just finished bathing in the clawfoot cast-iron tub Father bought for Mama at Christmas. There was no privacy in our one-room house. Agnes and I shared a cramped bed on one side of the room, next to Hilda's crib; Father and Mama's bed was on the opposite wall, a few feet from the kitchen table. It was the only home Agnes and I knew, and we couldn't imagine not bumping into each other every time we hunched over to tie a shoe. The two of us used the same towel to dry ourselves before slipping into our matching night-shirts—cut and sewed from the same bolt of blue flannel by Mama—and the smell of rye bread, fried onions, and boiled cabbage was still in the air from supper, three hours before.

"Oh," Agnes said, cocking her head. "I hear it now, too, Mama."

The winter cold was slithering like rattlesnakes through every crack in the walls and floors that night, and I tugged on gray wool socks and listened to the strange rumbling in the dark world beyond our walls. The only light in the room aside from the fire in the woodstove was from two candles on the kitchen table, flickering in the frigid draft blowing through the house. We lived in the Carr Fork area of Bingham with all the other Swedes, and nobody in Carr Fork had electricity. (Nor indoor plumbing, for that matter: For baths, Aggie and I had to cart in a few buckets from the outdoor water pump that Mama then heated on the stove.)

"The giant's getting closer," I whimpered.

Agnes rolled her eyes. "There's no such thing as—"

"HUSH!" Mama cried, rising from the rocking chair, and it bronco-bucked on the floor behind her.

The entire population of Bingham, Utah, lived in a deep, narrow canyon in the Oquirrh mountains, and all of us—fifteen thousand bipedal moles in a massive nest—were stuffed down together in the earth. Ramshackle wooden houses, tenements, and stores all piled on top of each other, lining both sides of the canyon walls, clear to the rim. The Kennecott copper mine was at one end of the seven-mile-long canyon, and the only reason for Bingham's existence. The canyon itself was less than a city block wide, so every time a new house was built it went to the end of the line like a naughty child, simply because there was no other place for it.

Father had come home for dinner that night, but he'd gone out again to play cards with his younger brother, Johan, and their friends. Mama had begged him not to drink any of Johan's bootleg gin. She feared he'd go blind from the stuff, like Cotter Jones who lived two houses down from us. Father was no stranger to hooch but he was also no Cotter Jones, who spent every waking moment of his life sucking at the teat of a dented tin flask he carried around in a hip pocket. Father was at least fully sober every Sunday, and rarely came home drunk from his card games, though his breath smelled like fermented pine from the juniper berries in the gin.

"Mama?" Agnes asked, now frightened herself. "What's wrong?"

"Everything's fine," Mama murmured, staring hard-eyed at the door, but even Agnes knew she was lying.

Until then, it was just a normal day. Father got up for work early in the morning, same as always, at four a.m. — he worked a ten-hour shift in the copper mine, six days a week — and Mama got up, too, to make his breakfast. They spoke softly, trying not to wake my sisters and me, but they needn't have bothered. We never failed to hear everything.

"That's the last of the sugar," Mama said, pouring coffee in his thermos. "If you want more before Friday we'll have to ask Fergus for credit."

Father was paid weekly. He gave his money to Mama and she ran the house. They bickered regularly over how little sugar she allowed him; she considered it a luxury, but Father had a sweet tooth and became irritable when none was left for his morning coffee.

"We're broke already?" His chair scraped on the wooden floor. "How come?"

Mama sighed. "Isaac needed new shoes. His toes were poking out of the old ones."

Before she became Mrs. Magnus Dahl, Mama's name was Hilda Gwozdek. Her folks and five ignorant, brooding siblings also lived in the canyon, but in the Highland Boy area with the rest of the Poles. Father always said Mama only married him to get away from her priggish mother and her short-tempered father, and there was at least a little truth to that: Mama undoubtedly loved Father for himself, but she loved him even more for not being a Gwozdek.

"That boy's growing too fast," Father said. I had my head under the covers but I knew he was looking at me. "He needs new clothes every damn day."

"You want me to bind his feet like a Japanese girl? Make him stay small forever?"

"You betcha." Father's voice was a rumbling growl, but I didn't need to see his face to know he was smiling. "So long as there's sugar in my coffee."

"Agnes is growing out of her clothes, too, by the way."

"So? Just give her a potato sack and let her run barefoot."

Agnes could never tell when Father was joking. She huffed indignantly beside me in bed, and I elbowed her to keep her quiet; she huffed louder and elbowed me back.

"How come you get new clothes and I don't?" she hissed.

"It's a *joke*, dummy," I hissed back, rubbing my rib cage. "Oh."

"Go to sleep, the pair of you," Mama ordered.

Father left for work and Mama returned to bed for a while, then rose again to get Agnes and me ready for school. Agnes got swatted for dawdling when Mama told her to get dressed, and she was still pouting when Mama kissed us and shoved us out the door. As usual, my best friend Bo was waiting on the porch, smiling as if somebody had just told him the funniest joke ever, even though his nose was running and his lips were blue from the wind.

"How many times have I told you not to stand outside in the cold, Bo Larsson?" Mama snapped. "Use the brain the good Lord gave you and come in the house next time, hear?"

"Yes, Mrs. Dahl," Bo stammered, teeth chattering.

She reached out in exasperation and roughly tugged his cap over his ears. "You're lucky you still have all your fingers and toes, child," she said. "Run along, now, all of you."

We obeyed, Agnes dragging her feet as a form of protest until we were well out of Mama's sight, then she brightened and sped by us. She pretended to dislike Bo, but not even Agnes could pull off a ruse like that. Bo was by far the most handsome boy we knew—his dimpled, freckled face and big green eyes made every girl in town dote on him, including my sister—but more than that, he was also the best-natured soul on earth, and there was nobody in the canyon who didn't adore him.

"You don't need to be afraid to come in the house, Bo," I told him. "Mama won't bite."

He flushed. I couldn't blame him for being scared: Everybody was scared of my mother. She wasn't mean—far from it—but she had a tongue in her head and wasn't shy of using it. (Agnes was sounding more like her all the time, and I dreaded the day the pair of them teamed up on me, one per ear.) Still, Mama loved Bo, just like the rest of us, and I think it bothered her to know he couldn't see that.

"You have any of your Valentine's candy left?" I asked. "Agnes stole all mine."

"I didn't either!" Agnes yelled over her shoulder.

Being different genders, my sister and I weren't identical twins, of course, but we may as well have been: We both had blond hair, blue eyes, thin faces, and square chins. We also liked a lot of the same things—books, music, stories, puzzles, card games—so people were surprised that we squabbled as much as we did. Part of it was simple jealousy: I was annoyed that she was smarter than me, and she resented that most people liked me better than her. I suspect the main reason we butted heads all the time, however, was that we were so much alike, and both of us enjoyed nothing more than yanking each other's chain.

Bo dug in the pocket of his thin brown coat and gave me a Tootsie Roll. He was shorter than me by a couple of inches, but I was skinny as a fishline and he was stocky and powerful. He already had a hint of his father's massive shoulders—his daddy Sven worked in the mine with Father, and Father said he'd never met a stronger man—as well as the beginning of Sven's barrel chest and thick calves. Bo could carry me on his back for blocks, and if I was dumb enough to wrestle him I'd end up facedown in the dirt and hogtied before I even knew how I got there.

Agnes drifted back, staring at the Tootsie Roll I'd just unwrapped. "Can I have half?"

"Sure." I popped the whole thing in my mouth and stuck out my tongue to show it to her.

"You're a *jackass*, Isaac," she said, running ahead again.

"You should be nicer to your sister," Bo said mildly.

"She should be nicer to me." We stepped around a drift of snow in front of Fergus's general store and a dried horse turd hit me in the face: Agnes had deadly aim. I stumbled and fell, but Bo caught me before I hit the ground.

"Dang you, Aggie!" I sputtered. She was already twenty feet ahead, laughing her fool head off.

I wiped my face with snow, swearing. A clump of slush had wormed its way inside my coat collar, too, and was wiggling down my chest, beneath my shirt. I could tell Bo was trying not to laugh and I almost said something mean, then realized he wouldn't think of laughing if I hadn't deserved it. He helped clean my face, his mittens gentle on my cheeks and forehead.

"I'll get even with her," I muttered, glaring after Aggie.

"You sure are a slow learner," he answered.

* * *

Our schoolhouse was small because it was only for the twenty or so kids who lived in the Carr Fork area of Bingham. There were almost a dozen other schools in other parts of the canyon—Highland Boy, Lark, Dinkeyville, Frog Town, Markham, Freeman, Heaston Heights, Copper Heights, Terrace Heights—but none of them, save for the main school in Bingham proper, was much bigger than ours. Since we were mostly Swedes in Carr Fork, there was a disproportionate number of blond heads in the room when our caps and hats came off. Bo was a vivid exception to the general rule: His hair was the color of an orange peel.

We sat side by side at our desks, as always, with Agnes directly in front of us, and the only thing out of the ordinary I remember happening that entire school day was when Erik Kalberg—a hapless boy with a lazy eye and a stutter—dropped his pencil in front of Agnes's desk and bent down to fetch it, attempting to peek up her skirt. The toe of her shoe caught him squarely on the forehead, sending him sprawling at our teacher's feet. Mrs. Sundberg made them both stand with their backs to the class, in separate corners of the room; Agnes kept glowering at me over her shoulder, feeling sorely ill-used and expecting me to do something about it.

I held up my hand. "Mrs. Sundberg?"

"Yes, Isaac?"

"I think Agnes would learn her lesson a whole lot faster if you put a bag over her head."

The class's laughter and my sister's outrage were equally gratifying, but the pleasure was short-lived. I saw Bo sadly shaking his head as Mrs. Sundberg dragged me from my chair to another corner of the room.

Other random memories from that day:

Bo walking Agnes and me home after school, then leaving for his own house as soon as our feet touched the boards of our porch; my baby sister Hilda's greedy blue eyes, coveting a wooden top spinning across the kitchen table between my hands; Mama teaching Agnes and me how to make *köttbullar*— meatballs with minced beef and pork, butter and black pepper—and letting us help her knead the dough for her crusty rye bread and cut up some cabbage and onions for supper; Agnes and I doing our homework at the table as the bread baked in the oven; Father coming home from work, tired and snappish, but cheering up after eating; Mama telling Agnes to never bother with a man before his stomach was full; Mama and Father arguing about him going out again to play cards; Agnes and I reading by candlelight until Mama made us stop, fearing for our eyes; Mama heating water for our bath; Agnes and I splashing each other in the tub as Mama sang to Hilda; three or four young Poles in the street outside, yelling and clowning in their blurred, baffling language as they passed our house, their voices fading as they made their way home, no doubt to Highland Boy.

Just another day in Bingham, Utah.

The rumble in the canyon grew louder, then all-encompassing, insupportable. Mama, still clasping Hilda in one arm, yelled something I couldn't hear, then fiercely seized my shoulder with her free hand and shoved me toward the door. In a panic, I ran smack into Aggie, still standing by the tub, and accidentally knocked her into the damn thing. I tried to help her out but just fell in on top of her, bruising my thigh on one rim of the tub and banging my head against the other. We'd already drained the bathwater but the cast-iron surface was still wet. I cried out in pain as Mama leaned over us with Hilda, screaming, "Get out, get out!" but before we could regain our feet, the world ended.

A mountain of snow ripped through the walls and ceiling of our home. Mama and Hilda vanished from sight as the tub was lifted on what felt like the back of a whale; it flipped end over end, Agnes and I tumbling around inside in a mad jumble of limbs, darkness, and snow, unable to hear ourselves scream. I caught a brief glimpse of a crescent moon, far overhead, and knew we were somehow outside; the moon disappeared, reappeared, and disappeared again, all in the space of a few heartbeats. God only knows how long this horrific carnival ride lasted—in retrospect, it couldn't have been more than fifteen seconds, but it felt like an eternity—yet it ended as abruptly as it had started: one second we were spinning out of control, the next we were completely still, and on solid ground again.

Entombed in an upside-down bathtub.

The avalanche, hungry for destruction, thundered away from wherever it had left us, and only then could I hear Agnes speaking. I couldn't see her or anything else, yet I could feel her arms wrapped tightly around my ribs, so tightly I was aware of her heart beating next to mine, much as it must have when we shared Mama's womb.

"Are you hurt?" she asked, shaking me. "Isaac? Are you hurt?"

I was in shock but her frantic voice brought me to my senses. I had blood in my mouth—I'd bitten my tongue—and from the wetness on the front of my nightshirt it seemed I'd peed myself, too, but other than that I was more or less intact.

"I'm okay," I gasped. We couldn't sit upright so we were forced to stay lying down. "What about you?"

"My ankle hurts."

For her to say anything I knew it was bad. Agnes complained about everything in life except physical pain. When she was smaller she got her hand caught in a door, snapping two fingers, and she barely even winced.

I shoved at the sides and bottom of the tub, knowing we'd never budge it. It outweighed both of us put together. I suddenly realized we were buried alive, under God only knew how many feet of snow, and my panic, on the ebb since Agnes spoke to me, returned with a vengeance.

"Mama?" My scream was deafening in the confines of our metal coffin. "Mama, WE'RE HERE!"

Agnes yelled, too, but after a couple of minutes she fell silent and made me stop as well. We listened intently for any noise aside from our own breathing but heard nothing.

"Nobody's there," Agnes said hoarsely.

"Shush. Mama will come."

She didn't argue but I could hear her sniffle and knew what she was thinking. We'd both seen Mama and Hilda swallowed by a white monster. I began crying, too.

"What do you think happened to Father?" Agnes asked, her voice hitching.

Uncle Johan—Father's clownish, happy-go-lucky, nineteen-year-old brother—lived alone in a small shack a couple of blocks away from us, which was why his home was the usual gathering place for card games and drinking. I couldn't imagine he and Father had fared any better than us when the slide hit, but then I remembered that one side of Johan's house butted up against a ridge of rock, right in the snow's path, which might've served as a shield from the worst of the avalanche. It was a faint chance, but still something, and I told Agnes so.

"No," she said. Her voice was grim in the darkness. "It got them, too."

Her breath caught in pain. Both of us were terribly cold—our hair, still wet from our bath, had ice crystals in it, and the urine on my nightshirt was freezing as well; I couldn't keep my teeth from chattering. I pulled her close, and we listened hopelessly for signs of life outside our shell. I don't know how long we lay there, saying nothing, but my feet and hands were numb and I had drifted into a deep, nearly impenetrable sleep when I felt Agnes pinching my arm, again and again.

"Quit, Aggie," I mumbled, "that hurts." I couldn't seem to wake up.

"Someone's out there," she husked. "Help," she croaked weakly. She sounded like she had sand in her throat. "Help!"

I shook my head, trying to rouse myself, and finally heard what she had: men's shouting voices, muffled by snow and distance, but definitely there.

"We're here!" I cried, managing more volume than Agnes. "Help us, please help us!"

There was an interminable silence, then the blessed sound of shovels plunging into snow. Agnes and I, alert again but cold beyond belief, banged on the tub with our fists and kept up a rolling broadside of screaming. At last a shovel struck our tomb, tolling it like a bell, and a moment later the lip of the tub at our feet lifted, inch by inch, then the whole thing was heaved aside by a group of men, standing around in the dim glow of a kerosene lamp. I couldn't make out the faces of any of our rescuers.

"It's Magnus Dahl's twins," someone said, then raised his voice and called to another group of men half a block away. "Hey, Johan, it's your brother's kids!"

A dark, thin, familiar form lurched toward us through chest-deep snow, followed closely by someone much more thickset. "Oh, thank God!" Uncle Johan said, stumbling into the lantern light with Sven Larsson, Bo's daddy, right behind him. Johan lifted me in his arms as Sven draped a coat around Aggie. "Where's your mother? Where's Hilda? Do you know?"

I was shaking so badly I couldn't talk. I sobbed with relief as he hurried back through the narrow lane he'd created to get to us, rushing toward warmth and shelter with Sven right at his heels, carting Agnes. I tried to tell Johan what happened but nothing came out of my mouth.

"The snow got Mama and the baby," Agnes said. "She tried to get us out of the house but Isaac and I fell in the tub."

Over Johan's shoulder I saw Sven Larsson half-turn without slowing; I heard his powerful voice ordering the rescue parties to hurry up and keep searching for Mama and Hilda.

"Where's Father?" I finally managed to stammer through clacking teeth.

Johan didn't answer. The heavens had burst open that night,

like a piñata, spilling stars all over the sky, and I tilted back to see his face in their light. There were tears on his cheeks, and a cold hand squeezed my heart. Watching Sven Larsson carrying Agnes reminded me there was someone else I loved unaccounted for.

"Bo?" I rasped. "Where's Bo?"

Sven gave me a reassuring smile. "Bo's fine, Isaac. The slide took our house but we got out in time. He and his mother are both safe."

I must've lost consciousness then, because the next thing I remember is waking in a large room full of people, sleeping on cots. I was nestled in stiff cotton sheets with a thick wool blanket over me, and I was blessedly warm; someone had dressed me in a clean nightshirt and clean socks as well, but the sleeves of the shirt were four or five inches longer than my arms. There was a smell of stale coffee in the air, and ammonia, but I had no idea where I was, and it was too dark—in spite of candlelight coming from an adjacent room—to make out anything that might help me get my bearings.

"Aggie?" I called out softly. Aside from a handful of nights I'd spent at Bo's house, I'd never slept in a bed without my sister beside me, and I was frightened. I raised my voice as much as I dared. "Aggie, where are you?"

"I'm here," came her whispered response. She was in the cot to my right, a foot away.

I relaxed slightly. "Where's Uncle Johan?"

"Looking for Father and Mama." She paused. "He's been gone a long time."

I didn't dare ask how long.

An older woman's voice over near the door interrupted us. "Hush now, children." Whoever she was, she sounded kind, but she spoke like someone used to obedience. "Other folks is tryin' to sleep."

I subsided for a moment, but I couldn't stay still. "What about Bo?" I murmured to Aggie. "Have you seen him?"

"Hi, Isaac." It was Bo himself, somewhere to my left. "I'm here."

I started to say hi back, but the older woman by the door cleared her throat and I bit my lip to keep from antagonizing her. A moment later I was startled by the silhouette of Agnes, standing by my cot. I pulled back my blanket and made room for her, and she crawled in next to me. Her right ankle was wrapped in some sort of splint.

"I'm really scared, Isaac," she whispered. "Are you scared, too?"

I nodded into her shoulder, unable to speak. A short, stocky figure appeared on the opposite side of the cot from where Agnes had materialized; it was Bo. For the first time in his life he was probably finding it difficult to smile, and I was glad I couldn't see his face. I lifted the blanket for him, too—Aggie and I curled up tighter to make room—and he joined us, crowding out every bit of the remaining space on the cot.

"Sorry 'bout your folks," he murmured. His breath smelled like hot cocoa. "And Hilda, too."

I started to cry, and a sob shook Agnes's whole body. Bo put his arm over us, and left it there until we both quieted again. I don't know how long he stayed with us before going back to his own bed, but the last thing I remember that night was the feel of his lips, dry and moth-light, brushing my forehead.

When I woke in the morning Agnes was still beside me, and Uncle Johan was sitting at the foot of the cot. In the light I was finally able to figure out we were in the back room of Fergus's general store, packed in with a few dozen other people who'd lost their homes. Johan didn't have to say anything about Father, Mama, and Hilda; we could see his despair in the shadows under his eyes, and the way he kept turning away from us as he spoke. He told us other things, though: How the avalanche had killed thirty-nine people for certain, but at least that many were still missing; how the snow had dropped from a thousand feet up in the mountains before cutting a deadly swath through the canyon; how Cotter Jones, blinded by alcohol and stumbling around the street in front of his home when the slide hit, was carried on its crest for half a mile, but had nothing wrong with him save for a few bruises.

We heard later that the avalanche had tossed Father on the floor in Uncle Johan's house and crushed the life out of him. Uncle Johan was closer to the door and got out before the slide hit; he was still buried in snow but somehow managed to fight his way to the surface before suffocating. Mama and Hilda weren't so lucky; they were found together right where Aggie and I last saw them. They were both blue and frozen solid, Mama clutching Hilda to her breast.

At the time, Aggie and I weren't aware how miraculous our escape had been; the bathtub that almost became our coffin not only saved us from the mortal weight of the snow, but also allowed us to breathe until we were found.